A Special Kind of Crime

EDITED BY LAWRENCE TREAT

PUBLISHED FOR THE CRIME CLUB BY

DOUBLEDAY & COMPANY, INC.

GARDEN CITY, NEW YORK

1982

Library of Congress Cataloging in Publication Data
Main entry under title:
A Special kind of crime.
  1. Detective and mystery stories, American.
I. Treat, Lawrence, 1903–
   PS648.D4S6   813'.0872'08
   ISBN 0-385-17993-6   AACR2
Library of Congress Catalog Card Number 81-43452

First Edition

"*I'm Sorry, Mr. Griggs*" by Stanley Cohen. Copyright © 1974 by Stanley Cohen. First published in *Ellery Queen's Mystery Magazine*, under the title "That Day on Connally." Also appeared in *Best Detective Stories of the Year, 1975*, under the current title. Reprinted by permission of the author.

"*Sugar and Spice*" by James Cross. Copyright © 1981 by Hugh J. Parry. Published by permission of the author.

"*The Nine-to-Five Man*" by Stanley Ellin. Copyright © 1961 by Stanley Ellin. Reprinted by permission of the author.

"*Intruder in the Maize*" by Joan Richter. Copyright © 1967 by Davis Publications, Inc. First published in *Ellery Queen's Mystery Magazine*. Reprinted by permission of the author.

"*Shooting Lines*" by Gerald Hammond. Copyright © 1982 by Gerald Hammond. Published by permission of the author.

"*The Nine Eels of Madame Wu*" by Edward D. Hoch. Copyright © 1980 by Davis Publications, Inc. First published in *Alfred Hitchcock's Mystery Magazine*. Reprinted by permission of the author.

"*Payoff on Double Zero*" by Warner Law. Copyright © 1971 by Warner Law. Originally appeared in *Playboy*. Reprinted by permission of Carol Russell Law.

"*Blurred View*" by John D. MacDonald. Copyright © 1966 by John D. MacDonald Publishing, Inc. Reprinted by permission of the author.

"*The Love of Money*" by J. I. Mwagojo. Copyright © 1982 by J. I. Mwagojo. Published by permission of the author.

"*The Man Who Collected 'The Shadow'* " by Bill Pronzini. Copyright © 1971 by Mercury Press, Inc. First published in *The Magazine of Fantasy and Science Fiction*. Reprinted by permission of the author.

"*The Adventure of Abraham Lincoln's Clue*" by Ellery Queen. Copyright © 1965, 1968 by Ellery Queen. Reprinted by permission of the author and his agents, Scott Meredith Literary Agency, Inc., 845 Third Ave., New York, N.Y. 10022.

"*Counselor at Law*" by Al Nussbaum. Copyright © 1981 by Renown Publications, Inc. Reprinted by permission of the author and his agent, Alex Jackinson.

"*The Iron Collar*" by Frank Sisk. Copyright © 1965 by Frank Sisk. First published in *Alfred Hitchcock's Mystery Magazine*. Reprinted by permission of the author.

"*The Poisoned Pawn*" by Henry Slesar. Copyright © by HSD Publications, Inc. Reprinted by permission of the author.

"*The Canarsie Cannonball*" by Gerald Tomlinson. Copyright © 1977 by Gerald Tomlinson. First published in *Ellery Queen's Mystery Magazine*. Reprinted by permission of the author.

"A Matter of Kicks" by Lawrence Treat and Richard Plotz. Copyright © 1979 by Davis Publications, Inc. First published in *Alfred Hitchcock's Mystery Magazine*. Reprinted by permission of the authors.

Contents

Preface

BY LAWRENCE TREAT

As Francis Bacon remarked some years before I was born, "reading maketh a full man," and I hope that all who read this book will emerge a little fuller—not only filled with bits of miscellaneous information and replete with the pleasure of learning, but enriched by meeting a group of top-flight authors and sharing the joy of some of their interests. What, for instance, do most of us know about kite fighting in Bangkok, or about the Mexican garotte or the fine points of arson?

This book originated in a conversation I had with a mystery writer and MWA member who had been a flier, airline executive, industrial designer, fisherman, and gadgeteer, besides being a writer and a chef. It occurred to me that mystery writers know a great deal and have usually done many things. They've been editors and teachers and ad men and cowboys and soldiers and lab technicians and policemen and gamblers and jockeys and athletes and practically everything else. In the light of so rich an agglomeration of experience, a collection of stories reflecting some of these specialties would have to be absorbing.

I was flooded with contributions, and in reading the stories I learned something about how to manufacture dog food, how to decipher a diplomatic code, how to burgle a suburban house, how to pass counterfeit money, how to tell when a gun had been reconstituted, and whether a Spanish grandee will kiss the hand of a married woman. I only regret that I can't edit a few more anthologies with all the fascinating stories that had to be rejected.

There is a nice mix here, between the lighthearted and the somber, but I incline to the lightsome. There is a singular lack of blood and pain in these pages. Most of the victims who have died have done so in good cheer, aware that they expired in the best of prose. I maintain that style is part and parcel of a good story, and that unless you write well, there's no point in dropping your fingers on a typewriter key. And these stories are well written.

Nevertheless this was not an easy anthology to edit, because so many of the stories submitted were very good. How could I select from such an extraordinary wealth of material?

At first I was baffled by the problem, but being a writer I'm inventive. Have to be. It's in the nature of my calling. I took each story and gave it a number, and I put all those numbers in an old, felt hat, the kind that nobody has worn in twenty or thirty years. (One respects a hat like that; it has acquired wisdom and experience.) So, once all the numbers were in the hat, I mixed them up and reached in, and a miracle occurred. Only the numbers of the very best stories came to hand . . .

One more note concerning this book. My wife, Rose, read all the stories and we discussed them in detail and eventually reached a consensus of two. Our choices were ratified by the Crime Club editors at Doubleday, Michele Tempesta and Terry Rafferty, whose good judgment is reflected in this volume.

I'm Sorry, Mr. Griggs

STANLEY COHEN

Sighting through the heavy snowfall, he lined up the cross hairs on her chest as the cable brought her into view. He focused on a brightly colored emblem on her parka, perfectly and conveniently located, and after following it for a second or two he squeezed off the shot. The girl heaved against the safety bar, then slumped back into the ornate seat. Another perfect hit.

How many was that? Eleven? An even dozen? Maybe even thirteen. He had lost count. All clean kills. Only one had required two shots. A big man who had shifted in the seat just as he fired. The man began struggling after the first bullet hit and he fired a second with greater concentration, instantly stopping the man's wild thrashing movements. But he'd hated having to fire a second time—it was a blow to his otherwise perfect score.

He leaned the rifle against the wall of the shed and pressed the handle of the chair-lift drive. A little farther. Another twenty feet or so. As the chair glided into the landing area beneath the shed he cut the power, just as the ski-patrol attendant would have done to help a skier out of the seat.

He moved quickly up to the chair, pushed the sagging body backward, raised the safety bar, and pulled the man onto the platform. Then, turning him over, he gripped the man under his armpits and dragged him along the planked floor to the back of the platform and toward the convenient little hollow behind the shed. When he reached the drop-off into the hollow, he gave the body a push and then a kick and watched it slide on its own, downward and into the pile with the others.

He hustled back into the shed and grabbed the ski poles out of the holder on the lift-chair. He wheeled and hurled them toward the array of bodies, skis, and poles. Then he returned to the lift drive control and started it again. Time to bring another nice live target into view.

The girl in the seat still some fifty feet out showed no signs of life. Why should she? Fish in a barrel. A human shooting gallery. A helpless human form moving slowly in a set path at fifty yards or less. And with a scope sight. Almost unsportsman-like.

He thought about snipers who'd made the news in recent years. Kids with .22s, popping at cars on parkways near big cities, never hoping to score a clean kill. Or butchers, hauling an arsenal to the top of some tall building and blasting away at everybody in sight. Suicidal exhibitionists! Morons! With no hope whatever of walking away from it. No imagination. No planning. No class. He'd show the world how it was done by a master. A real master. And in the process he'd return a small favor to the ski community.

His mind riffled back through the countless interviews he'd had with the honchos of all the ski mountains.

"I'm sorry, Mr. Griggs, but we've completed our recruiting for this year's ski patrol."

"But, sir, I'm no ordinary skier. Look, I can make these guys you've been hiring look like beginners."

"I'm afraid we're just full up at this time."

"All I ask is a chance. Before Vietnam I was the lead instructor at Stratton. I taught the advanced classes. I even trained most of the ski patrol. All the college hotshots. Don't you understand? I'm a pro. The best."

"I can appreciate that, Mr. Griggs, but we're just not taking on any more men this season."

"Look, somebody's got to give me a break. Skiing's my life . . . It's because of my war record, isn't it?"

"I'm sorry, Mr. Griggs, we're just not hiring."

"You've been running ads, looking for guys."

"We've finished filling our roster."

"You know, this isn't a fair shake. I couldn't help all that publicity. I had no way of stopping it. I didn't want it. Besides, I was acquitted. Completely. They let me go clean. I was only a noncom. I was acting under orders at all times."

"I'm sorry, Mr. Griggs."

"Look, if you'd been over there as long as I was, you'd have reacted the same. All I wanted was to stay alive and get back. It got to where you couldn't tell the women from the men, or the kids, either, for that matter. There were even instances where our guys *did* get it from kids or women. That was a mess, over there. You've got to have been there to know about it."

"I'm sorry, Mr. Griggs."

"Look, I was given a clean bill and all I ask is to get back into skiing. I couldn't help all that publicity. You can't keep me out forever. I want to make my living on skis."

"I'm sorry, Mr. Griggs, I'm sorry, Mr. Griggs, I'm sorry . . ."

He set himself and took a breath and followed the next target that moved into view and fired and smiled at the whispered crack of the silenced rifle and at the way the young man lurched in the seat and then collapsed. Another clean hit. And he watched the chairs move closer. Almost time to stop the lift and take off the chick with the plugged emblem.

He was a master at two skills. Skiing wasn't his only area of expertise. He could shoot. And he liked shooting. Back in Nam he had become his company's cleanup man. As the unrelenting tension of the hide-and-seek fighting worked on him, he found he could best keep his head by taking pleasure in doing what he did well. If he was to kill to survive, he might as well be good at it. And to be good at it he had to like doing it.

His C.O. had recognized his instinctual capacity and had given him all the "special assignments." He soon grew to feed on them. He liked good clean kills because they were a challenge. Tough to pull off in the jungle. But he also liked those "special assignments," the closer-range "less competitive" jobs. And he had liked doing them with neatness and finesse.

He stopped the lift and began struggling with the dead girl's body. She'd been good-looking. A dish. He would have liked knowing her a little better before she decided to take the chair lift up Old Imperial that particular morning. But too bad. There would be other chicks.

Since she was light and feminine, he put his shoulder into her waist and hoisted her up and carried her to the edge of the little pocket where he had been piling the bodies. He dropped her onto the incline and she slid down among the others. Too bad about her. She was nice. Really nice. She'd picked the wrong day to ski Old Imperial.

How many more should he take before skiing down and driving away? He probably had enough already to leave his mark on the ski world for a long time. How many people would start thinking twice and maybe just stay home and watch TV before planning a weekend of skiing? A weekend of being a helpless target, dangling from a lift-cable, moving slowly toward the top of a mountain? The operators were going to pay for keeping him out.

He'd returned from Nam in the summer and could hardly wait for the snow. But that one sticky morning when the story broke about the incident in the town by the river marked the beginning of a nightmare even greater than all those he'd had in the stinking jungle. Who the hell ever heard of locking somebody up for defending his country? "Everything I did I did under orders, sir."

"Some of our witnesses feel that you seemed to have more than just a desire to carry out orders on the morning in question."

"Sir, I was doing as I was told. We were at war, regardless what college kids might say. I was mainly interested in survival. It could have been them or me."

"That's for the court to decide."

The punishing uncertainties of the trial and the confinement dragged out for months, during which he was restricted inside the base, and he watched the season come and go, reading the daily ski reports when he could get a paper. He was finally acquitted and released but his name, Wesley Griggs, had become a familiar phrase, almost a synonym for the senseless excesses of the war.

As soon as the next season approached, he began his tour of the Northeastern ski areas, looking for a job, a full-time skiing job, ready at last to begin living again, to buckle on the new boots and the gleaming new Mark IIs and hit the slopes and let the ski air with its exhilarating clarity flush the glooms and stenches of jungles and army posts out of his head.

He sensed he was a marked man after the first job interview.

He was apprehensive on the second and the turndown came without surprise. Thereafter he went from mountain to mountain, playing out the complete dialogue, all the way to the final, repeated, "I'm sorry, Mr. Griggs." Anticipating each rejection, he would become so antagonistic the operators found him oppressive, almost frightening.

After he was completely certain no operator would have the likes of him with his record and reputation working their precious mountain, he decided to spend a little time hunting. Get out his rifle, his other love, and get off a round or two at a deer. After watching the animal drop with a single, clean, perfect shot he suddenly made up his mind about what he was going to do. He immediately began planning details.

He had been a ski fanatic even as a child, a scrawny kid, often cutting school, always skulking around one or another of the mountains near his home in Vermont, listening to instructors teach rich kids, sneaking onto the lifts or stealing lift passes off jackets in the main lodge and skiing the slopes from sunup to dusk on a progression of stolen skis. He dropped out of high school in his junior year, bought an old heap, and drove from mountain to mountain, all over New England, satisfying himself that he was master of every slope. Having become a brilliant skier, he managed to get into a ski patrol the following year and within the two more years was the youngest No. 1 ever in the patrol at Stratton, one of his favorite mountains with its profusion of runs. Then he was drafted.

When he began planning his payoff to the operators for their kindness and consideration, he remembered the Old Imperial run at Connally Mountain, a tough isolated slope with an antiquated lift, bucket-like seats strung out some seventy-five feet apart, slow-moving, the patrol member in the shed at the top stopping the lift and helping each skier out of the bucket. The run was steep in places, and long, a challenging and satisfying run for even the best skiers, which explained its popularity despite the time-consuming ride to the top.

And he also remembered the bend in cable direction as the run approached the summit so that only two chairs at a time were in view from the shed. He had only to get a rifle with a removable stock, ride to the top of Old Imperial with the dismantled weapon strapped under his coat, shoot the attendant in the back, and take over the mountain. After making a good solid kill he'd simply leave the lift stopped, ski down, get into his car, and drive away. He'd be gone before the patrol could get up to the summit on the "cat" to check out the problem . . .

He watched the next chair turn the corner and move into view with another target, a guy in a fancy sweater and stocking cap. No heavy jacket. Probably a good skier. This would be the last one. Pop him off and call it quits. He'd gotten enough to leave his mark, to make that day on Connally long remembered. No use taking unnecessary chances.

He sighted in on a couple of stripes in the sweater's design, a hair left of center. Perfect. Follow the target for a second or two, maintain concentration, squeeze. But a split second before he fired, the skier reached down to touch his boot. He'd missed completely!

The skier looked up abruptly, stared at the shed and at patches of woods to the right and to the left. Then he flipped up the safety bar on the chair and leaped quickly out of the seat, not even bothering to take his poles, dropping the ten or fifteen feet to the snow and falling over.

How had he missed? He had to get off another shot! Drop him quick before he got to his feet and skied around the bend and out of sight. He lined up on the skier as the skier struggled upright to start downhill. The same two stripes, from the back instead of the front. He squeezed but the gun clicked harmlessly. Damn! Why hadn't he reloaded? Why hadn't he kept count? How could he have been so stupid?

The skier, starting a little slowly without poles, moved downward, gaining speed, and finally swept to the right, around the crook in the slope and out of view.

No need to panic. Just get rid of the gun and ski down. No clues. Nothing. He didn't know from nothing. That's all. No, he didn't see or hear anything. No fingerprints, even if they found the gun. He'd handled it with glove-liners and had rubbed it carefully to make sure. No panic, no panic.

He ran a few yards along the path to the summit, a spot just beyond the little hollow. The bodies were becoming speckled with snow. He stuffed the rifle into a drift near the base of a tree and smoothed over the spot where the gun went in. A few minutes of fresh snow and there'd be no trace. Nothing to worry about.

He hurried back to the shed, set down his skis, and stepped into them. Grabbing his poles and gloves, he moved back along the path. The lift was motionless, the nearest chair containing a crumpled body wearing skis, the second chair empty except for poles. He pushed off, skiing down the slope with style and grace.

The long ride down gave him time to think, to anticipate questions and plan his responses. No, he hadn't seen anything unusual going on. Accidents? No. Anybody with a gun? You kidding me? No. And no, he didn't know of any reason why nobody'd come down the slope in the last little while. No, he didn't know why the lift wasn't moving—it was running fine when he got up there and he'd taken a bad fall on the way down and had stopped and rested a few minutes to get himself back together.

He began to feel strangely chilled and realized that despite the air temperature and the wind of skiing and the snow in his face, his body was steamy with sweat.

He glanced up at skiers stranded in the unmoving chairs and hoped they'd still be hanging there, freezing their noses off, when he drove away. He looked down and ahead. A good slope. One of the best. Let the people in the chairs watch a pro take it down.

As he reached the lower stretches of the run and the main lodge came into view, he saw the "cat" just starting up the slope, carrying two members of the patrol, each wearing his bright blue jacket and blue hat. They had a long ride to the top. He was moving a lot faster. He had plenty of time. More than enough. He'd had much closer calls than this in Nam.

He continued down toward the area around the main lodge where all the lifts took on their loads and headed up the mountain. Lots of skiers. They'd remember this day at Connally. They might even lose some of their interest in skiing. He had only to get through the crowd unnoticed, over to the parking lot, then get the hell out of here.

As he drew nearer he was able to separate the crowd into individuals. He picked out the skier in the fancy sweater, the one he'd missed with his last shot. The guy was standing in a group, right where the slope leveled out, watching him approach. Nothing to worry about. They couldn't possibly know anything yet.

Several in the group wore the mountain's bright blue jackets. He recognized the honcho who ran the mountain, a big overage college Joe. He thought about the interview with him several months back and wondered if the creep would remember him. Then he spotted the fat guy who ran the ski school. And one or two more from the patrol. And a cop, the trooper, the big one with the mustache who'd been directing traffic, wearing his shiny, navy-blue jacket with the big badge and the fur collar, and the hat with the fur-lined earmuffs tied up and sticking out like wings. When it became obvious the group was waiting for him, he began plowing and slowed as he reached them.

"Excuse me," the honcho said, "but did you notice what's wrong at the top? The operator has stopped the lift and we don't know why."

No look of recognition. The creep didn't remember him. Still, his heart was pounding. This was it. The last hurdle. The parking lot was less than a hundred yards away. "Uh, everything looked okay to me when I was up top. I noticed the lift stopped, too. Why is that?"

"We thought you might be able to tell *us*. You just came down."

"No, as a matter of fact I left the top some time ago. Had a fall about halfway down. Stopped and rested awhile. Sprained my ankle a little." He felt dizzy from his churning pulse and wondered if they could tell.

"You seem all right, now."

"Yeah, it's a lot better."

"This man says someone took a shot at him up there. Did you hear anything that sounded like a shot?"

"Shot? You kidding? What kinda shot? Hell, don't say that. I'll be scared to go back up. No, I didn't hear any shot."

"Did you see anyone with anything that might have been a gun of any kind?" the cop asked. "Anything at all?"

He hesitated, to appear to be trying to remember. "No. Not a thing."

"Well, we've sent up two members of the patrol," the manager said. "We should know something in a few minutes."

"Probably nothing serious." He started to ski slowly out of the group and toward the parking lot.

"Hey," one of the ski patrol said. "What's that all over the shoulder of your jacket? Blood?"

He stopped and froze. His mouth fell open and he looked at all of them, his eyes going from face to face. The chick! He dropped his poles and clutched at his right shoulder with his left hand, still looking from face to face. As he did, his right arm dropped against his side and he felt the box of shells, still about half full, in his jacket pocket. He'd forgotten to bury them with the gun.

"Well? What about it?" The cop studied his face, then reached out and tugged at his shoulder to look at the stain.

He didn't answer.

"I think you'd better wait here with us till the patrol gets to the top," the cop said.

"Uh, I can't. I gotta get going. I really got to go." He thought about trying to run but he was on skis and he'd dropped his poles. And he was surrounded by blue jackets.

"So early?" the cop said. "You've got an eight-dollar lift ticket there and it's not even time to break for lunch yet. You'd just better wait here with us till we hear from the patrol."

The manager squinted at him and said, "You look very familiar. Have we met before?"

But he hadn't even heard the question. He'd just remembered something funny. The blood on his jacket wasn't fresh. He had worn the jacket hunting and had messed it up lifting the doe he'd shot. A silly grin spread across his face and he began to snigger and then laugh uncontrollably.

Sugar and Spice

JAMES CROSS

"Please send for M. Pierre," the Baron said. "We would like to congratulate him."

The Baron was a small, fat, arrogant man. Below a wispy mustache, over-red, over-full lips normally oscillated between sensuality and disdain. But this time he spoke politely, warmly, almost respectfully.

"At once, M. le Baron," the young waiter Étienne said. "M. Pierre will be honored."

He walked quickly toward the kitchen at the end of the rectangular dining room, with its high ceilings and gilded walls. Turner, the British solicitor, watched him disappear. Then he looked at the third man, his French colleague, Maître Suffren. Over Suffren's shoulder he caught sight of the Louis Quinze gilded clock. Already three, he thought, the business unfinished and the evening plane to be caught back to London.

"Briefly speaking," he said to Suffren, "our Treasury's position is this: the Treaty of Commerce and Amity gives preferential treatment to still French wines, bottled in France. However . . ."

"Then what is the trouble?" the Baron asked. "They *are* bottled in France. It can be proven. Not at the chateau, of course—I would not want my name on such swill—but not five kilometers away in the Commune of St. Fiacre. Very aptly named," he went on, "considering the travel these poor, helpless, little wines must undergo."

"That is precisely the point the Treasury make. They feel that the term 'bottled' implies 'produced,' and they further feel that the term 'France' is sufficiently clear so as to exclude the wine produced in your extensive Algerian holdings, transported from Algiers in ships like oil tankers, pumped into tank trucks at Marseilles and thence driven to St. Fiacre to be bottled. Good Lord, if you want to fool the consumers, send them bottled to the colonies. They wouldn't know the difference there."

"They are already going to Washington," the Baron replied, "by the ton. We have outlets there—one or two 'exclusive' liquor stores. You are right; they probably do not know the difference, only the label. But even that outlet cannot soak up the production of my Algerian vineyards."

"I have examined both the French and English versions of the Treaty," Maître Suffren added. "The wording is crystal clear: 'Mis en bouteilles—bottled.' There is nothing about where the wine is produced."

Turner shook his head. He wondered whether he would ever succeed in convincing continental clients, bred under quasi-Napoleonic law codes, that the British Common Law was a little different.

"The Treasury have been aware of this for some time. When Algeria was, in law, a department of France, there was naturally no trouble. But now to import wine from a third country, bottle it here, and seek to qualify it for preferential duty, well, the Treasury feel that this is a bit too much. You have brought me to Paris, gentlemen, to get my opinion. Now you have it. The Treasury are not going to budge, and you will lose your case—and get a good deal of unfavorable publicity into the bargain."

"Perhaps," Maître Suffren said, "perhaps some compromise rate of duty could be . . ."

"Shh," the Baron hissed imperiously, "here he comes."

The man who approached them was in clean and bright chef's cap and apron and white trousers—ones that had obviously been changed, since no working chef could keep that clean. He was short, but not really short like the Baron; he was stout but not really stout; he had blond hair but not really blond; his features were good but not really good—only even and unassuming. Turner knew something of the Baron's arrogance, so he was completely taken aback when the Baron, while the chef was still ten feet away, rose to his feet and applauded silently. Turner was still more surprised when the dry, Voltairean man of the law, Maître Suffren, did the same. He got up awkwardly himself, but he could not quite bring himself to silent applause. In a split second, the Baron and the lawyer resumed their seats and Turner followed them.

"As usual, my dear M. Pierre," the Baron began, "no, no— not as usual, better than usual, if that is possible. Those *quenelles de brochet*—I have never eaten the like in my life."

"M. le Baron is too generous," Pierre Chaptal replied, "but also impossible to deceive. There was a slight difference today, one that not one in a hundred caught. It is in the powder that goes in the sauce, the powder made from the shell of the *écrevisse*. Today, I added to it a touch of the powdered shell of the *homard*."

"I thought there was a difference," the Baron said genially. "You can't fool an old dog like me. But by all means do not change back. You have reached perfection."

"With the permission of M. le Baron," Chaptal replied, "I had considered that the changes I have made justify giving the dish a new name. I and the Restaurant Chaptal would both be honored if . . ."

"Not after me, my dear Chaptal," the Baron said, "but rather after the organization which has honored me with its presidency, the Companions of Lucullus."

"*Entendu*, M. le Baron. From now on, it shall be *quenelles de brochet* Companions of Lucullus. And now, with your permission, I must return to my post."

Turner looked at the Baron. His personal view was that the quenelles were nothing more than elongated Swedish fish balls (which he detested) swamped in a pinkish-reddish sauce. And crushed crayfish shells!—so that's how they got the color—not with tomato sauce, wonder if the stuff is really digestible. Next time, he thought, old Suffren's going to come to London, and we can have something decent for lunch—steak and kidney pie, not this molded fish stuff.

"Companions of Lucullus?" he said questioningly to Suffren. The Baron looked at him coldly.

"You have no doubt heard of Michelin, M. Turner," he said.

"By all means, chaps put out tires. Rather clever advertisement, sort of a man made out of tires. Very good product; I've used them myself."

"They also," the Baron said slowly, as if talking to one of his

Algerian grape-pickers, "publish a guide to the restaurants of France. Merely to be listed in Michelin is an honor. To be starred is to be ennobled. It is like your nobility, and at the very top are the greatest—the Dukes—the handful of restaurants that gain three stars. The Restaurant Chaptal and its chef and owner, Pierre Chaptal, have been so honored for seven successive years. My own title goes back to Hugh Capet; nevertheless, I rise to applaud Pierre Chaptal."

"It is a very serious matter, the Michelin ratings," Maître Suffren broke in. "And not merely financially—though that is important; a restaurant proprietor can go from penury to wealth and then down again to the dustbin in a matter of months or weeks, all depending upon the stars. He can be a name to rank with de Gaulle or Picasso and then a nobody. I tell you there have been men driven to death or madness by the Michelin ratings. And there is no resting on the oars—the ratings are for a single year and are subject to revision. An investigator may be sitting at the next table at this moment."

Turner looked nervously to his left, expecting a uniformed official with a notebook. All he could see was an enormously fat man eating what appeared to be the head of a small calf with evident relish.

"But the Companions of Lucullus?" he asked.

"I have told you about Michelin," the Baron said, "and how powerful their ratings are. Well, that is merely for the bourgeois. The Companions of Lucullus also publish ratings of restaurants—in a small edition of some hundred-odd copies at a thousand francs and available only to the elected members. Believe me, my dear M. Turner, compared to the Lucullan's guide that of Michelin is like the wine I have transported in tankers from Algeria compared to that which I grow at my chateau for my own use. Not that we can ever prove it," he went on, "but it is my belief that, despite all of their talk of inspectors, the Michelin somehow gets a peek at our ratings before they make their own."

"Most amazing," Turner said. What a fuss to make over food, he thought.

"When I rose for M. Chaptal," the Baron said, "it was the tribute of birth to genius. But ten years ago Chaptal was less than nothing, and ten years from now he might be nothing again, while even bankrupt or in prison, I still remain the Baron de Coutras. The difference, M. Turner, between birth and genius."

Good God, Turner thought, the man's halfway round the bend. He was relieved when the Baron signed the bill in a lordly manner and after having walked with them to the door, left Turner to the relatively simple Cartesian legalism of Maître Suffren.

Back in the kitchen, Pierre Chaptal breathed deeply, feeling his heart pumping crazily. He had been through such scenes a thousand times by now—discussing advance menus with wealthy gourmets, accepting congratulations, even—on rare occasions—discussing *haute cuisine* in his kitchen while from the corner of his eye he stood sentry over his assistants: the vegetable boy dicing carrots and scallions and leeks; the soup cook stirring the pot; the *pâtissier* peering into the pastry ovens and superintending the icing and glazing of fantastic pyramids and cones and hexagons. One day, he thought, they will catch me. He glanced up to see the young waiter Étienne staring at him.

"Yes," Chaptal said brusquely, "yes, what is it?"

"It is what we talked about last week, M. Chaptal. I would like to start in the kitchen. I realize that the pay will be less and that there will be a long apprenticeship, but I wish someday to be a great chef."

Chaptal screwed his face into something approaching a kindly smile.

"Impossible," he said sadly. "You are already ten years too old. Your career is set. Concentrate on the service and one day we will see you as *sommelier* or even *maître d'hôtel.*"

The young man walked away gloomily and Chaptal, putting his hands behind his back, took his pulse surreptitiously. Just as he thought, it was racing. The whole thing was impossible. He could keep it up no longer. One day, he would start screaming and give the whole thing away; and it would be the padded cell for him or, with more luck, the quick leap from the tall building. But either would be better than the laughter and the scorn.

It was really quite simple. Pierre Chaptal could discourse on food and wines like Brillat-Savarin; he could plan a dinner as well as Escoffier; he could visualize a new dish with the genius of the unfortunate Vatel. He simply could not cook. Like Einstein with simple arithmetic; like a genius of chemistry who cannot conduct a simple test-tube experiment; like Wagner forcing his guests to listen to him play the piano—when it came to basic simple jobs that the rawest apprentice could manage, Chaptal turned into a culinary idiot. Under his clumsy fingers, the gently firm quenelles became soggy or friable; the hollandaise curdled; wine corks broke in the bottle; the tenderest beef, the true Charolais, toughened under the flame; the finest asparagus broke in half.

Such a situation is not as rare as one might believe. There are many small restaurants in France where the man of the house is proprietor and apparent chef (since it is a folk belief that only men can cook seriously) while in fact the wife does the cooking. For a modest family business, with the daughter behind the *caisse* and the son-in-law waiting on tables, it is quite acceptable. But not for a three-star restaurant in Michelin and accolades from the Companions of Lucullus. There, it is the chef who makes the restaurant, who gains the stars. For such things as decor and service and price, Michelin uses not stars but forks and not three but four; but a restaurant marked in the guidebook with three or four forks but no stars is simply an overpriced tourist trap. Without Chaptal's reputation as one of the best, the Restaurant Chaptal would simply have forks, not stars.

He glanced around the kitchen, noting that all the apprentices and under-chefs were working assiduously. Then he opened the door that led to the inner kitchen, where his wife, Marie-Claude, translated his thoughts and words and commands into food. She was putting a brisket of beef into the great *fonte d'acier* cooking pot. The dish had been ordered in advance for a party of six for the next day. For about twenty-four hours the beef would simmer in little more than its own juice plus spices and a little wine. At rare intervals, the close-fitting lid would be lifted while carrots, turnips, parsnips, and potatoes would be deftly slipped in, and then at precisely noon the next day the deceptively simple peasant dish would be ready to serve. If the guests came early, they would have to wait; if they were a little late, they would have to suffer M. Chaptal's pained disgust; if they were really late, the pot-au-feu would be served to the kitchen staff and the guests would still be charged for it and asked to order something else, or to leave.

He looked at his wife. She was still remarkably attractive. The golden hair had faded a bit; the strong, Grecian features had coarsened imperceptibly; there was the suspicion of an *embonpoint;* but she was still a sensually handsome woman. If during one of his buying trips, Chaptal had picked the equivalent up at some café, he would go to bed with her at once. Logically, there was no reason why Marie-Claude herself did not attract him, but there it was. Perhaps it was Solange, the new girl at the cashier's desk, with her long black hair and the miniskirt and the black net stockings and the green eyeshadow and the near-white lipstick. The first time, three months before, at the room-by-the-hour hotel off the Élysées, she had run her lips and tongue over him from foot to brow and then wrapped her long, sinuous legs around him, biting his neck and tearing his back with her sharp nails when she came twice to his carefully nurtured spasm. It was after that that he no longer felt for Marie-Claude. Whatever suspicions she may have had, it was not necessary to question him or to speak; she knew and Chaptal was aware that she knew.

"The Baron has invited us to name the new quenelles after the Lucullans," Chaptal said.

"He has good taste, the Baron," Marie-Claude replied, "though personally I would like to see him and all his Companions sneezing in the basket. Titles," she went on, "in a Republic, what a farce."

"We make our living from them, my dear," Chaptal said.

"I am quite aware of that, Pierre. Did you speak to Étienne? He was looking for you. I think he has a real talent."

Chaptal laughed.

"Perhaps if he had started at the age of ten. As it is, he is quick, intelligent, handsome, soft-spoken—the ladies are most appreciative—we can bring him on, and one day he may qualify for *sommelier* or even *maître d'hôtel.*"

"He's a good young man," Marie-Claude said, "and he has his heart set on it."

"Then let him go somewhere else."

For a moment, Chaptal wondered whether Marie-Claude had taken Étienne as a lover. But the thought almost made him laugh. She was twenty years older, she was dedicated to the restaurant and to the income and prestige it gave them; she was more interested in a perfect *boeuf en daube* or *jambon en croûte* than a roll in the hay. If she had any feeling for Étienne, it was in terms of the male child she had lost, who would have been almost the age of Étienne. Let her feed Étienne, let her mother him—anything, just so long as she attends to her cooking.

Marie-Claude was staring at him coldly, and for a moment Chaptal felt afraid. This woman could ruin me. It was true that she would ruin the Restaurant Chaptal and herself into the bargain, but women were notoriously emotional and sentimental.

He smiled at her.

"Look," he said, "Étienne is doing well. Let him stay as he is, learning, up front for the next six months. Then we can consider the kitchen. But let's not go too far; he's not a member of the family. There's no point teaching him how to be a proprietor; that way we just lose a good waiter and gain a possible rival."

"I know it very well," Marie-Claude said calmly.

The weeks passed, and the months. From time to time, individual members of the Companions of Lucullus lunched or dined at the restaurant, and always went away happy. Chaptal himself was by no means purely happy. On the one hand, the hours with Solange seemed to renew his youth and vigor; on the other hand, he was no longer as young as he felt. The gorgeous hours, as Voltaire had pointed out two centuries before, were paid for with lassitude, muscle pains, sharp twinges in the lower abdomen. Moreover, Solange, for all her sexual abandon, never forgot that she worked at the cash register: there were three raises, innumerable trips to Italy. It was not that she made much of a dent in profits; it was the fear that Marie-Claude might question the accounts someday. As a matter of course, Chaptal kept two account books: one for the tax collectors, the other for himself. Now, under the importunities of Solange, he was forced to keep a third—for Marie-Claude.

When the annual dinner of the inner circle of the Companions of Lucullus—some ten out of a hundred members—came around, Chaptal had almost a feeling of relief. It had always gone well; it would go well this year; he would keep his Lucullan rating and his Michelin rating. The Restaurant Chaptal would continue to wear the three stars.

Perhaps it was Solange, perhaps it was the champagne and brandy, perhaps it was the waiting and the tension, perhaps it was just middle age—whatever it was, just two days before the Lucullan dinner, Chaptal felt gnawing pains in his side—*"maladie de foie,"* the disease of the restaurant proprietor, the doctor called it; and blazing agony in his left big toe—*"la maladie anglaise,"* the gout. The doctor recommended one of the innumerable hot-springs cures of France, but Chaptal could not be that far away from the restaurant. He stretched out on the twin bed in his upstairs apartment and followed the Évian regime of abstinence and mineral water. Nothing could go wrong, but if anything did, he would be within easy call.

His first intimation that something had indeed gone wrong was when Marie-Claude came up after the dinner.

"How was it?" Chaptal asked.

Marie-Claude looked at him and sighed. Then she took off her shoes, sprawled flat across the other twin bed, and lit a cigarette.

"A disaster," she said. "If we keep a single star, we're lucky."

Chaptal felt his heart beating fast and a cold pang in his stomach.

"What the hell went wrong?"

"Everything. First of all, this is the time of my period. You know what your old grandmother believed: women in that state turn the cream sour, curdle the sauces, make the meat tough, ruin the meal. Well, that was just the beginning. The pastrycook, Abdul the Algerian, got in a fight with Hamid, the other Algerian, the vegetable apprentice. So they had it out with kitchen knives and we had to call the police. Then one of the *flics* gave us a summons into the bargain—it appears that our exhaust fans from the kitchen are bothering a neighbor. Then Tino was bringing up the Corton-Charlemagne for the fowl course and he broke the bottles, so we had to serve new bottles only half chilled. I tell you if I hadn't brought Étienne into the kitchen to help out, it would have been a complete *sauve qui peut*."

"The Baron," Chaptal gasped, "what did he say?"

"Not a thing; he just looked gloomy. Oh yes, he did say he'd get in touch with you."

"Oh God," Chaptal said, "we're finished."

"Wait awhile; see what the Baron has to say."

The next day, the Baron made it very clear. The immediate reaction of the subcommittee of the Companions of Lucullus was to remove the Restaurant Chaptal from their listings completely—not a matter of moving down from three stars, but of utter ostracism. He, the Baron, on the basis of the meal they were served, must admit that he had to agree with the harsh verdict. Nevertheless, because of the honored reputation of the Restaurant Chaptal for seven years, and because of Chaptal's unavoidable absence, he had convinced the Companions that it deserved another chance. In precisely one week, he, the Baron, and three companions would give the restaurant one final test. He was warning Chaptal because he respected him and because he wanted to give him the opportunity to put everything in order.

For the second visit of the Companions of Lucullus, Chaptal took no chances. He closed the restaurant to the public. He hired additional backup under-chefs. He contributed heavily to the local police charity to ward off any complaints. He was at the restaurant at 7 A.M. writing out the menu that he had worked on for a week, running over every point with his staff, and conferring frequently with his wife. His attention was so focused that when he stood by the cashier's desk, warning Solange that the bill would be signed for and not paid in cash, he was cold and unreactive when she ran her hand slowly up his leg.

The subcommittee arrived at precisely eight. Instead of four, there were five. For some unknown reason, the Baron had invited the English lawyer, M. Turner. The first course went well. With the caviar, Chaptal provided the driest of champagnes. The oysters—it was hard to ruin oysters on the half shell—were equally successful. The trouble began with the *quenelles de brochet*, a specialty of the house. From his vantage point, Chaptal saw the Englishman, Turner, remove a large piece of *écrevisse* shell from the sauce and put it carefully on the side of his plate; he saw Maître Suffren hold up a forkful of the thick sauce, taste it, then put it aside; he saw two others of the members leave the quenelles half eaten; and finally he saw the Baron push the dish away after one mouthful.

For the main course, Chaptal had ordered beef Wellington. Before it was served, he personally poured the Grands Échézeaux. He extracted the cork carefully, poured off the cork in a quarter glass. Then he poured the first glass for the Baron. The Baron sipped slowly, then a look of disgust came over his face as he removed a piece of cork from his mouth.

"My dear Chaptal," the Baron said, "it is very hard to say whether your Échézeaux is good or bad, with cork in my mouth. All I can say is that it is perhaps slightly better than the tanker wine I grow in Algeria."

Chaptal stood immobile. Then he took the Baron's glass and gave him a new one.

"A thousand pardons, M. le Baron," he said nervously.

The Baron tasted and wrinkled his lips in disgust.

"I was mistaken," the Baron said, "it is worse than the Algerian."

The beef Wellington arrived and Chaptal prepared to slice it: to cut through the crisp pastry, through the layer of pâté, into the true filet of beef with its dark crusty shell and its inner juicy redness. *Merde alors*, he thought. The pastry shell was not cooked; there was a floury sogginess as he drew the knife through it. Inside, the beef did not give him the expected resistance as the knife went through the crisp outer layer into the heart of the filet. It was rubbery. He finished the carving of the five servings like a man in a trance. He already knew what the rest of the meal would be like. The haricots would be mushy and stringy; the salad would be drab and flat; the sherbet half melted and acid; the fruit overripe; the pastry dry; the coffee weak *and* bitter; the brandy soapy. That bitch, he thought, she's ruined me.

He fled to the living quarters upstairs. It was too much. Somewhere in a desk drawer was the last souvenir of his father who had been in the Resistance and had been decorated posthumously: a little capsule, cyanide enclosed in gelatin, one quick bite and all his troubles were over. When he lay down on the bed, the first thing he felt was like a hard blow to the head; then a clutching hand on his throat, and then a sharp pain near his heart; and then nothing but a little froth of spittle at his mouth.

In the kitchen, there was a complete confusion and dismay. A vegetable apprentice had actually lit a cigarette; the pastrycook was pouring himself a large glass of cognac. Even the young waiter, Étienne, who had come in from the dining room, stood there helplessly, looking miserable. Marie-Claude suddenly came out of the inner kitchen. She walked up to the apprentice and knocked the cigarette from his lips, grinding it under her toe on the floor; she took the cognac glass away from the pastrycook and poured it down the drain.

"When it's all over," she said, "you can have the whole bottle; but right now, all of you get back to your posts. It can still be saved. Where is M. Chaptal?"

"He ran upstairs, madame. He looked terrible."

Madame Chaptal raced up to the apartment, opened the door quietly. A small bed lamp was still on. She moved closer to the bed and looked down at her husband. A few days, she thought. I thought he would stick it out until the actual ratings appeared; but he couldn't even last three courses. She smiled coldly on the dead man; then she returned to the kitchen.

"M. Chaptal is indisposed," she told the staff. "We are going to carry on without him. Léon, Benoît, start clearing the table. Étienne, stand by for a new serving of quenelles. I'll have them for you by the time you return. The rest of you continue as planned, but hold everything back about half an hour."

She went outside to the table.

"M. le Baron," she said, "I am Madame Chaptal. I come to tell you that my husband is again indisposed. I also come to tell you that he was aware of his sickness and feared that something like this might happen. Thus, arrangements were made that any dishes found to be deficient should be duplicated. M. le Baron," she went on, "messieurs, I beg of you, do not judge us yet. In a matter of minutes, you will have the quenelles again, newly created as they should have been, and then the beef; and with them the good wines. Be just, messieurs, and judge us on our best."

As she spoke, one of her hands reached out to a serving table and retrieved the cork from the Échézeaux—the cork she had carefully grooved twenty-four hours before to let in the air; the bottle she had opened and to which she had added pieces of cork and then resealed.

The Baron smiled. A damned attractive woman, he thought; no wonder Chaptal kept her locked away in back. He turned to his guests.

"I feel it's only fair to give them a chance."

"Hear, hear!" Turner said, wondering what all the fuss was about. True, the dinner was rather poor, with all its sauces and pastry crusts; but then so had the lunch been, and the Baron had literally raved about it.

The others nodded.

"Very well, then," the Baron said. "It is very irregular, but still . . . Madame Chaptal, we are in your hands."

Before the new quenelles were served, the Baron carefully refreshed his palate with a little bread and water. He held the forkful in his mouth like a baby refusing to swallow. He chewed, more with his tongue than his teeth. Then he swallowed and beamed ecstatically. He turned to Étienne.

"So far," he said, "you may tell Madame that all goes well. The quenelles are, if anything, better than the memorable lunch."

After that, it was all triumph. The wines were superb. The substitute beef Wellington was better even than the quenelles. There was nothing that was not perfection. After the coffee and his first Armagnac, the Baron excused himself and asked Étienne to bring him out to the kitchen. Marie-Claude was there to greet him.

"I must have a word with Chaptal," he said. "God knows

what went wrong, but the real meal more than made up for it. We are exacting, but to genius, we can be generous. I'd like to tell him that he need fear no more about losing his stars."

"He would be honored to hear it from you, M. le Baron, but he appears to be asleep. He is a very nervous man, and the tension and the first failure were too much."

The Baron looked at her sharply.

"Do you cook yourself, madame?"

"A little, M. le Baron; my husband has instructed me."

"Tell me honestly, did you cook the second meal tonight?"

"Under my husband's instructions that he gave me in advance."

The Baron looked at her steadily.

"Perhaps we can discuss the matter later," he said. "Over lunch. I cannot offer you a meal to match tonight; but I do myself tolerably well in my apartment, and there is a penthouse and a view."

"I should be honored, M. le Baron."

"I like pretty women to call me Albert," the Baron said. *À bientôt.*"

Marie-Claude walked slowly upstairs for the second time. When she arrived at the bedroom, she looked carefully at Chaptal. She leaned down to listen for the heartbeat again, but all she could sense was the faint smell of bitter almond. She looked at the dead man for a long moment; then she covered him with a sheet and blanket. She would call the police in the morning.

By the time she arrived downstairs, the Companions of Lucullus were putting on their coats. Marie-Claude saw them to the door. In a few minutes the table was cleared, the dishes were washed. She dismissed the waiters and the kitchen help. Then she turned to Solange at the cashier's desk.

"After today," she said calmly, "we won't be needing you."

The girl started to reply; then she shrugged her shoulders, put on her coat, and started for the door. She paused for a moment before leaving.

"M. Chaptal is going to have something to say about this," she said.

"I think you will find that M. Chaptal will not argue with me over a skinny little *poule,*" Marie-Claude said calmly.

When the restaurant was finally empty except for Étienne, Marie-Claude locked the doors and walked slowly up to the young man. She kissed him very hard on the mouth, feeling him straining against her. After a minute, she pushed him slowly away.

"Be patient, Tiennot," she said. "There's all night for us, but first we're going to have a real meal—my God but cooking's a hungry business. We're going to have the meal I could have cooked the first time if I had wanted to. And then we're going to talk about your future. By the way," she went on, "I never asked you your last name."

"Sarraut," he said, "Étienne Sarraut."

"Restaurant Sarraut," she said, almost to herself, "no, it would never do." She turned to Étienne. "M. Chaptal is a very sick man, so sick that I don't think he will ever cook again. But there is the name, and the name means something. And the stars, too. We are safe for a year, but we're going to have to work very hard. Poor Pierre, despite everything, he never has had the right temperament for this business."

The Nine-to-Five Man

STANLEY ELLIN

The alarm clock sounded, as it did every weekday morning, at exactly 7:20, and without opening his eyes Mr. Keesler reached out a hand and turned it off. His wife was already preparing breakfast—it was her modest boast that she had a built-in alarm to get her up in the morning—and a smell of frying bacon permeated the bedroom. Mr. Keesler savored it for a moment, lying there on his back with his eyes closed, and then wearily sat up and swung his feet out of bed. His eyeglasses were on the night table next to the alarm clock. He put them on and blinked in the morning light, yawned, scratched his head with pleasure, and fumbled for his slippers.

The pleasure turned to mild irritation. One slipper was not there. He kneeled down, swept his hand back and forth under the bed, and finally found it. He stood up, puffing a little, and went into the bathroom. After lathering his face he discovered that his razor was dull, and discovered immediately afterward that he had forgotten to buy new blades the day before. By taking a few minutes more than usual he managed to get a presentable, though painful, shave out of the old blade. Then he washed, brushed his teeth carefully, and combed his hair. He liked to say that he was in pretty good shape since he still had teeth and hair enough to need brushing.

In the bedroom again, he heard Mrs. Keesler's voice rising from the foot of the stairway. "Breakfast, dear," she called. "It's on the table now."

It was not really on the table, Mr. Keesler knew; his wife would first be setting the table when he walked into the kitchen. She was like that, always using little tricks to make the house run smoothly. But no matter how you looked at it, she was a sweetheart all right. He nodded soberly at his reflection in the dresser mirror while he knotted his tie. He was a lucky man to have a wife like that. A fine wife, a fine mother— maybe a little bit too much of an easy mark for her relatives— but a real sweetheart.

The small annoyance of the relatives came up at the breakfast table.

"Joe and Betty are expecting us over tonight, dear," said Mrs. Keesler. "Betty called me about it yesterday. Is that all right with you?"

"All right," said Mr. Keesler amiably. He knew there was nothing good on television that evening anyhow.

"Then will you remember to pick up your other suit at the tailor's on the way home?"

"For Betty and Joe?" said Mr. Keesler. "What for? They're only in-laws."

"Still and all, I like you to look nice when you go over there, so please don't forget." Mrs. Keesler hesitated. "Albert's going to be there, too."

"Naturally. He lives there."

"I know, but you hardly ever get a chance to see him, and, after all, he's our nephew. He happens to be a very nice boy."

"All right, he's a very nice boy," said Mr. Keesler. "What does he want from me?"

Mrs. Keesler blushed. "Well, it so happens he's having a very hard time getting a job where—"

"No," said Mr. Keesler. "Absolutely not." He put down his knife and fork and regarded his wife sternly. "You know yourself that there's hardly enough money in the novelties line to make us a living. So for me to take in a lazy—"

"I'm sorry," said Mrs. Keesler. "I didn't mean to get you upset about it." She put a consoling hand on his. "And what kind of thing is that to say, about not making a living? Maybe we don't have as much as some others, but we do all right. A nice house and two fine sons in college—what more could we ask for? So don't talk like that. And go to work, or you'll be late."

Mr. Keesler shook his head. "What a softie," he said. "If you only wouldn't let Betty talk you into these things—"

"Now don't start with that. Just go to work."

She helped him on with his coat in the hallway. "Are you going to take the car today?" she asked.

"No."

"All right, then I can use it for the shopping. But don't forget about the suit. It's the tailor right near the subway station." Mrs. Keesler plucked a piece of lint from his coat collar. "And you make a very nice living, so stop talking like that. We do all right."

Mr. Keesler left the house by the side door. It was an unpretentious frame house in the Flatbush section of Brooklyn, and like most of the others on the block it had a small garage behind it. Mr. Keesler unlocked the door of the garage and stepped inside. The car occupied nearly all the space there, but room had also been found for a clutter of tools, metal cans, paintbrushes, and a couple of old kitchen chairs which had been partly painted.

The car itself was a four-year-old Chevrolet, a little the

worse for wear, and it took an effort to open the lid of its trunk. Mr. Keesler finally got it open and lifted out his big leather sample case, groaning at its weight. He did not lock the garage door when he left, since he had the only key to it, and he knew Mrs. Keesler wanted to use the car.

It was a two block walk to the Beverley Road station of the IRT subway. At a newsstand near the station Mr. Keesler bought a New York *Times,* and when the train came in he arranged himself against the door at the end of the car. There was no chance of getting a seat during the rush hour, but from long experience Mr. Keesler knew how to travel with the least inconvenience. By standing with his back braced against the door and his legs astride the sample case he was able to read his newspaper until, by the time the train reached 14th Street, the press of bodies against him made it impossible to turn the pages.

At 42nd Street he managed to push his way out of the car using the sample case as a battering ram. He crossed the platform and took a local two stations farther to Columbus Circle. When he walked up the stairs of the station he saw by his wristwatch that it was exactly five minutes to nine.

Mr. Keesler's office was in the smallest and shabbiest building on Columbus Circle. It was made to look even smaller and shabbier by the new Coliseum which loomed over it on one side and by the apartment hotels which towered over it on the other. It had one creaky elevator to service its occupants, and an old man named Eddie to operate the elevator.

When Mr. Keesler came into the building Eddie had his mail all ready for him. The mail consisted of a large bundle of letters tied with a string, and a half dozen small cardboard boxes. Mr. Keesler managed to get all this under one arm with difficulty, and Eddie said, "Well, that's a nice big load the same as ever. I hope you get some business out of it."

"I hope so," said Mr. Keesler.

Another tenant picked up his mail and stepped into the elevator behind Mr. Keesler. "Well," he said, looking at the load under Mr. Keesler's arm, "it's nice to see that somebody's making money around here."

"Sure," said Mr. Keesler. "They send you the orders all

right, but when it comes to paying for them where are they?"

"That's how it goes," said Eddie.

He took the elevator up to the third floor and Mr. Keesler got out there. His office was in Room 301 at the end of the corridor, and on its door were painted the words KEESLER NOVELTIES. Underneath in quotation marks was the phrase *"Everything for the trade."*

The office was a room with a window that looked out over Central Park. Against one wall was a battered rolltop desk that Mr. Keesler's father had bought when he himself had started in the novelties business long ago, and before it was a large, comfortable swivel chair with a foam-rubber cushion on its seat. Against the opposite wall was a table, and on it was an old L. C. Smith typewriter, a telephone, some telephone books, and a stack of magazines. There was another stack of magazines on top of a large filing cabinet in a corner of the room. Under the window was a chaise longue which Mr. Keesler had bought secondhand from Eddie for five dollars, and next to the rolltop desk were a wastepaper basket and a wooden coatrack that he had bought from Eddie for fifty cents. Tenants who moved from the building sometimes found it cheaper to abandon their shopworn furnishings than to pay cartage for them, and Eddie did a small business in selling these articles for whatever he was offered.

Mr. Keesler closed the office door behind him. He gratefully set the heavy sample case down in a corner, pushed open the desk, and dropped his mail and the New York *Times* on it. Then he hung his hat and coat on the rack, checking the pockets of the coat to make sure he had forgotten nothing in them.

He sat down at the desk, opened the string around the mail, and looked at the return address on each letter. Two of the letters were from banks. He unlocked a drawer of the desk, drew out a notebook, and entered the figures into it. Then he tore the receipts into small shreds and dropped them into the wastepaper basket.

The rest of the mail was easily disposed of. Mr. Keesler took each of the smaller envelopes and, without opening it, tore it in half and tossed it into the basket on top of the shredded deposit slips. He then opened the envelopes which were thick and unwieldy, extracted their contents—brochures and catalogues—and placed them on the desk. When he was finished he had a neat pile of catalogues and brochures before him. These he dumped into a drawer of the filing cabinet.

He now turned his attention to the cardboard boxes. He opened them and pulled out various odds and ends—good-luck charms, a souvenir coin, a plastic key-ring, several packets of cancelled foreign stamps, and a small cellophane bag containing one chocolate cracker. Mr. Keesler tossed the empty boxes into the wastepaper basket, ate the cracker, and pushed the rest of the stuff to the back of the desk. The cracker was a little bit too sweet for his taste, but not bad.

In the top drawer of the desk were a pair of scissors, a box of stationery, and a box of stamps. Mr. Keesler removed these to the table and placed them next to the typewriter. He wheeled the swivel chair to the table, sat down, and opened the classified telephone directory to its listing of dentists. He ran his finger down a column of names. Then he picked up the phone and dialed a number.

"Dr. Glover's office," said a woman's voice.

"Look," said Mr. Keesler, "this is an emergency. I'm in the neighborhood here, so can I come in during the afternoon? It hurts pretty bad."

"Are you a regular patient of Dr. Glover's?"

"No, but I thought—"

"I'm sorry, but the doctor's schedule is full. If you want to call again tomorrow—"

"No, never mind," said Mr. Keesler. "I'll try someone else."

He ran his finger down the column in the directory and dialed again.

"This is Dr. Gordon's office," said a woman's voice, but much more youthful and pleasant than the one Mr. Keesler had just encountered. "Who is it, please?"

"Look," said Mr. Keesler, "I'm suffering a lot of pain, and I was wondering if the doctor couldn't give me a couple of minutes this afternoon. I'm right in the neighborhood here. I can be there any time that's convenient. Say around two o'clock?"

"Well, two o'clock is already filled, but I have a cancellation here for three. Would that be all right?"

"That would be fine. And the name is Keesler." Mr. Keesler spelled it out carefully. "Thanks a lot, miss, and I'll be there right on the dot."

He pressed the bar of the phone down, released it, and dialed again. "Is Mr. Hummel there?" he said. "Good. Tell him it's about the big delivery he was expecting this afternoon."

In a moment he heard Mr. Hummel's voice. "Yeah?"

"You know who this is?" asked Mr. Keesler.

"Sure I know who it is."

"All right," said Mr. Keesler, "then meet me at four o'clock instead of three. You understand?"

"I get it," said Mr. Hummel.

Mr. Keesler did not continue the conversation. He put down the phone, pushed aside the directory, and took a magazine from the pile on the table. The back pages of the magazine were full of advertisements for free gifts, free samples, and free catalogues. *Mail us this coupon,* most of them said, *and we will send you absolutely free—*

Mr. Keesler studied these offers, finally selected ten of them, cut out the coupons with his scissors, and addressed them on the typewriter. He typed slowly but accurately, using only two fingers. Then he addressed ten envelopes, sealed the coupons into them, and stamped them. He snapped a rubber band around the envelopes for easier mailing and put everything else in the office back into its proper place. It was now 10:25, and the only thing left to attend to was the New York *Times*.

By twelve o'clock, Mr. Keesler, stretched comfortably out on the chaise longue, had finished reading the *Times*. He had, however, bypassed the stock market quotations as was his custom. In 1929 his father's entire capital had been wiped out overnight in the market crash, and since that day Mr. Keesler had a cold and cynical antipathy to stocks and bonds and anything connected with them. When talking to people about it he would make it a little joke. "I like to know that my money is all tied up in cash," he would say. But inwardly he had been deeply scarred by what his father had gone through after the debacle. He had been very fond of his father, a gentle and hard-working man, well-liked by all who knew him, and had never forgiven the stock market for what it had done to him.

Twelve o'clock was lunchtime for Mr. Keesler, as it was for almost everyone else in the building. Carrying his mail, he walked downstairs along with many others who knew that it would take Eddie quite a while to pick them up in his over-worked elevator at this hour. He dropped the letters into a mailbox on the corner, and banged the lid of the mailbox a couple of times for safety's sake.

Near 58th Street on Eighth Avenue was a cafeteria which served good food at reasonable prices, and Mr. Keesler had a cheese sandwich, baked apple, and coffee there. Before he left he had a counterman wrap a cinnamon bun in waxed paper and place it in a brown paper bag for him to take along with him.

Swinging the bag in his hand as he walked, Mr. Keesler went into a drugstore a block away and bought a roll of two-inch-wide surgical bandage. On his way out of the store he surreptitiously removed the bandage from its box and wrapper and dropped the box and wrapper into a litter basket on the street. The roll of bandage itself he put into the bag containing the cinnamon bun.

He repeated this process in a drugstore on the next block, and then six more times in various stores on his way down Eighth Avenue. Each time he would pay the exact amount in change, drop the box and wrappings into a litter basket, put the roll of bandage into his paper bag. When he had eight rolls of bandage in the bag on top of the cinnamon bun he turned around and walked back to the office building. It was exactly one o'clock when he got there.

Eddie was waiting in the elevator, and when he saw the paper bag he smiled toothlessly and said as he always did, "What is it this time?"

"Cinnamon buns," said Mr. Keesler. "Here, have one." He pulled out the cinnamon bun wrapped in its waxed paper, and Eddie took it.

"Thanks," he said.

"That's all right," said Mr. Keesler. "There's plenty here for both of us. I shouldn't be eating so much of this stuff anyhow."

At the third floor he asked Eddie to hold the elevator, he'd be out in a minute. "I just have to pick up the sample case," he said. "Got to get to work on the customers."

In the office he lifted the sample case to the desk, put the eight rolls of bandage in it, and threw away the now empty paper bag into the wastepaper basket. With the sample case weighing him down he made his way back to the elevator.

"This thing weighs more every time I pick it up," he said to Eddie as the elevator went down, and Eddie said, "Well, that's the way it goes. We're none of us as young as we used to be."

A block away from Columbus Circle, Mr. Keesler took an Independent Line subway train to East Broadway, not far from Manhattan Bridge. He ascended into the light of Straus Square, walked down to Water Street, and turned left there. His destination was near Montgomery Street, but he stopped before he came to it and looked around.

The neighborhood was an area of old warehouses, decaying tenements, and raw, new housing projects. The street Mr. Keesler was interested in, however, contained only warehouses. Blackened with age they stood in a row looking like ancient fortresses. There was a mixed smell of refuse and salt water around them that invited coveys of pigeons and sea gulls to fly overhead.

Mr. Keesler paid no attention to the birds, nor to the few waifs and strays on the street. Hefting his sample case, he turned into an alley which led between two warehouses and made his way to the vast and empty lot behind them. He walked along until he came to a metal door in the third warehouse down the row. Using a large, old-fashioned key, he opened the door, stepped into the blackness beyond it, and closed it behind him, locking it from the inside and testing it to make sure it was locked.

There was a light switch on the wall near the door. Mr. Keesler put down his sample case and wrapped a handkerchief loosely around his hand. He fumbled along the wall with that hand until he found the switch, and when he pressed it a dim light suffused the building. Since the windows of the building were sealed by metal shutters, the light could not be seen outside. Mr. Keesler then put away the handkerchief and carried the sample case across the vast expanse of the warehouse to the huge door of the delivery entrance that faced on the street.

Near the door was a long plank table on which was a time-stamper, a few old receipt books, and some pencil stubs. Mr. Keesler put down the sample case, took off his coat, neatly folded it and laid it on the table, and placed his hat on top of it. He bent over the sample case and opened it. From it he took the eight rolls of bandage, a large tube of fixative called Quick-Dry, a four-inch length of plumber's candle, two metal cans each containing two gallons of high octane gasoline, six paper drinking cups, a two-yard length of fishline, a handful of soiled linen rags, and a pair of rubber gloves much spattered with drops of dried paint. All this he arranged on the table.

Now donning the rubber gloves he picked up the length of fishline and made a series of loops in it. He fitted a roll of bandage into each loop and drew the string tight. When he held it up at arm's length it looked like a string of white fishing bobbers.

Each gasoline tin had a small spout and looked as if it were tightly sealed. But the lid of one could be removed entirely and Mr. Keesler pried at it until it came off. He lowered the line of rolled bandages into the can, leaving the end of the string dangling over the edge for ready handling. A few bubbles broke at the surface of the can as the gauze bandages started to soak up gasoline. Mr. Keesler observed this with satisfaction, and then, taking the tube of Quick-Dry with him, he made a thoughtful tour of inspection of the warehouse.

What he saw was a broad and high steel framework running through the center of the building from end to end and supporting a great number of cardboard boxes, wooden cases, and paper-covered rolls of cloth. More boxes and cases were stacked nearly ceiling-high against two walls of the room.

He surveyed everything carefully, wrinkling his nose against the sour odor of mold that rose around him. He tested a few of the cardboard boxes by pulling away loose pieces, and found them all as dry as dust.

Then having studied everything to his satisfaction he kneeled down at a point midway between the steel framework and the angle of the two walls where the cases were stacked highest and squeezed some fixative on the wooden floor. He watched it spread and settle, and then went back to the table.

From the pocket of his jacket he drew out a finely whetted penknife and an octagon-shaped metal pencil which was also marked off as a ruler. He looked at his wristwatch, making some brief calculations, and measured off a length of the plumber's candle with the ruler. With the penknife he then sliced through the candle and trimmed away some wax to give the wick clearance. Before putting the knife back into his pocket he cleaned the blade with one of the pieces of cloth on the table.

When he looked into the can which contained the bandages soaking in gasoline he saw no more bubbles. He picked up the can and carried it to the place on the floor where the fixative was spread. Slowly reeling up the string so that none of the gasoline would spatter him he detached each roll of wet bandage from it. He loosened a few inches of gauze from six of the bandages and pressed the exposed gauze firmly into the fixative, which was now gummy.

Unspooling the bandage as he walked he then drew each of the six lengths of gauze in turn to a designated point. Three went among the boxes on the framework and three went into the cases along the walls. They were nicely spaced so that they radiated like the main strands of a spider web to points high among the packed cases. To reach the farthest points in the warehouse Mr. Keesler knotted the extra rolls of bandage to two of those which he had pulled out short of the mark. There was a sharp reek of gasoline in the warehouse now, added to its smell of mold.

Where the ends of the bandages were thrust between the boxes, Mr. Keesler made sure that the upper box was set back a little to provide a narrow platform. He took the paper drinking cups from the table, filled each with gasoline, and set it on top of the end of the bandage, resting on this platform.

The fixative was now put to work again. Mr. Keesler squeezed some of it over the juncture of the six bandages on the floor which were sealed there by the previous application. While it hardened he went to the table, took a handful of rags, and brought them to the open gasoline can. He lowered each rag in turn into the can, squeezed some of the excess gasoline back into the can after he pulled it out, and arranged all the rags around the fixative.

Then he took the stump of plumber's candle which he had prepared and pressed it down into the drying fixative. He tested it to make sure it was tightly set into place, looped the gasoline saturated fishline around and around its base, and pushed the rags close up against it. He made sure that a proper length of candle was exposed, and then stood up to view his handiwork. Everything, as far as he could see, was in order.

Humming a little tune under his breath, Mr. Keesler took the two cans of gasoline and disposed of their contents among the boxes. He handled the cans expertly, splashing gasoline against the boxes where the bandages were attached, pouring it between the boxes wherever he detected a draft stirring in the dank air around him. When the cans were empty he wiped them thoroughly with a rag he had reserved for the purpose and added the rag to the pile around the candle.

Everything that needed to be done had now been done.

Mr. Keesler went back to the table, tightly sealed the gasoline cans, and placed them in the sample case. He pulled off the rubber gloves and put them and the remnant of plumber's candle into the case, too. Then he locked the case and put on his hat and coat.

He carried the case to a point a few feet away from the candle on the floor, set it down, and took out a book of matches from his pocket. Cupping a hand around the matchbox he lit one, and walking with great care while shielding the flame, he approached the candle, bent over it, and lit it. The flame guttered and then took hold.

Mr. Keesler stood up and put out the match, not by shaking it or blowing at it, but by wetting his thumb and forefinger in his mouth and squeezing out the light between them. He dropped the used match into his pocket, went to the back door, switched off the electric light there with his handkerchiefed hand, and drew open the door a few inches.

After peering outside to make sure no one was observing

him, Mr. Keesler stepped through the door, locked it behind him, and departed.

He returned to his office by the same route he had come. In the elevator he said to Eddie, "All of a sudden my tooth is killing me. I guess I'll have to run over to the dentist," and Eddie said, "Your teeth sure give you a lot of trouble, don't they?"

"They sure do," said Mr. Keesler.

He left the sample case in his room, washed his hands and face in the lavatory at the opposite end of the hallway, and took the elevator down. The dentist's office was on 56th Street near Seventh Avenue, a few minutes' walk away, and when Mr. Keesler entered the reception room the clock on the wall there showed him that it was two minutes before three. He was pleased to see that the dentist's receptionist was young and pretty and that she had his name neatly entered in her appointment book.

"You're right on time," she said as she filled out a record card for him. She handed him the card. "Just give this to Dr. Gordon when you go into the office."

In the office Mr. Keesler took off his glasses, put them in his pocket, and sat back in the dentist's chair. His feet hurt, and it felt good to be sitting down.

"Where does it hurt?" said Dr. Gordon, and Mr. Keesler indicated the back of his lower right jaw. "Right there," he said.

He closed his eyes and crossed his hands restfully on his belly while the doctor peered into his open mouth and poked at his teeth with a sharp instrument.

"Nothing wrong on the surface," Dr. Gordon said. "Matter of fact, your teeth seem to be in excellent shape. How old are you?"

"Fifty," said Mr. Keesler with pride. "Fifty-one next week."

"Wish my teeth were as good," said the dentist. "Well, it might possibly be that wisdom tooth under the gum that's giving the trouble. But all I can do now is put something soothing on it and take X rays. Then we'll know."

"Fine," said Mr. Keesler.

He came out of the office at 3:30 with a sweet, minty taste in his mouth and with his feet well-rested. Walking briskly he headed for the BMT subway station at 57th Street and took a train down to Herald Square. He climbed to the street there and took a position among the crowd moving slowly past the windows of R. H. Macy's Department Store, keeping his eyes fixed on the windows as he moved.

At four o'clock he looked at his watch.

At five minutes after four he looked at it with concern.

Then in the window of the store he saw a car coming up to the curb. He walked across the street and entered it, and the car immediately drew away from the curb and fell in with the rest of the traffic on the street.

"You're late, Hummel," said Mr. Keesler to the driver. "Nothing went wrong, did it?"

"Nothing," said Mr. Hummel tensely. "It must have started just about 3:30. The cops called me ten minutes ago to tell me about it. The whole building's going, they said. They wanted me to rush over right away."

"Well, all right," said Mr. Keesler. "So what are you so upset about? Everything is fine. In no time at all you'll have sixty thousand dollars of insurance money in your pocket, you'll be rid of the whole load of stuff you were stuck with—you ought to be a happy man."

Mr. Hummel awkwardly manipulated the car into a turn that led downtown. "But if they find out," he said. "How can you be so sure they won't? At my age to go to jail—!"

Mr. Keesler had dealt with overwrought clients many times before. "Look, Hummel," he said patiently, "the first job I ever did was thirty years ago for my own father, God rest his soul, when the market cleaned him out. To his dying day he thought it was an accident, he never knew it was me. My wife don't know what I do. Nobody knows. Why? Because I'm an expert. I'm the best in the business. When I do a job I'm covered up every possible way—right down to the least little thing. So quit worrying. Nobody will ever find out."

"But in the daytime," said Mr. Hummel. "With people around. I still say it would have been better at night."

Mr. Keesler shook his head. "If it happened at night, the Fire Marshal and the insurance people would be twice as suspicious. And what do I look like, anyhow, Hummel, some kind of bum who goes sneaking around at night? I'm a nine-to-five man. I go to the office and I come home from the office like anybody else. Believe me, that's the best protection there is."

"It could be," said Mr. Hummel, nodding thoughtfully. "It could be."

A dozen blocks away from the warehouse thick, black smoke could be seen billowing into the air above it. On Water Street, three blocks away, Mr. Keesler put a hand on Mr. Hummel's arm.

"Stop here," he said. "There's always marshals and insurance people around the building looking at people, so this is close enough. You can see all you have to from here."

Mr. Hummel looked at the smoke pouring from the building, at the tongues of flame now and then shooting up from it, at the fire engines and tangles of hose in the street, and at the firemen playing water against the walls of the building. He shook his head in awe. "Look at that," he said, marveling. "Look at that."

"I did," said Mr. Keesler. "So how about the money?"

Mr. Hummel stirred himself from his daze, reached into his trouser pocket, and handed Mr. Keesler a tightly folded roll of bills. "It's all there," he said. "I had it made up the way you said."

There were fourteen hundred-dollar bills and five twenties in the roll. Bending low and keeping the money out of sight, Mr. Keesler counted it twice. He had two bank deposit envelopes all filled out and ready in his pocket. Into one which credited the money to the account of *K. E. Esler* he put thirteen of the hundred-dollar bills. Into the other which was made out in the name of *Keesler Novelties* he put a single hundred-dollar bill. The five twenties he slipped into his wallet, and from the wallet took out the key to the warehouse.

"Don't forget this," he said, handing it to Mr. Hummel. "Now I have to run along."

"Wait a second," said Mr. Hummel. "I wanted to ask you about something, and since I don't know where to get in touch with you—"

"Yes?"

"Well, I got a friend who's in a very bad spot. He's stuck

with a big inventory of fur pieces that he can't get rid of, and he needs cash bad. Do you understand?"

"Sure," said Mr. Keesler. "Give me his name and phone number, and I'll call him up in a couple of weeks."

"Couldn't you make it any sooner?"

"I'm a busy man," said Mr. Keesler. "I'll call him in two weeks." He took out the book of matches and inside it wrote the name and number Mr. Hummel gave him. He put away the matches and opened the door of the car. "So long, Hummel."

"So long, Esler," said Mr. Hummel.

For the second time that day Mr. Keesler traveled in the subway from East Broadway to Columbus Circle. But instead of going directly to his office this time, he turned down Eighth Avenue and dropped the sealed envelope which contained the thirteen hundred dollars into the night-deposit box of the Merchant's National Bank. Across the street was the Columbus National Bank, and into its night-deposit box he placed the envelope containing the hundred dollars. When he arrived at his office it was ten minutes before five.

Mr. Keesler opened his sample case, threw in the odds and ends that had come in the mail that morning, shut the sample case, and closed the rolltop desk after throwing the New York *Times* into the wastebasket. He took a magazine from the pile on the filing cabinet and sat down in the swivel chair while he looked at it.

At exactly five o'clock he left the office, carrying the sample case.

The elevator was crowded, but Mr. Keesler managed to wedge himself into it. "Well," said Eddie on the way down, "another day, another dollar."

In the subway station Mr. Keesler bought a *World-Telegram*, but was unable to read it in the crowded train. He held it under his arm, standing astride the sample case, half dozing as he stood there. When he got out of the station at Beverley Road he stopped at the stationery store on the corner to buy a package of razor blades. Then he walked home slowly, turned into the driveway, and entered the garage.

Mrs. Keesler always had trouble getting the car into the garage. It stood there now at a slight angle to the wall so that Mr. Keesler had to squeeze past it to get to the back of the garage. He opened the sample case, took out the piece of plumber's candle and the tube of Quick-Dry, and put them into a drawer of the workbench there. The drawer was already full of other bits of hardware and small household supplies.

Then he took the two gasoline cans from the sample case and a piece of rubber tubing from the wall and siphoned gasoline from the tank of the car into the cans until they were full. He put them on the floor among other cans which were full of paint and solvent.

Finally he took out the rubber gloves and tossed them on the floor under one of the partly painted chairs. The spatters of paint on the gloves were the exact color of the paint on the chairs.

Mr. Keesler went into the house by the side door, and Mrs. Keesler who had been setting the kitchen table heard him. She came into the living room and watched as Mr. Keesler turned the sample case upside down over the table. Trinkets rolled all over the table, and Mrs. Keesler caught the souvenir charm before it could fall to the floor.

"More junk," she said good-naturedly.

"Same as always," said Mr. Keesler, "just stuff from the office. I'll give them to Sally's kids." His niece Sally had two pretty little daughters of whom he was very fond.

Mrs. Keesler put her hand over her mouth and looked around. "And what about the suit?" she said. "Don't tell me you forgot about the suit at the tailor's!"

Mr. Keesler already had one arm out of his coat. He stood there helplessly.

"Oh, no," he said.

His wife sighed resignedly.

"Oh, yes," she said. "And you'll go right down there now before he closes."

Mr. Keesler thrust an arm out behind him, groping for the sleeve of his coat, and located it with his wife's help. She brushed away a speck on the shoulder of the coat, and then patted her husband's cheek affectionately.

"If you could only learn to be a little methodical, dear," said Mrs. Keesler.

Intruder in the Maize

JOAN RICHTER

She waited until the churning of the Land-Rover's heavy wheels on the long gravel drive had faded into the softer sound of tires against murum and then she got up and quickly began to dress. She was annoyed that she had wasted the last hour in a pretense of sleep, but it had been preferable to a confrontation with Jack.

She had heard him get up while it was still dark and go outside. And she had imagined him as he crouched on the rise overlooking the field of maize, waiting, as he had been waiting and watching every dawn for the last two weeks. Sometimes she wondered if he remembered any longer what it was he was waiting for.

She threw a sweater over her suntanned shoulders and left the house by the veranda door, passing the kitchen as she went to tell Kariuki all she wanted this morning was coffee and she would fix that herself later. She walked across the dew-soaked lawn, past the bottle brush tree from whose rose-colored flowers the sunlight birds drank their morning fill, to where the shrubs thinned and she could look out across the green valley to the opposite ridge.

Overhead the East African sky was an intense blue, spreading endlessly, with high clouds that rose like white mountains asking to be climbed. Sometimes she wondered if Jack saw any of this, if he realized at all how much beauty there was just outside their window.

She breathed deeply of the cool air. It was dry, but it did not strike her as thin, not even on that first day, a year ago, when they had just arrived. The only time she felt the altitude was when she walked uphill, and then her breath came in quick, short pulls and her chest felt hard and tight.

A cracking of a twig caused her to look down the near slope into the valley where, among the trees and brush, the smoke of cook fires rose. She saw a man making his way up along one of the paths, his dark head bent, so that she could not see his face; but from his dress—the short-sleeved white shirt and the dark trousers—she was sure it was Molo, one of the few farmers in the area who had adopted European dress.

He had a small *shamba* on the other side of the valley where in previous years he had raised potatoes and maize, but this season he had set out his first real money crop—a half acre of pyrethrum, a silver green plant from whose daisy-like flowers an insecticide was extracted. She wondered what the occasion was for his leaving his *shamba* so early in the day.

"*Habari,*" she said, using the Swahili greeting.

"*Mzuri,*" he replied, but the look on his face did not seem to agree that everything was good.

There were a few more prescribed words for them to exchange before they exhausted her knowledge of Swahili. Then they would switch to English and slowly Molo would come to the point of his visit.

He looked up at the sky. "The rains come soon."

She looked too, but saw nothing that resembled a rain cloud. But, then, both night and day the skies were strange to her. The stars were not the ones she knew, nor were the clouds. She knew only that they were beautiful, more so than any she had ever seen anywhere.

"Is the Bwana at home?"

He called her Memsab Simon, but he never called Jack anything but Bwana.

"He left early this morning on safari." She smiled, still not used to the East African meaning of the word; only rarely did it mean sun helmets and bearers and trekking through the bush; most often it referred to any trip out of town, whether for a day or a week.

"Did the Bwana Red go with him?"

Lately Jack almost never went anywhere without Red, and she did not know whether that made her angry or relieved, whether it was an indication of Jack's lack of trust in her, or lack of confidence in himself. She liked Red—perhaps too much—but she had done nothing to cause Jack to be jealous. Whether Red returned her admiration she had no idea, for he showed no sign; but her ego was mollified by the knowledge that Red was no fool. He had to work with Jack (another sticky point—Jack was the boss, but Red, having lived in East Africa for the last ten years, knew all there was to know).

"Yes, Bwana Red went with him. Is something wrong, Molo? Do you need more seed?"

Jack had come to East Africa on a two-year contract as an agricultural adviser, and one of the things for which he was responsible was the parceling out of seed. It was given on a loan basis, to be paid for when the crop was harvested. It was a precious commodity, doled out on the basis of past records of repayment. Jack had been concerned about stealing, so he kept the sacks of seed locked in a storehouse at one end of the maize field.

That was the one thing she didn't like, the one thing that marred the beauty of the land and the sky; barred windows, locked doors—not just outside doors, but all inside doors, to closets and pantries, doors that sealed one section of a house off from another.

"It's different with the seed," she had said to Jack, though she had not really meant it—but the seed was not her affair. "But I'll be darned if I'm going to lock up the pantry every time I leave the house, just so the houseboy won't help himself to a spoonful of sugar!"

She had pointed to a peg board on the wall. "Look at that! There must be fifty different keys there. I won't live that way."

"The house is yours to run as you want," Jack had said. "But don't come crying to me the day one of them"—and he had nodded in the direction where Kariuki and his helper were preparing lunch—"walks off with something that can't be replaced."

After that she had put the silver that Jack's family had given them in the wall safe behind the mirror in the bedroom and left it there. It was too much bother taking it out in the morning and locking it up again at night.

One day when Red was with them, Jack brought up the topic again, thinking he would have his colleague's support; but Red had said, "If I bothered to check, I suppose at the end of each month I'd find I was out a pound of sugar and maybe some tea. On a day to day basis Jinja helps himself to a banana or toast that's left over from breakfast. The banana would rot before I'd get around to eating it—and what would I do with leftover toast but throw it away?"

"That isn't the point," Jack had countered. "They ought to be taught that what's yours is not theirs."

"There's a difference between stealing money and things of value—and taking scraps of food." Red's voice had been patient, but not condescending. "When Jinja washes my trousers, he checks the pockets because I'm always leaving things in them—cigarettes, screws, keys, a few shillings. He keeps a basket on the shelf above the tub for all that stuff. I find the shillings there too, along with everything else."

Jack had looked at him narrowly. "Have you ever checked? Have you ever left an odd bunch of change—"

"You mean have I ever tried to trap him?"

Jack nodded.

Red shook his head. "If I did that it would mean I didn't trust him. And he would know, and then the whole thing would break down and I *couldn't* trust him."

Jack had continued the discussion, long after Red would have been happy to let it go. In a final effort to win a point Jack had flashed, "The Africans wanted freedom, now they have to accept the responsibility that goes with it!"

"I couldn't agree with you more," Red had said, "but I don't go along with your methods. You want to *police* them—and that isn't freedom. Sure there are thieves among them—but show me a society that hasn't any. Just once suspect them of thievery without cause, and you will create a thief."

After Red had left them, she had not been able to keep silent. Perhaps she had been too strong in stating her position, for Jack had said unpleasantly, "So you think the Bwana Red is a great hero too." And Jack had turned away . . .

Now Molo shook his head. No, he had not come for seed.

What does he want, she wondered. What has brought him

up from the valley at a time of day when he should be working his *shamba?* Although she was better at it than when they had first come, she still found it difficult to read the African face. Joy she could identify, but other emotions—anger, fear, distrust—eluded her.

She prepared herself for more small talk. "The tomato plants you gave me are doing very well, Molo. Would you like to see them?"

A sudden though almost imperceptible change in his expression made her realize that accidentally she had hit on what he had been waiting for. He had been waiting for her to invite him onto her land.

"I would like to see maize. Bwana says wild pig is coming and eating."

So even Molo had heard of Jack's morning excursions. "You can have my gun," Red had offered. "I bet, whatever it is, comes around dawn. From that rise over there it would be an easy shot."

"I'll get him," Jack had said, "but I won't use a gun."

"Suit yourself, but setting traps can be slow. That's a big field."

"Traps?" She remembered the arrogance in Jack's voice. "I intend to use a bow."

Red had looked up quickly and perhaps the look that crossed his face *had* been one of admiration, though she had not seen it as such. But Jack's satisfied face had been evidence enough of his own interpretation.

"I'm a fair marksman," he had said. "I had some practice in the States."

Silently she recalled the country club's manicured lawn, the steady bull's-eye target.

"A couple of weeks ago I bought a bow from one of Molo's brothers and a dozen arrows. It's a different kind of weapon from what I've been used to, but it sure has zing."

"A little light to do in a pig," Red said, "unless you're an incredibly good shot."

Jack had given him a smug look. "I've got something else that will help it along."

She remembered the frown that had creased Red's brow.

"I'd be careful with that stuff. It's not something to fool with."

"Thanks for the advice. I never did have a wet nurse, and I hardly need one now."

Just the recollection of his retort made her blush . . .

Molo led the way along the ridge toward the maize. She knew that the polite palaver was over. They were getting to the reason for his visit. He turned when they reached the edge of the green field and continued along the north side of the planted area, moving in the direction of the rise, the lookout Jack went to every morning, where she knew he had gone this morning before he'd left to meet Red.

At the rise Molo stopped, and for the first time she noticed that he had his *panga* with him, the machete-like knife whose broad blade was used to cut grass, chop roots, dig potatoes, prune trees, and sever the heads off chickens. It was as much a part of the African farm scene as was the hoe in the States before mechanization. Usually when Molo came to pay a social call or to see Jack or Red on business, he left his *panga* behind. Idly, she wondered why he had it with him now.

He was pointing with it and she followed the dark line of his arm to the end of the blade.

"Pig come out of forest and walk low on belly through maize."

For a moment she could not see the slight furrow in the sea of green stalks, but then her eyes discovered the thin line that traveled straight across the otherwise untouched field.

"You stay here, Memsab Simon."

There was something in the tone of his voice that she reacted to. He was not being rude, but rather protective, and she wondered against what. Or was she misunderstanding completely? Was this like an expression she could not read?

"Molo, you don't think the pig is there now?"

"No, pig is gone."

"Then why, what—"

"It is better you stay. Let me see."

She nodded. Molo might be a guest on her land, but she was still a stranger in his country. With an uneasiness—of what she was not sure—she stood watching him as he descended the small hill and entered the maize. Overhead the sky was the same blue it had been minutes ago, before she had seen him coming up from the valley, with the same white, climbing clouds. There was still no visible sign of rain. It was something else that had thrown a shadow over the day.

The maize was shoulder high, so that when Molo paused and looked at the ground she could not see what it was he was looking at.

What had he found? What *was* he looking for?

He straightened and walked forward, stopping again after a few paces. Then he walked quickly on as though he had seen ahead of him what he had been looking for.

He had entered the field from the side bounded by the forest and was following the path that had been broken for him. As she studied the larger picture she saw that the parting in the maize seemed to lead to the storehouse.

Oh, God, she thought. Some animal found a way into Jack's burglarproof store! Had Jack come here every morning for the last two weeks and not discovered this for himself?

Molo had almost reached the wooden building. As she watched his movements a thought began to form in her mind. Had an animal made that path? Or had it been a man? A man trying to find a way to break into the seed store?

Molo had said something earlier that now made her wonder. "Pig come out of forest and walk low on belly through maize." It was an odd way to describe an animal's foraging.

Molo had reached the storehouse and was standing with his eyes cast down. Then he raised his head and called in Swahili. "Come now."

Hurriedly she started down the slope, slipping as she went, but driven by an impatience that came of waiting, curiosity, and a mounting concern that something was wrong. Her sweater slipped off her shoulders, but she did not stop to pick it up. At the edge of the maize field she put her arms up in front of her face to shield it from the slashing leaves.

She stumbled and looked down at the ground and saw what Molo had seen—a stone smeared with blood and more blood on one of the low leaves. Ahead there were drops of blood, hardly visible on the red brown earth, but unmistakable and vivid against the pale green of the maize.

Had Jack hit his target this morning? Had he only wounded it? She looked around her, trying to see into the impenetrable maize. The wounded animal might be hidden, crouching, waiting to spring at her, or to charge. How could Molo be so sure it was gone? Already she had thrust the thought from her that her husband's quarry might have been human.

Her breath was coming in quick shallow gasps when she reached Molo who was standing in the shadow of the storehouse. Her eyes fell to the ground and she saw a pile of dirt and a hole dug under the foundation; beside them a sack of seed and an abandoned *panga* that had been used to dig the hole.

She took all this in, and more, for at Molo's feet lay an arrow, its shaft bloody, its sharp triangular point sticky. Her hands flew to her face and she heard herself moan. An animal could not use a *panga*, nor could it tear an arrow from its stricken body! The succeeding thought made her cringe and her head twisted between her hands. Jack had shot a man!

All arrows looked the same. Perhaps it wasn't Jack's at all. He had marked his, scoring the shaft. But from where she stood she could not see—the shaft was partially covered with the loosened earth.

With a supreme effort she slid her hands down from her face and brought them to her sides. She had to find out. She had to know. She hesitated, and then with horrified determination she took a quick step forward, her hand outstretched. But almost before she moved, Molo's shadow was upon her and his arm caught her across the chest and threw her to the ground.

A scream choked in her throat as she stared up at him, a black man standing over her, his *panga* raised. It sliced through the air and caught the blood-smeared arrow and tossed it aside.

She saw him stab his *panga* in the ground and turn to her. "I am sorry, Memsab, but the arrow is poison."

He held out his hand and helped her to her feet.

"Even a scratch brings death."

A residue of terror filled her throat and she did not trust herself to speak, for she could not let Molo know what she had thought. She looked at him and pointed to where the arrow lay. The question formed slowly on her lips. "Is it the Bwana's arrow?"

"Yes," he said. "It killed my brother."

Her hand reached out and then fell to her side. What was there for her to say?

"I am sorry, too," Molo said and then she knew that her face did not present the enigma to him that his did to her. "I am sorry that my brother became a thief—and that your husband must die."

Oh, God, she thought, what did that mean? Tribal vengeance? Could she reason with Molo? If not, she would have to get word to Jack somehow. It was possible that he and Red had not yet left town.

She turned to Molo, hoping she could find some words to reach him, but he had already begun to speak. The words came slowly, thoughtfully, half in English, half in Swahili.

"Before the Bwana came, my brother was watchman for the Bwana Red. He slept at night outside the seed store, the old one which we do not use any more. No one stole or they would know my brother's *panga*."

Molo's eyes fell to the ground where the multipurpose knife lay. Then he looked at her again. "But then the new Bwana came and everything changed and my brother became a thief." He stopped. It was as much as he could say.

"But why did your brother sell my husband a bow? Why did he give him the poison?"

"The bow he sold because he needed money, and because he thought the Bwana could not shoot well. But he did not give him poison. He would not. The Bwana got poison somewhere far from here, from someone he pay a lot of money."

Suddenly Molo cocked his head, in response to some distant sound. She heard it too. It was the Land-Rover returning. She heard it leave the murum road and turn into the gravel drive.

"It is the Bwana Red," Molo said.

She looked, but it was too far for her to recognize who was in the vehicle. It bore down on them coming as close to the field as it could. Then she saw that it was Red driving and that the seat beside him was empty.

She ran toward him. "Where's Jack?"

"In town. What's going on? He sent me out here, said there was something for me to see."

"There was no wild pig in the maize—it was Molo's brother. He'd dug a hole under the storehouse."

Red frowned as he climbed out of the Land-Rover. "I guess that's one for Jack's side. I'd have said it would take a lot to make Molo's brother turn thief." A flicker of hope crossed his clouded face. "I suppose Jack caught him in the act?"

She took a breath. "Jack didn't catch him. He killed him."

Red's face went blank with disbelief. "Why? He was a man, not an animal. Why did he kill him?"

Tears seared her eyes, but she fought against them. It was past the time for weeping. She had no answer to Red's question. It was what she had been asking herself.

Molo had come up and was standing with them. Red turned to him. "How did he do it? He wasn't that good a shot with the bow."

"The arrow came here." Molo touched the fleshy part of his thigh. "It would not have killed him—but it was poisoned."

"Poisoned!" Red turned to her. "Where did he get poison?"

"I thought he'd gotten it from Molo's brother. But Molo says no, that he got it somewhere far from here."

"That arrogant—this can only mean trouble for all of us—whites and blacks."

Molo shook his head. "No, Bwana Red. There will be no trouble. My brother is dead. And the Bwana will die. It will end there."

"Molo, old friend," Red said in Swahili, "the viper eventually spends itself. Do not put yourself in danger by seeking its death."

"Do not worry, Bwana Red. The viper has felt its own sting."

She looked from one man to the other. What had they said? She had caught the proverb, but did not understand its application. She turned to Red. "Why didn't Jack come back with you? Where is he?"

"I left him at the dispensary. He cut himself on one of those damn arrowheads—not bad, but enough to need a couple of stitches. I wanted to wait with him, but he didn't seem to want me around. Now I understand why."

She listened to each word, each progressive syllable, and her realization grew until the horror of it was evident in her face.

Red caught her hand. "God, I'm sorry. I know what you're thinking. But he's all right. It's just a simple cut. You see the poison is applied to the shaft of the arrow, not the tip—for reasons just like this—it's so easy to get a scratch and that's all you need."

She looked at him and shook her head. Then she turned to Molo. "How did you know? How did you know the Bwana would die?"

"Many people were in town, waiting at the dispensary. They brought the news to my *shamba.*"

"What's this all about?" Red said, turning to her. "I just told you. He'll be all right."

"No," she said. "No, he won't. You see he didn't know about applying the poison to the shaft—he put it on the arrowheads."

Shooting Lines

GERALD HAMMOND

Keith Calder did not expect to be welcomed with open arms when he returned to the shop, for last night had been the occasion of his annual quarrel with Molly. The geese were in at last, arriving from their breeding grounds in the far north to overwinter in Scotland. Molly, who hated being left alone in a cooling bed and loathed opening the shop on her own, had nagged at Keith to wait for his partner's return from holiday; but by then the geese would have learned to fly a dozen gunshots high. Keith had promised to be back in good time.

But the morning flight had been late and had lasted until the sun was well up, and the firth was a long hour's drive away. Even the presence of two fat greylags and a number of mallard in the bag might not be a sufficient peace offering. Keith parked in the Square of Newton Lauder and entered his shop with an ingratiating smile fixed painfully on his face, and walking very softly. At first he thought that the shop, crammed as it was with shooting and fishing gear, was bare of customers. His spirits rose . . . for the duration of half a second or so.

"This gentleman has been waiting for *ages*," Molly said in a voice that jangled with falling icicles. "I told him that you'd surely be back by ten, and then I said the same thing about ten-thirty and eleven. He has a gun to sell."

A large man got up out of the customer's chair, holding a leather, leg-of-mutton gun case.

Keith's heart sank. If there was one thing that Molly detested, even worse than being deserted before dawn, it was making polite conversation with strangers. "Traffic was terrible," he said, slipping behind the counter. "Let me get my coat off and we'll see what you've got."

The customer drew the parts of a double-barreled shotgun out of the case and assembled them clumsily. Keith took it from him and turned away to the working table against the wall—ostensibly to use the brighter light that hung above, but in truth because he never let a seller see his eyes while he appraised a gun. A gentle shake and a quick dropping and closing of the barrels assured him that the action was tight and sound. He stood looking down for a second or two, and took a deep breath. On the note pad beside him he jotted the number of the gun from the rib. "Did Molly make you a cup of coffee?" he asked.

"An hour ago," Molly snapped.

"I expect you could do with another. And," Keith said deliberately, "I would very much like a cup of coffee myself." He looked round and met her eye.

Molly was ready to refuse any favors, but the words were a long-established signal. They had been offered many a stolen gun in the past. With a snort of exasperation she squeezed past, palming the slip of paper and managing to bump Keith's buttocks so that he caught his midriff painfully against the corner of the table.

When the pain had abated a little, Keith disassembled the

gun and gauged the barrels. He studied the number on the action and the fore-end, and compared them with those on the top rib. "Have you had it long?" he asked, turning.

"Only a day or two," the man said. His voice was totally accentless, like that of a newsreader or, Keith thought, one of the upper stratum of secondhand-car salesmen. He had a frank and open face and he met Keith's eyes squarely. "My uncle had it made for him, but now the poor old chap's losing the sight of his right eye. He won't be shooting again, so he gave it to me. Well, I only shoot clay pigeons, and I've got a perfectly good Miroku which suits me fine, so this one would be no more than a wall ornament to me, and a constant worry. I thought I'd rather sell it and put the money into something else, something I need more."

"Very sensible," Keith said.

Molly put her head round the door from the back shop. "The kettle's on," she said with an almost imperceptible headshake. So the gun was not on the list of stolen guns.

"Darling," Keith said, "I've left the dogs shut in the car. Would you mind letting them out for a minute?"

Molly's eyebrows shot up. This was another signal. The telephone could not be used without every word being heard throughout the shop, but Divisional Headquarters of the police was just across the square. "I suppose so," she said. She sounded grudging, but Keith knew his Molly. There was a spring in her step, and the spark in her eye had changed from exasperation to excitement and curiosity. She closed the door after her and the ring of the shop bell marked the cutting-off of the street noises. It was quiet again in the shop, echoes muffled by the hanging coats and waders that almost filled the ceiling space.

"You have the receipt?" Keith asked.

The man pulled an envelope from his pocket. "My uncle couldn't find the receipt, but he gave me a letter confirming the gift. You're welcome to phone the makers, who'll vouch for the name of the original customer."

"I never doubted," Keith said wryly. "But could I phone your uncle?"

"If you want. The number's on the letter."

The letter was typewritten, all but a sprawling signature, and on plain paper. The address, which was typed like the rest, was in Edinburgh. Keith could visualize the district—enormous old houses now divided into very expensive flats, occupied by lawyers and successful businessmen.

"What brought you to me?" Keith asked.

The man shrugged. "The price I was offered in Edinburgh seemed too low. I'd heard your name as a dealer in guns. I'm on my way to Newcastle on business, so I thought I'd stop and let you make me an offer. But I'll be back in Edinburgh to-night. If you don't want it, I'll take what I was offered."

Keith hid a smile. The story hung together almost too well. "Would you leave it with me to examine?" he asked. "You could collect it again on your way back."

"Sorry. If you can't make me an offer, I'll try my luck in Newcastle. I'm afraid this is take-it-or-leave-it time."

Keith put out his hand, not for the letter but for the telephone directory. "I think I'll try your uncle's number," he said.

For the first time the man's expression of bland honesty slipped and Keith glimpsed the ruthlessness beneath. But the voice was kept steady. The man looked at his watch. "I can't wait any longer, I've a business lunch to attend in Newcastle. Give me back the gun."

Keith sighed, and surreptitiously fumbled two small objects from a drawer. He had never been one to run away from a fight, but violence in the cluttered shop, among the glass cases and the trout rods, would do too much damage to be contemplated. He slipped round the end of the counter and set his back against the shop door. He dropped in the two cartridges, closed the gun and snicked off the safety catch. "Stay where you are," he said. "The police will be here in a minute."

The man stood very still, but a change came over him that reminded Keith of a bull preparing to charge. "Ye'll no' dare tae shoot, Jimmy," he said, and the Scots of the industrial West lay heavily on his tongue. "They'd hae youse for murder."

"You take one step toward me," Keith said, "and I'll have reason to believe you mean violence. Especially after the threats you've been making. That makes it self-defense."

"I've no' made ony threats."

"But you won't be around to deny it. I'll blow your head off, and whistle while I wipe up the blood and brains. This gun's been used in a serious crime, and I'm taking no chances with you."

For a full minute they stood, locked in a clash of wills, until a large sergeant and an even larger constable came to the shop door. Keith stepped aside to let them in.

The man had recovered his poise and his accent. "I think this fellow's lost his mind," he said loftily. "He's been threatening me with a loaded gun. You'd better get it off him, very carefully, and take him in until he's come to his senses."

"It's not loaded," Keith said. He pulled both triggers and was rewarded by two dull clicks. He dropped the barrels and caught the two objects which the ejectors flipped into his hand. "Snap caps," he said. "Dummy cartridges. It doesn't do a gun any good to pull the triggers when the chambers are empty."

The man struggled all the way across the square, but what he said about Keith is best forgotten. Very little of it was true.

In the afternoon of the following day Molly and Keith were invited, politely but firmly, to visit Chief Inspector Munro in his lair—a soulless room which always managed to look gloomy despite large windows and bright lighting. The functional elegance of the gun lying on Munro's desk sprang into enhanced beauty against the plainness of the room.

Munro's scrawny figure was drooping with tiredness and his slow West Highland speech was broken by yawns, but he was still freewheeling on the nervous energy which had carried him through the night. "We have the story," he said, "or as much of it as we're going to get from those so far in custody. Two out of the six are talking, which is a wee bit above average for the type. Make it three out of seven, Mr. Calder, and tell me how you knew."

Keith stretched lazily. He felt fulfilled—not only by the verification of his hunch but because Molly had been asking the same question with all the blandishments at her disposal—and, when it came to blandishments, Molly had plenty to dispose. To punish her for yesterday's contrariness he had left her curiosity unsatisfied.

"You could say that I was reading between the lines," he said.

Molly snorted with indignation.

"Come away now," Munro said. "I've reports to finish and I've been up all night, liaising with the Regional Crime Squad and with the Strathclyde force. Very pleased they are, too, but I am just about ready to drop. So let's have no more riddles."

"All right," Keith said. He leaned forward and picked up the gun. "This was obviously a top-class gun, handmade, side-by-side, Best English. But as soon as I had it in my hands it felt wrong, muzzle-heavy. So maybe I looked at it a bittie more critically than usual. And what I meant about reading the lines, there were just a few lines where none should be. Firstly round the barrels, just in front of the chambers."

"You mean it's been sleeved?" Molly said. "I had it in my hands and I didn't see anything."

Munro stifled a yawn which dwarfed all the others. "What's sleeved?" he asked.

"The expensive part of a pair of barrels is all at the breech end," Keith explained. "So when barrels are damaged or rusted, it's cheaper to take them apart, turn them off about six inches from the breech and renew the rest. It's been very neatly done and some engraving's been added to camouflage it and the whole lot's been re-blued. But, sure as hell, three quarters of each barrel's length is new, only the breeches and the rib are original. And the next thing to hit me in the eye is that it should have been marked as having been sleeved, and it isn't.

"Then I noticed a faint shadow line across the stock. There's a join hidden by the last line of the checkering, and by the top tang and the trigger guard, just leaving four places where it crosses an eighth of an inch of wood. It's been cleverly joined, and filled over with transparent resin, but the grain didn't quite run through and somebody's had to add a few lines to disguise it.

"Lastly, there's one little line on top of the rib, and two wee dots."

Molly was leaning against Keith's shoulder and following

every word. "I noticed that," she said, "but I couldn't make it mean anything."

"You would have," Keith said, "if it had still been inlaid with gold. Or if they hadn't added the second dot." He paused. "No? Well, maybe if it had been in the shape of a Two."

Molly put a hand to her face. "You mean it's a One? Number One of a pair?"

Munro was still plodding along behind. "But guns do have repairs to stocks, and have their barrels—what did you call it?—sleeved?"

"Aye, they do. But this gun bears a name. It's a famous name, but used on its own it's either very old or very new. A famous firm came to grief a few years ago, and it was set up again under a shortened title that hadn't been used on its own for a hundred years. The first guns under the new name haven't been in use for more than a year or eighteen months. So how, I wondered, did such a pair get separated, and one of them badly damaged at both ends, in such a short space of time?"

"Just as a matter of interest," Munro said, "no more than that, what do you think happened?"

"Tell me where I go wrong. It seemed to me that it must have started with a burglary; and one that hasn't been discovered yet because the gun isn't on the stolen list. The thieves didn't realize that they'd got hold of something worth five figures easily, or that they could have bought something good enough for their purpose for fifty quid. They, or their mates, sawed the guns off to use in a robbery. There was a security van held up and robbed in Hamilton a fortnight back, and I wondered if that would be it."

"It was," Munro said tiredly.

"The other one probably went into the Clyde," Keith said. "But maybe the man who used this one gave it to a friend or a relative to get rid of. And the friend, or whatever, realized that this was the most expensive part of a very expensive gun. So I'd guess that it's been in and out of the back door of one of the bigger gunsmiths. I could even guess at the name."

"You'd likely be right," Munro said. "It'll come out in court, so you can just wait. I suppose you could guess at the original owner's name?"

"Henry Graham," Keith said. "The letter was signed Henry Graham, and the man was quite willing to have me ring up and check on the purchaser of the gun. And he didn't mind me phoning the number at the head of the letter, where I suppose a friend would have been waiting. Did you catch the friend through the phone number?"

"We did."

"But he didn't like it when I picked up the directory to check the number. Maybe because the number's different from the one on the letter, and the penny might have dropped. It could be any of a dozen Henry Grahams, of course, the name's common enough. But I was hearing on the car radio that one of that name, the chairman of the Scottish Oils Exploration Trust, is on his way back from the States after a successful tour selling British oil technology for deep-sea exploration. They said that his work was done, and that he only wanted to get back for the pheasant season. I think he'll maybe have a nasty shock when he opens his front door."

"He has had the shock already," Munro said. "We telegraphed to him, and he telegraphed back with permission to open the flat. It had been stripped of pictures, silver, everything."

"But why," Molly said plaintively, "why would they come to you to sell the gun? You drive the hardest bargain this side of the Official Receiver. Why come to you?"

"With Henry Graham on the way home," Keith said, "they couldn't hang about. And I dare say they thought that an innocent country gunsmith mightn't look too closely if he was getting a bargain."

"Innocent!" Molly snorted. "When were you innocent?"

"Not for a wheen of years," Keith admitted.

The Nine Eels of Madame Wu

EDWARD D. HOCH

Madame Wu's shop on a small street in East Bangkok was crowded with tourists that April afternoon, and so she had to get the teenaged neighbor girl to watch the place while she went to the canal to release her eels. It was a ritual which had not varied in Madame Wu's life since the American, Sid Crawford, had moved in with her. That had been nearly ten years ago now, during those crumbling final years of the Vietnam War.

While Madame Wu tended her shop of Chinese curios, Crawford made his living from February to June of each year by engaging in the traditional Bangkok sport of kite fighting. The events were usually held in the early evenings at the Pramane Ground near the Grand Palace, where a strong southerly wind provided fuel for the sky battles. And on the afternoons before Crawford's especially important fights Madame Wu went to the Klong Maha Nak, the canal near her shop, to release the traditional eels. Nine was a lucky number in Thailand, and setting free that number of eels was considered to bring good fortune.

Madame Wu bought the eels in a water-filled plastic bag from a street urchin who sold them for that purpose. She often suspected he later recaptured some of the same eels from the canal to sell all over again, but that was not her concern. She was interested only in assuring Crawford's victory in the kite fight above the Pramane Ground.

She went to the lily-strewn waters of the canal alone and dumped the writhing mass of eels into it, watching them splash and swim away, darting through the dark masses of lily pads until they disappeared from view. Then she returned to the little apartment above her shop, where Crawford was putting the finishing touches on his kites.

"I have released the eels," she told him. "You will have good luck."

He looked up at her and smiled. He was a slim man now in his middle forties, with a streak of gray knifing through his otherwise black hair. The handsome American, they had called him when he first came to Bangkok—but, if he was no longer quite so handsome, then neither was Madame Wu herself. They had both drifted uncertainly into middle age.

"I have little faith in your eels," he admitted, "but if the ritual pleases you that's enough. Will you be coming with me this evening?"

"Of course. I will close the shop early."

"That is good, Anna," he said, attaching another barb to the string of his star-shaped kite.

She had told him once how she came to be called Anna. Her Chinese parents, newly settled in Bangkok, had chosen to name her after Anna Leonowens, the Englishwoman who'd journeyed to Siam in 1862 to instruct the king's many children. Crawford still called her that, though to the customers of her shop and the other merchants on the street she had long been Madame Wu.

No one ever used Crawford's given name either. When they arrived together at the Pramane Ground, a large open space just north of the Grand Palace, she heard several men calling out, "Crawford!" He waved each time but did not stop, walking through the gathering crowd of spectators with Madame Wu at his side, striding purposefully, like the champion he was.

The Pramane Ground was used regularly for events as diverse as weekend markets and royal cremations, and every May the king himself inaugurated the planting season by sponsoring a plowing ceremony on the site. But on these spring evenings when the south wind blew strong and free it was given over to the kite fights.

Madame Wu could not remember now the sequence of events that had propelled Crawford to the forefront in the sport. It had started in a bar, certainly, as had so many events in her life. A drunken challenge, a large bet made in haste, and then they had gone across to the open space by the palace. She remembered only one thing about that first evening. She had tugged at Crawford's sleeve and pointed across the street and said, "There is where Anna's second house stood, when she was governess for the king's children."

The battle in the sky was waged between two kites—a five-foot-long "male" kite in the shape of a star with a thick barbed string, and a much smaller "female" kite with a thin unbarbed string but a long tail able to ensnare the points of the star kite. The star kite could tangle or cut the smaller kite's string with its barbed cord and win, or it could lose the battle by being dragged to the ground by the smaller kite.

That first evening, Crawford flew a small kite, and he took naturally to the sport, maneuvering his kite so skillfully that the star kite was pulled ignominiously to the ground. But in the years that followed he had become an expert at flying both types. Whenever there was a challenger with money to bet, Crawford took him on. Now he mainly flew the larger star kites, often cutting through an opponent's string in a matter of minutes.

On this night, in a contest important enough for Madame Wu to have freed nine eels, Crawford was being challenged by a Pakistani youth who'd built a solid reputation in the sport since his recent arrival in Bangkok. Already she could see that the betting was heavy, and Crawford himself had wagered a large amount of cash on the outcome. Spectators were lining up, waving tight wads of money.

"Will you win?" she asked him, experiencing an uncharacteristic twinge of doubt.

He glanced around at the faces in the crowd, as he always did. "Why not? You freed your eels, didn't you?"

"Yes, but—"

"Then I'll win," he said with a smile. "It is written in the heavens."

"You make fun of me now."

"After so many years? I would be a fool!"

She'd asked him once, years ago, why he always studied the faces in the crowd so carefully. "Because," he had replied, "someday someone will come to kill me." His answer had terrified her, and all that night she'd lain awake sobbing, unable to accept even the remote possibility of his death. She'd never asked him the question again, though he still gazed out at the gathering crowds each evening before a kite fight as if anticipating some danger that never arrived.

This evening the south wind was perfect, and the young Pakistani launched his kite easily while the crowd cheered. Many of them came, Madame Wu realized, hoping to see the American defeated. She'd told Crawford that once, but he didn't seem to mind. It only made the bets against him larger and increased his own winnings.

Now, gauging the wind by the movement of his opponent's kite, he released his own star kite and ran with the heavy barbed string until he could position it for the attack. For several minutes the rival kites maneuvered close to one another. Then the smaller kite managed to snare Crawford's star with its long tail. Madame Wu drew a sharp breath and waited while Crawford yanked his barbed string again and again. He had to get free quickly, before he could be dragged to earth.

Madame Wu thought of her eels flashing free through the lily-covered waters of the canal.

Then Crawford gave a final jerk to his kite string and the crowd cheered. He was free. Even those who had wagered against him applauded his skill. Madame Wu wanted to add her praise but she knew better than to speak to him during a match. There would be plenty of time to replay the details back at their apartment over the curio shop while he relaxed with a pipe.

Now there was still the match to be won. Crawford released more of his barbed string, and let the star kite climb gently with an updraft. His kite was positioned well above the challenger, in a near classic posture for attack. The heavy barbed string moved in, but the Pakistani still had a few tricks left. He sent his smaller kite into several dipping spins, bringing it almost to the ground, each time managing to avoid the cutting barbs.

The kites maneuvered in the wind for another ten minutes before the end came quite quickly. Crawford saw his opportunity and took it, swooping down to loop his string around that of the smaller kite. Then he pulled it in and the barbs sliced easily through the Pakistani's string. The small kite, freed of its mooring, rose with the wind and drifted over the trees as the crowd cheered. Crawford allowed himself a slight smile as he began pulling in his own kite. Then he went around collecting on his bets as Madame Wu trailed behind.

Later, over drinks at a nearby outdoor nightclub, one of the other gamblers conceded, "Crawford, you're the best there is! You're better than any of these local lads, and better than the Pakistanis too." His name was Bates and he was a British merchant who often made big wagers on the kite fights.

Crawford smiled his sleepy smile and said, "It was Madame Wu's eels that did it for me. I'm a great believer in local customs."

"I can see that." Bates drained his glass and ordered another drink. "There's a young American in town," he said casually. "Have you met him yet?"

"Who would that be?" Crawford asked.

"His name's Michael Fleet. He says he was in Vietnam, like you were."

Crawford merely grunted. A great many young Americans had passed through Bangkok in the years he'd been there. But Madame Wu sensed there was some other purpose to the Englishman's inquiry. "What is so special about this American?" she asked.

Bates toyed with his empty glass while awaiting a refill. "He says he wants to learn kite fighting. I thought he might look you up."

"Maybe he will," Crawford conceded. He put down his glass and stood up. "Come on, Anna. It's time we were getting home."

"When will you be fighting again?" Bates wanted to know.

"When the south wind is right and the bets are big." Crawford picked up the star kite, which was leaning against the wall, and went out with Madame Wu behind him.

She carefully filled the long pipe and handed it to him as he lay on the bed. "What are you thinking of?" she asked.

"Lots of things. How it was back home—and in Vietnam."

Madame Wu took a deep breath. "You said once, a long

time ago, that someday a man would come to kill you. Do you
remember that?"

"I remember," he said.

"You are different tonight—since the Englishman mentioned
this young American. Do you fear him?"

He turned away from her on the bed. "I don't want to talk
about it now."

"Why would anyone come after all these years?"

"Some people have long memories," he said simply.

"Is that why you never went home to America?"

"That, and other reasons."

She sighed and changed the subject. "How much money did
you win tonight?"

"About six thousand bahts," he said and turned back to her
with a smile. "That's around three hundred American dollars.
Very good for an hour's work."

She smiled too. It was very good. But it reminded her that
she had not checked the day's receipts in the curio shop. "I
will be back," she told him. He nodded and drew on his pipe.

Downstairs she went quickly about the task of counting the
cash in the register and adding up the credit-card purchases.
While she was working she happened to glance out the big
front window and saw a man standing in the shadows across
the street. Though she could not see his face, she thought he
was watching the building.

When she went back to the apartment she did not mention
the man to Crawford.

The following morning over breakfast she asked, "Why do
we stay in Bangkok, Crawford? We could go to Australia and I
could open a new shop there."

"Australia? What gave you that idea?"

"Perhaps it is time for a new beginning."

He grunted and sipped his coffee.

"I'd better go down and open the shop," she decided.

The sign over the front read MADAME WU'S CURIO EMPORIUM.
Crawford had christened it that when she opened the place
with money he'd supplied. She'd never asked him about the
money, which somehow had come with him out of the jungles

of Vietnam. She had learned long ago to accept without question whatever life had to offer her.

But now there was a man waiting for her to open the shop. Instinctively she knew it was the man she'd seen in the shadows across the street last night. She tried to smile as she unlocked the door and said, "Come right in. We're open for business."

"Does Sidney Crawford live here?" he asked.

She studied his tanned face and saw a young, innocent expression that might have belonged to an angel in an old painting. Surely that face could hold no danger for Crawford. "Yes," she said. "He lives here. Who are you?"

"Name's Michael Fleet. Mike Fleet. I want to learn kite fighting."

She recognized the name as the one Bates had mentioned the previous evening. "Were you there last night?" she asked.

"I sure was! But afterward you all went off in a crowd to the nightclub and I didn't want to intrude. An Englishman named Bates said I should see Crawford. He said he's the best kite fighter in the city."

"I suppose he is," she admitted. "But why would you want to learn such a sport? It is not like boxing or *takraw* or sword duels, our more traditional sports. Some even say that kite fighting is only a game for boy-men who have never grown up."

"There's money in it. I won a hundred bahts myself last night, betting on Crawford!"

The idea of winning a five-dollar bet seemed to excite him so much that she knew she had to let him meet Crawford. His innocence was genuine. "Wait here," she told him, and disappeared into the back of the shop to climb the stairs to their apartment.

When she told Crawford he eyed her with suspicion. "It's the boy Bates mentioned," he said.

"Yes. He is harmless. He only wants to kite fight, to learn from the master. He won five dollars betting on you last night."

Crawford snorted. "He mustn't consider me much of a master if that's all he bet!" He buttoned his shirt and tucked it into his pants. "All right. Send him up."

But as she went back downstairs she saw him reach into the drawer where he kept his Beretta pistol beneath a pile of underwear.

Mike Fleet was twenty-six years old, a young man from California who'd gotten to Vietnam just as the Americans were withdrawing. "I never did get to see enough of this part of the world," he told them when they'd welcomed him upstairs, "so I decided to stay over here and bum around for a few years."

"It's a long few years," Crawford pointed out. "The war ended in '75."

"Yeah. The time does pass quickly when you're havin' fun." For just an instant Madame Wu thought she saw the mask of innocence slip. Then it was back in place as the young American said, "I want to learn to kite fight like you, Mr. Crawford."

"I'm just Crawford here, son. And if you stay you'll just be Fleet. The locals don't have time for two names—not when they're making bets before a match."

"Then you'll teach me?"

Crawford eyed him for a moment before replying. "Maybe." He got to his feet. "Come on—I'll take you along to the Pramane Ground while I try out a new kite."

It was some time before Madame Wu could close her curio shop for an hour and join them. When she reached the open space north of the palace she saw that Crawford had turned the kite string over to Mike Fleet, who was guiding it well, listening while Crawford coached him on every movement.

As Madame Wu stood watching from the edge of the field she was joined by the Englishman, Bates. "I see that young American found Crawford."

"Yes," she replied. "He came to my shop this morning."

Bates nodded. "Seems like a nice chap."

Presently the two Americans ceased their sport and walked over to Madame Wu and the Englishman. "He's got the makings of a champ," Crawford conceded, patting the younger man on the shoulder. "Come back tomorrow, Fleet, and we'll put up both kites at once and spar a bit."

"You mean that?"

"I mean it."

Mike Fleet left with a grin on his face.

"Where do all these young Americans come from?" Bates wondered aloud. "What in God's name brings them to Bangkok? Is it drugs, or women, or what?"

"We have plenty of both," Crawford replied. "He sure didn't come all this distance to learn kite fighting."

Later, back at the apartment, Madame Wu asked, "Do you want me to prepare your pipe?"

Crawford shook his head. "Not yet. Come here. I want to talk. I want to tell you about Vietnam."

"There is no need."

"I want you to know about it in case anything happens to me."

"Crawford—you will live forever!"

He laughed and took her in his arms. "I believed that myself once, when I was younger."

"All right," she agreed. "Tell me about it."

"When I was in the Army," he began, "in 1970, right before I came here and met you, I was given a great deal of American money and sent on a mission into the jungle. I was to meet a man and pay him to assassinate one of the North Vietnamese leaders. The assassination would have been carried out by powerful explosives which would also have killed a great many innocent people. It was war, they told me—and innocent people die all the time in war.

"I knew it was true. I'd seen a village destroyed by napalm just the week before. Well, I went off on my mission, but somewhere along the line I decided it was time for the killing to stop. I never met the man in the jungle. I crossed over into Cambodia and kept going until I reached Thailand. I moved along the coast, sometimes paying native fishermen to take me short distances by boat."

"But why would they want to kill you for that?" Madame Wu asked. "What you did was a good thing, not bad."

"That depends on how you look at it. I imagine there are people back home who figure I betrayed my country and lost the war all by myself."

"It was a long time ago, Crawford."

"Nearly ten years now," he agreed.

"Why are you telling me now? Because you fear this boy who has come looking for you?"

"He's no boy. He's twenty-six years old. Old enough to be a trained assassin."

"Why would they send a trained assassin when any one of a hundred persons in the crowd could kill you at a kite fight?"

"I don't know," he admitted.

"And if you fear him so much, why have you agreed to teach him to kite fight?"

"Maybe I've got some crazy idea of winning him over. Maybe I figure if he gets to know me well enough he won't be able to kill me."

"And maybe you're wrong about him."

"We'll see," he said quietly.

They held a mock kite fight the following evening and though Crawford cut up the younger man's kite quite badly Fleet managed to stay in the contest for nearly an hour. Then they switched kites and Crawford demonstrated the techniques of soaring and gliding by which the smaller kite's long tail could be used to entangle the star points of the larger kite. The young man learned fast, with an intensity Madame Wu could only admire.

But at the end of the evening she had a question for Fleet while Crawford gathered up the fallen kites. "The other morning when you came to my shop—I saw you watching it the night before."

"Yes," he admitted. "I was trying to work up my courage. Finally I decided to wait till morning."

"I see."

"He's a great man, Crawford is."

"I think so," Madame Wu said. "I don't know what I'd do if anything happened to him."

"You speak English quite well," Fleet observed, studying her closely for the first time. "Did Crawford teach you?"

"The Americans taught me. Crawford was the last of many, but the most important one. After Crawford, I want no more teachers."

"What about this man Bates?"

"He was a doctor once, but when he came here a few years back he was a merchant, employed by a British company. He doesn't talk much about his past. No one does in Bangkok."

"Does Crawford?"

Her eyes searched his face. "He talks to me. Why do you wonder?"

Mike Fleet shrugged. "I don't know. I asked him about Vietnam and he changed the subject. Hell, we were both there! I thought he'd want to talk about it."

"Some things are better left in the past."

Bates had appeared from somewhere to speak with Crawford and when they parted Crawford came over with the kites to where Fleet and Madame Wu stood waiting. "Bates says the Pakistani wants a rematch."

"Will you give him one?" Fleet wanted to know.

"It's customary. One rematch—like in championship boxing."

"When?" Madame Wu asked.

"Tomorrow evening."

"I will need to free more eels."

Crawford's eyes twinkled. "What's the matter? The last batch run out of steam already?"

"For the major kite fights a new ritual is needed."

He smiled at Fleet. "I taught her everything I know about business but she still can't face a decision or a kite fight without releasing her eels."

"She's a fine woman," the younger man said. "I wish I could find one half as good in this city."

"There are new ones arriving every day from the rural areas. Some say there might be as many as two hundred thousand prostitutes in Bangkok."

Fleet blushed at his words. "I don't mean a prostitute."

Crawford turned to Madame Wu. "Tell him what you were when I found you, Anna."

She sucked in her breath and said, very quietly, not looking at either of them, "I was a bar hostess at the Café of Floating Lights. Crawford took me away from that and set me up in business."

"You're a lucky man, Crawford. With a woman like this I wouldn't have gone back home either."

"Let's hope you find one," Crawford said.

They parted then, and Madame Wu fell into step beside Crawford. "What do you think of him?" she asked.

Crawford pondered a moment. Then he said simply, "I think he's been sent to kill me."

Over breakfast the next morning Crawford made plans for the day. "I need to fix up the kite a bit for tonight. Fleet will be there and I have to put on a good show for him."

"Even if he plans to kill you?"

"I could be wrong. Maybe he's as innocent as you think. Anyway, I can't go through the rest of my life looking over my shoulder."

She went downstairs to the shop with him. He needed to buy more heavy kite string so she unlocked the door to let him out. It was not yet nine o'clock, and the little street of shops was still nearly deserted. As he stood in the doorway she heard something like a muffled cough. He stepped back into the shop and slammed the door. He was holding his side and when he took his hand away Madame Wu saw the blood.

"Crawford—what is it?" She tried to keep her voice calm, though her heart was racing.

"Someone just took a shot at me from across the street. Either he used a silencer or it was a small-caliber target pistol."

"Did you see anyone?" she asked, pulling away his shirt to expose the wound.

"No. Don't bother with that. It just grazed me."

"You're bleeding. You need stitches."

"He's a damned lousy shot."

"Lucky for you! I must get you to a doctor."

"No. A little tape will close the wound."

"You will bleed to death!" She was insistent now. Though there was not much blood, his face was very pale.

She helped him upstairs and brought some tape, but after an examination of the wound in a mirror he was forced to agree with her. "All right," he said. "Call Bates. He used to be a doctor."

"Why not go to a hospital?"

"I'd just as soon the word didn't get around quite yet. Right now, whoever tried to kill me doesn't know how badly I'm hurt. That could be an advantage for the next few hours."

She tried Bates's number three times before he answered. When his voice finally came on the line she said, "Mr. Bates, someone tried to kill Crawford. Could you come here right away, please?"

"What? How badly is he hurt?"

"Not too bad, I think."

"I'll be right over."

When she hung up she started thinking about the eels. Now, it seemed, they were more important than ever. It was no longer merely a kite fight that was at stake, but Crawford's life.

She went to him and said, "When Bates comes I must go out for some eels."

He tried to laugh, but she could see he was in pain.

"Is it bad, Crawford?"

"A scrape. I'll be good as new."

She went downstairs to wait for Bates. When he arrived he was carrying a small black medical bag she'd never seen before. For the first time she believed the story that he had been a doctor once.

"Who shot him?" he demanded.

"We don't know. We saw no one. Go up to him, Bates, and patch his wound. I must do some shopping, but I will be back."

She made her way down the street, past the other shops that were just opening their doors. The morning mist was burning off early and the sun would quickly warm the air.

At the great outdoor market there was no sign of the boy who sold the eels, and for a moment she panicked. Then she saw him across the field near one of the dried-up canals. He had a pushcart full of brown plastic bags that seemed to writhe even as she watched. "Quickly, boy!" she called out. "Sell me nine eels for luck!"

Clutching her purchase close, feeling the eels move against her as if anxious for their coming freedom, she was tempted to go immediately to the Klong Maha Nak. But then something stirred in her memory. Something dangerous.

Crawford was in danger.

She hurried back to the shop, still clutching the plastic bag. She climbed the stairs to the kitchen and listened.

Bates and Crawford were talking in the bedroom. The Englishman laughed about something and then come out to the kitchen with his black bag.

He saw Madame Wu by the table and smiled. "He'll be as good as new. I took a couple of stitches and taped him up well."

"That's fine."

"I'll go now," he said. "Let him get a bit of rest."

"Mr. Bates—"

"Yes?"

"When you arrived you asked who shot Crawford. But on the phone I only told you someone tried to kill him. How did you know it was by shooting?"

"I—"

"I think it was you, Mr. Bates, hiding across the street when he came out this morning."

"What? What are you talking about?" His black bag had come open and he was reaching inside.

Madame Wu saw the bread knife on the table, just out of reach. She knew she had made a terrible mistake. Even as she tried to speak again, Bates raised the silenced pistol and fired three times.

Crawford opened his eyes. Bates was coming back into the room. "What was that noise?" Crawford asked.

Then he saw the gun in the Englishman's hand. It was a hit man's weapon—a .22 caliber target pistol with a silencer.

"I had to kill her, Crawford, so I might as well finish you off too. I can make it look as if you killed each other."

"It was you across the street this morning!"

"Yes," Bates said, raising the pistol until Crawford was looking down the barrel. "You always knew someone would come, didn't you?"

"You came three years ago. Why did you wait so long?"

"My position was too safe here. I didn't want to jeopardize it with a foolish killing. Once I knew it was you I spent some time trying to find out what you did with the money."

"It's downstairs in the curio shop."

"I know that now."

"What business is it of yours whether I live or die?"

Bates shrugged. "None, personally. It wasn't my war, after all. But I'm an arms merchant, selling to various factions in Southeast Asia. There are people who still remember you—who say you lost the war. They told me I had to kill you if I wanted to stay in business. So I waited for the right opportunity—the appearance of a young American I could pin it on. That's why I patched you up when Madame Wu phoned. It wouldn't do to kill you here, where Fleet might not be blamed. I planned to have another try tonight after the kite fight. She forced my hand—so now you'll die together."

"Wait—" Crawford began, trying to rise from the bed.

"I'll miss you, Crawford," Bates said, his finger whitening on the trigger. "I won a great deal of money on you."

That was when Madame Wu plunged the bread knife into his back.

"You made a terrible mess," Crawford told her. "There's blood all over the place."

Madame Wu sat trembling in the chair while they waited for the police. "I never killed anyone before. Is that what it's like?"

"That's what it's like. You saved my life, Anna."

"It was the eels," she told him. "I was holding them to my chest when he shot me. The bullets knocked me over, but they hit the eels."

"I guess I'll never doubt you again when you say that they bring good luck."

"Will there be others like Bates who come to kill you?"

"Perhaps."

"What will you do now?"

He touched his side and winced. "I may not be able to handle the kite this evening. I'll have to see if young Fleet can carry on for me."

Payoff on Double Zero

WARNER LAW

Although she was typing from her shorthand notes, the middle-aged secretary kept sneaking glances at Sam Miller across the outer office. He was waiting to see her boss, Mr. Collins, who was the owner and manager of the casino in the Starlight Hotel. This is a relatively old establishment, not far out of town on the Las Vegas Strip.

To women in general, and to middle-aged secretaries in particular, Sam was almost surrealistically handsome, too all-American to believe in one look. He was in his early twenties, well over six feet tall, broad in the shoulders and lithe below. His blond hair was cut short, his face was tanned, his nose perfectly straight, his teeth white, his smile a gift of pleasure. His eyes were true blue and his gaze was of such clear and steady honesty that it made even a secretary with a pure conscience and a fine Methodist background feel somewhat shifty and sinful when she met it. She knew that Mr. Collins would be eager to hire Sam—though he'd pretend he wasn't and he'd give the boy a little hard time first. The Starlight needed dealers and rarely did they find one who was such a poster picture of integrity. More than that, Sam's looks would draw most of the women gamblers in Vegas, the younger ones with an urge to bed him and the older ones with an impulse to mother him. Then the intercom buzzed and Mr. Collins said that he was ready to see Mr. Miller.

Sam went in and carefully shut the door behind him. Mr. Collins posed behind his massive desk, right hand extended, a smile of limited cordiality on his face. Sam had heard that Mr. Collins was Balkan by birth, with a name of many jagged syllables that had been carefully naturalized and neutralized. He was a man in his sixties, olive in coloring, wearing a light-gray silk suit exactly shaded to match his hair.

Sam shook his hand and smiled and said, "How do you do, sir?"

"It's a pleasure to meet you, Sam Miller. Sit down. Tell me the story of your life." Mr. Collins had only a trace of a foreign accent.

Sam sat. "All of it?"

"Well, it can scarcely have been a very long life. How old are you?"

"Twenty-two, sir."

"Might I see your driver's license?"

"Sure." Sam took it from his wallet and handed it over the desk and Mr. Collins gave it a quick glance and passed it back.

"Have you ever been arrested?"

"No, sir."

"Be certain, now. The rules of the Nevada Gaming Commission require me to check."

"No, sir. I've never been arrested for anything."

"Why do you wish to be a dealer?"

"To make some money and save it, so I can go to college full time."

"Where do you come from originally?"

"I was born in Los Angeles and I went to Hollywood High, and then I enlisted in the Marine Corps, rather than be drafted."

"What did you do in the Marine Corps?"

"I got sent to Vietnam."

"Did anything happen to you?"

"Yes. I got shot three times."

"You have my profound sympathy. Were they serious wounds?"

"One was. It was in the stomach. The others were just flesh wounds. Anyway, I finally got discharged last summer."

"Do you happen to have your discharge papers on your person?"

Sam produced them and Mr. Collins looked them over and handed them back.

"And after your discharge?"

"My uncle had a liquor store in Hollywood and I went to work for him. But we were held up four times. Twice I got clobbered with revolver butts and once I was shot in the foot, and finally my uncle was pistol-whipped and he said the hell with it and sold the store and I was out of a job."

"You've crowded a good deal of action into your short life."

Sam smiled. "Not intentionally. And then somebody suggested I might get a job dealing up here in Las Vegas, and my math was always pretty good, and so I came up and took a course at Mr. Ferguson's Dealers' School and, as you've seen from the diploma your secretary brought in, I graduated yesterday."

Mr. Collins picked up the diploma and handed it to Sam. "Why did you come here—that is, instead of to some other casino?"

"Mr. Ferguson said he thought you might be hiring dealers and that you were a good man to work for. He also said that you were the smartest man in Vegas."

"Did he, now? It's the first I've heard of it. As it happens, however, I've just been talking to Ferguson on the phone about you. He says you were one of the best students he's had in a long time. How is your roulette?"

"Pretty fair, I think."

"We shall see. A little test. Thirty-two has come up," Mr. Collins began, and then rattled on with, "and a player has two chips straight up on it, one split, two chips on corners, four chips on three across, and three chips on the first column. How many chips do you pay this player?"

It took Sam four seconds to answer, "A hundred and forty-seven."

"You forgot the column bet."

"No, sir, I didn't. You said the first column. Thirty-two is in the second column." Sam smiled a little. "Which you very well know."

Mr. Collins did not smile. "These are quarter chips. How much has the player won?"

"Seven stacks plus seven. Thirty-six seventy-five."

Now Mr. Collins smiled. "Can you start work this afternoon at four? That's the middle shift—four till midnight."

"Yes, sir."

"You'll get forty dollars per shift, plus your share of the

dealers' tips. Like most casinos, we pool them and whack them up evenly. You'll average around two-fifty, two-seventy-five for a forty-hour week. Is that satisfactory?"

"Yes, sir." Sam rose as if to leave.

"Sit down. I have something to tell you. I and I alone own the gaming license here. I am not answerable to anyone. I have no connection with the Mafia nor any other bunch of criminals. We do not cheat our players, we do not cheat the Nevada Gaming Commission, and we do not cheat the Internal Revenue Service. Furthermore, if any dealer tries to cheat the house in favor of himself or a player, he gets no mercy from me."

"Mr. Ferguson told me you ran an honest game."

"It is *more* than an honest game. A little test. Number seven has come up. Having made sure that the number is not covered, you clear the board of chips. But then a player says, 'Just a minute, here! I had a chip on seven, but you took it away!' You know for certain that this player is lying through his teeth. What do you do?"

"Well . . . I'd send for my pit boss."

"No. You apologize to the player and you pay him. Only if the player does this more than once do you call for your pit boss—who will have been at your side by that time, anyway. The point I am making is that as far as *you* are concerned, every player is honest and he is always right. You are not a policeman and you are not a detective. That is the job of your pit boss and it is also my job. *It is not yours.*"

"Yes, sir."

Mr. Collins rose and extended his hand. "Nice to have you with us. Keep your hands off our cocktail waitresses. There are plenty of other pretty girls in this town."

At 3:45 that afternoon, Sam walked again into the Starlight Hotel. Being one of the older Strip hotels, it was not a large one. The casino itself was a separate wing. People came to play there because it was neither noisy nor garish, like the newer and much larger Strip casinos. The slots were in a separate room, so their clatter did not disturb the serious gamblers. On the depressed oval that was the casino floor, there were two crap tables, three 21 tables, and three roulette tables. There was no wheel of fortune and no bingo and no racetrack betting. This was a casino for players who appreciated quiet. Even the stickmen at the crap tables kept their continuous chatter down.

Sam didn't know where to report for work, but he found a small bar through an archway on the upper level of the room and went in and inquired of the barman, whose name turned out to be Chuck. He told Sam how to find the dealers' room.

Sam followed a corridor to the rear of the building, where he found a room with some wall lockers and a few easy chairs and tables. Other dealers were there, hanging up their jackets and putting on their green aprons. A scrawny little man in a dark suit came up to Sam. He looked fifty and had a sour, sallow face.

"Sam Miller?"

"Yes, sir."

"I'm Pete and I'm your pit boss on this shift." He turned to the other dealers. "Boys, this is Sam Miller." They grunted friendly greetings. "You'll get to know 'em all," Pete told Sam. "But this is Harry." He took Sam over to meet a tall man of seventy with weary eyes. "You'll be working together. You can begin by stacking for Harry tonight."

"Pleased to meet you, sonny boy," Harry said and shook Sam's hand and looked at him and reacted. "My God—you look fifteen years old."

In the casino, Sam found that his roulette-table setup was almost identical with the one in Ferguson's school. There were six stools along the players' side of the table. By the wheel on the dealer's right were stacks of chips in different colors— white, red, green, blue, brown, and yellow. They were all marked STARLIGHT but had no stated value. Since the minimum bet was a quarter, their value was so presumed.

Past the colors were stacks of dollar tokens. These were of base metal, minted for the casino. To the right of the tokens were stacks of house checks, with marked denominations of five dollars ranging upward to fifty dollars. The casino also had house checks worth one hundred dollars and five hundred dollars and one thousand dollars, but these were seldom seen in any quantity at a roulette table.

In front of the dealer was a slot in which rested a plastic

shingle, and when players bought chips with currency, the bills were shoved down through the slot and into the locked cashbox under the table.

Since this was now the end of a shift, Mr. Collins came up with his keys and an empty cashbox. He exchanged one box for the other and walked off with the full one toward the cashier's office, followed by an armed and uniformed security guard.

For the first hour, Sam merely stacked the chips and the occasional checks that Harry shoved over to him. It was a quiet game, without plungers or cheaters or arguments. Then Harry went off for a break and Sam took over the dealing.

Not long after, a woman came up to Sam's table. She was in her fifties, tall and scrawny, and her mouth held more than her share of the world's teeth. She was wearing a gold-lamé blouse over orange slacks. She sounded rather drunk as she said, "Gimme a coupla stacksa quarters." She handed Sam a ten-dollar bill. He slotted the money and passed her two stacks of red chips. "I don' like red," she said. "It doesn't go with my slacks. You got another color?"

"How about green?" Sam asked her, smiling.

"Green is jus' fine," she said and soon picked up the two stacks Sam put in front of her.

Sam started the ball whirring.

"I been playin' this roulette for years and years," the woman announced to the table at large, "an' there's no such thing as a system. No such thing as a system! You just gotta let the chips fall where they may, as the fella said!"

She then turned her back to the table, with twenty chips in each hand, and tossed them all over her shoulders onto the board. They clattered down every which way and knocked other bets out of position, and a great many of the chips rolled off the table and onto the floor. The other players cried out in annoyance. Sam removed the ball from the wheel. Pete started over, pausing to push one of several buttons on a small table in the center of the enclosure.

"I'm sorry, ma'am," Sam told the woman, "but we can't bet that way."

She giggled. "I'm jus' lettin' the chips fall where they may!"

"Even so," Sam said with an engaging smile, "if your bets aren't in correct positions, I won't know how to pay you when you win."

The other players had been patiently bending over and retrieving green chips from the floor. Sam gathered them and stacked them for her and made sure they were all there.

"I'm real sorry to make all this trouble," the woman said, smiling at Sam. "Let's see, now. Most of 'em fell around twenny, so that's where I'll kinda put 'em. Around twenny." With drunken carefulness, she began to slather her chips around number 20.

In the distance, Sam saw Mr. Collins approaching from his office—where he had just heard the warning buzz from Pete. He walked up and stood at the head of the table, but said nothing.

Sam put the ball in motion. The woman watched it spin. "It's just got to be twenny," she said. "Or else I am bankrupt!"

The ball fell into number 20. "Ooooooh!" She jumped up and down and clapped her hands. "I won! I won!"

Sam counted the green chips on the board. "Six straight up on twenty, nine splits, ten on corners. That's four hundred and forty-three chips, plus these twenty-five left on the board."

"How much is that in money?" the woman asked.

"One hundred and seventeen dollars," Sam said.

Mr. Collins had come up behind her. "My congratulations, Mrs. Burke," he said.

She turned. "Oh, dear Mr. Collins. How are you?"

"It's always such a pleasure to see you here," Mr. Collins said. "As a matter of fact, I've been meaning to call you. Before you break the bank, why don't you cash in and come and have a drink with me? I need your advice about a piece of real estate."

In moments, Mrs. Burke had been paid her winnings and was walking off happily on Mr. Collins' arm. Under the chatter of the players, Pete murmured to Sam, "Very nicely handled, son. What Howard Hughes and Kerkorian don't own in Vegas, Mrs. Burke does."

On Sam's second night of dealing, nothing whatever happened. But on his third night, there was trouble.

A fat-faced young man with a sullen mouth and pimples had been betting regularly on 14 and losing. He was playing with ten-dollar house checks, but he didn't look as if he could afford them, and he kept increasing his bets until he was up to fifty dollars a spin, straight up on 14. Despair came into his eyes.

This time, 15 came up. There was no bet on it. Sam cleared the board.

"Hold on, there!" the young man said. "What about my fifty on fifteen?"

Sam smiled politely. "I think it was on fourteen, sir."

Pete had already pushed a button and was at Sam's side.

"Not this time it wasn't!" the young man said. "I finally got tired of fourteen and bet on fifteen. You were just so used to seeing me bet on fourteen that you made a mistake, that's all."

Eighteen hundred dollars was involved. Sam glanced over at Pete, but before the pit boss could speak, a distinguished-looking white-haired man at the very end of the table called to Sam, "I'm afraid the young man up there is right." His manner was reluctant and apologetic. "I'm sorry to be difficult, but I did see him bet on fifteen. I wondered at the time if he'd made a mistake or was changing his number after all this time."

The smartest man in Vegas had by now come up behind the bettor. "Pay the bet, Sam," he said. "I want no arguments here."

"Yes, sir," Sam said and reached for some checks.

Pete stopped him with a hand and said, "We don't have that much here at the table, Mr. Collins."

This was not true.

"Oh?" said Mr. Collins. "Well, let's go to my office, then. If you and your friend would come with me, I'll see that—"

"My *friend?*" the young man asked. "I've never—"

The older man said from the foot of the table, "I've never seen that young fellow before in my life!"

"Oh?" Mr. Collins looked surprised. "I'm sorry. I'd presumed you two were friends."

"I never laid eyes on that gentleman before in my life!" the young man said.

"I understand," said Mr. Collins. "However, sir," he said to the older man, "I'll need a brief statement from you affirming that you saw the bet being placed. It's required by the Nevada Gaming Commission in these instances."

This was rubbish.

The older man sighed and picked up his chips and came round the table and offered his hand and a smile to the young man and said, "My name is John Wood."

"I'm George Wilkins and I'm real sorry to put you to all this trouble, but thank you for sticking up for me. What I mean"— he nodded toward Sam—"young fellows like this are obviously so new they make normal mistakes."

Sam wished he could knock this young man down and kick his teeth out. The two walked away with Mr. Collins. They did not return to the casino floor. When midnight came and Sam went off duty, he passed Mr. Collins on the upper level and asked him, "What happened to those two cheaters?"

Mr. Collins smiled. "Why do you so presume, Sam?"

"Because there was no bet on fifteen and anybody who said otherwise is a liar."

Laughing, Mr. Collins said, "Sam, you wouldn't believe how stupid some people can be. I asked to see their driver's licenses, as a matter of form. Without thinking, they showed them to me. What do you think I learned?"

"Don't tell me they have the same name?!"

"No, no. But their addresses showed that they live two houses apart. In Van Nuys, California."

"My God! What did you do to them?"

"Nothing. I left them alone in my office for a minute and when I came back, they were gone. I presume they're well back in California by now." The smartest man in Vegas patted Sam on the shoulder and said, "Good night, Sam," and walked off.

It was around eleven on Sam's fourth night that things really began to happen. Sam was dealing and Harry was stacking for him. The table was crowded and all the colors were in use. Behind the seated players, others stood, betting with coins and house checks. As the ball began to slow, Sam said, "No more bets, please."

A man started shouting, "Let me through! Here, now—let me through! Get out of the way, damn it!"

He was a tall man in his seventies and he wore a white Stetson. He had a white mustache under a long red nose. He shouldered his way through the standers. He held two packages of bank-strapped currency above his head and when he reached the table, he threw them both in the general area of number 23 and announced, "That's two thousand dollars right smack on twenty-three! Straight up!"

Sam quickly picked up the packs and tossed them off the betting area. "I'm sorry, sir." The ball fell into number 11.

The old man's reedy voice rose above the murmur at the table. "What's the matter, young fella? Something the matter with my money?" He was wearing a white-silk Western shirt and an apache tie with a gold tie slide in the shape of a nugget, and over all he had on a spotless white-buckskin suit with long fringes and with stitched patch pockets high and low. Sam had seen a similar suit in a Las Vegas store window for $295.

"This is perfectly good money!" the old man said, showing off the two packs. They contained hundred-dollar bills, which, as Sam knew, usually come from a bank strapped in units of ten. These looked to be fresh from the Bureau of Engraving and Printing.

Sam smiled at the old man. "Of course it is, sir. But, for one thing, you were too late for this roll; and for another, there's a two-hundred-dollar maximum bet on the numbers; and for still another, we don't use paper money on this table."

"Well, sell me some chips, damn it!"

"I will, sir, but we're out of colors and—"

Pete had come to the table and he now asked, "What denomination would you like to play with, sir?"

"Hundreds! Hundred-dollar chips, if you've got 'em." Everyone at the table was now listening and the old man turned and smiled and said, "My name's Premberton! Bert Premberton! From up Elko way! Pleased to make your acquaintance!" He shook hands with those whom he could reach.

"I'll have to get some hundred-dollar checks from the cashier, Mr. Premberton," Pete said. "How many would you like?"

"Well, now . . ." The old man pondered and brought out package after package of strapped hundred-dollar bills from his various pockets and stacked them on the table in front of him. Twenty thousand dollars was visible. There was a stunned silence around the table. "Sold a ranch today," Premberton told everyone simply. "Or it finally got through escrow, I should say." To Pete, he said, "Oh, hell. Let's jest start with two thousand. But get plenty, while you're at it." He handed Sam two packages of hundred-dollar bills and stuffed the others back into his pockets.

Sam handed them to Pete, who broke the paper straps and fanned the bills and nodded and said, "Two thousand. I'll be right back."

"Here, now!" the old man bellowed. "What if twenty-three comes up while you're gone, hey? I want two hundred on it, every time. Twenty-three is gonna be a hot one tonight, I can tell you for true!"

"You'll be covered on every roll, Mr. Premberton," Pete said, starting off.

"Take over for me," Sam told Harry and walked after Pete, catching up with him outside the roulette enclosure. "Pete?" The pit boss stopped and turned. "I don't like this old man," Sam said. "I've got a kind of feeling about him."

"Why?"

"Well, for one thing, he's been drinking, and I didn't like the way he butted his way to the table, and—well, I just don't trust him is all."

"It is not your job to trust people. As long as his money's good, I don't care if—"

"But maybe it isn't. Maybe it's—"

Mr. Collins had walked up to them. "Troubles?"

"Maybe it's counterfeit," Sam finished.

Pete smiled. "You have got to be kidding."

Mr. Collins took the bills from Pete and ruffled through them and handed them back and motioned the pit boss toward the cashier's window. Then he sighed.

"Sam you still have a good deal to learn. For all practical purposes—as far as we are concerned—there is no such thing as a hundred-dollar bill that is counterfeit. Oh, they do exist, but they're extremely rare, for the reason that printers don't bother with them because they're so difficult to pass. We get fives and tens and twenties and now and then a fifty. But I don't think I've seen a funny hundred in twenty years. In any case, there are two places in which no one but an idiot would deliberately pass even *one* phony hundred-dollar bill, and one is a bank and the other is a casino. Both places have smart cashiers and men with guns."

"I'm sorry," Sam said. "I didn't know that. I was only trying to protect the house."

"It is not your job to protect the house. I thought I'd made that perfectly clear when we first met. Would you get back to your table now, please?"

"Yes, sir."

Pete came up to them, carrying a plastic rack nearly full of one-hundred-dollar house checks. "I got quite a few, just in case," he said. "And to make our boy detective here happy, I asked both Ruth and Hazel to check out those bills; they're both experts in the currency department, and they assure me that the twenty hundreds are the genuine article, with the serial numbers in sequence, just as they left the Bureau of Engraving and Printing."

"I'm sorry to be so stupid," Sam said and followed Pete back to the table, where he and the pit boss piled the checks neatly in stacks of twenty. Harry reached for one stack, knocked off four checks and handed the remaining sixteen to Premberton, saying, "Two thousand, sir, less four hundred for the last two rolls."

The old man grunted his understanding and placed two checks on 23. He then began looking around the casino as if for someone, finally saw her, put two fingers into his mouth and produced a shrill whistle. He waved a hand and shouted, "Over here, honey!"

A girl came toward the table and tried to get through the crowd. "Let her through, there!" the old man cried. "That's my little bride, there! Let her through, damn it!"

People gave way and the girl soon joined Premberton, who hugged and kissed her. The girl blushed and said, "Oh, Bert! Not here!"

The girl was spectacularly lovely. She was in her early twenties and had golden hair and large young breasts. Her mouth was full and sensuous, but her wide blue eyes gave her an expression of innocence.

"Folks! I want you to meet my sweet little honeybunch, Vikki!" He kissed her again and hugged her and then ran his hand up and around her buttocks. "We got hitched this very mornin'!" There was a silence around the table, partly of incredulity and partly of disapproval. "And the reason twenty-three is goin' to be a hot number tonight is that today is February the twenty-third and it's also my own little hot number here's birthday, and she's twenty-three this very day! What do you think of that?" Premberton turned to Harry and asked, "You're sure, now, that two hundred is all I can bet at a time?"

"Yes, sir," Harry said as the ball slowed. "That's our limit." The ball dropped once and bounced about and finally fell into 23 and remained there. "Twenty-three," Harry announced and smiled at Vikki. "Happy birthday, young lady."

"Hey, now!" the old man shouted and clapped everyone he could reach on the back. "What'd I tell you? Twenty-three's goin' to be a hot number tonight!"

Harry pushed three and a half stacks over to the old man. "Seventy checks, sir. Seven thousand dollars."

The other players started exclaiming in excitement and people who heard the commotion began to crowd around the table to watch. Premberton told Vikki to open her shoulder bag and he dumped the seventy checks into it. "You'll get that Rolls-Royce automobile for a weddin' present yet, honeybunch!" Then, to Harry, "Say, now! My little bride here can play, too, can't she?"

"Surely, sir," Harry said.

"Well, you jest do that, Vikki honey! You put two hundred on twenty-three along with me, you hear?"

After the old man had bet his two checks, Vikki added two more from her purse. Harry turned to Sam. "Take over for a couple of minutes, would you?" Harry walked off and Sam stepped into his place and Pete came up to stack for Sam. Other players began piling chips onto 23. Sam sent the ball spinning. It eventually fell into number 5.

"You got to do better 'n that, young fella!" the old man shouted.

Sam smiled at him. "I'm trying, sir. I really am."

"I sure wish we could bet more than four hundred," the old man said. "Twenty-three is sure goin' to be a hot one tonight!"

A man standing next to Premberton volunteered: "You can also play splits if you want to, sir, and corners and three across."

"How's that?"

Using his finger as a pointer, the man showed him what he meant.

"Well, I'm jest goin' to bet that way, then!" He started to cover the board all around 23 and then said, "I'm goin' to need some more chips, young fella." He brought out three more packs of hundred-dollar bills and handed them to Sam, who broke the straps and counted the bills.

"Three thousand," Sam announced and slotted the money. Then he reached for the stack and a half Pete had ready for him and passed the checks to the old man, who finished covering 23 and its surrounding numbers. As the ball whirred, Sam figured that if 23 came up, the Prembertons would win $20,200. The number turned out to be 22, but the old man had five thousand dollars coming to him because of his bets on splits and corners and three across. When Sam passed his winnings to him, the old man dumped them into Vikki's purse and bet again as before. The next three numbers were losers for Premberton, who was then almost out of visible checks.

"Better give me five thousand this time, young fella," he said, bringing five packages of money from his pocket. It was slotted and Sam gave him two and a half stacks. Harry returned and took over the stacking from Pete. The ball fell into 24. Sam paid the old man another fifty checks and these, too, went into Vikki's purse.

"Start thinkin' what color you want that Rolls-Royce automobile painted, honeybunch."

The next two numbers were 0 and 36 and Premberton was down again in checks. "Five thousand more, young fella." The money came out and was counted and sent down into the cashbox and the old man got his two and a half stacks.

"Take over for me?" Sam asked Harry. To Pete as he passed, Sam said, "Got to take a leak." He crossed the casino floor and went up to the upper level, where Mr. Collins was standing, his eyes in constant motion as he surveyed and studied the activity below.

"How is it going, Sam?"

"Mr. Collins, I don't like what's going on at my table."

"Oh? Troubles?"

"Well, whenever that old man wins, he dumps his checks into his wife's bag, but when he loses, he cashes some more of his hundred-dollar bills."

"So?"

"She has close to seventeen thousand in there right now."

"So?" Mr. Collins shrugged. "Sam, some players feel luckier when they're playing with house money and others prefer to pocket our money and play with their own. It's their business. It is not yours."

"I know. But I keep getting the feeling there's something phony about the old man. I mean, as if he were Walter Brennan, playing a rich old rancher. Except that Walter Brennan would convince me and this Mr. Premberton doesn't. It's like he's overacting his part. And the way he fondles that pretty little girl who's young enough to be his granddaughter—well, it makes you kind of sick."

Mr. Collins smiled. "I see. It's not just a roulette dealer I've hired. I have in addition a drama critic and an arbiter of morals." His smile faded. "Has this old gentleman tried any funny business with his bets?"

"Well, no. Not yet, anyway."

"Nor will he. Sam, I'll tell you how to spot a potential cheater on sight. When an ordinary player comes into this casino, he will glance around casually and then decide where he wants to go and go there. But when a cheater comes in—and by this I mean someone who has cheated before elsewhere and may well do so here—he will stop and look carefully at the face of every dealer and pit boss on the floor, for fear he'll be recognized from the past. When I see this, I make sure that this player is watched every minute he's here."

"That's very interesting," Sam said. "I'd never thought of that."

"I saw this old man walk down from the bar. He looked

around for the nearest roulette table and hurried to it. In addition, it happens that Chuck the bartender knows him. He's from up near Elko and he recently sold one of his ranches, which is why he has all this bank cash on him. Also, he got married this morning and he's celebrating."

"He told us, at the table."

"All right. Sam, I will tell you one more time and only one more time: the overall problems involved in running this casino are mine. They are not yours. Please don't make me lose my patience with you."

"No, sir. I'm sorry." Sam walked off and into the men's room and in a couple of minutes came out. As he passed the archway leading to the bar, he paused and then went in. There were few customers and Chuck was drying glasses.

"Hi, Sammy boy."

Sam said, "Chuck—this old man—this Mr. Premberton. Mr. Collins says you know him."

Chuck nodded. "He's a rancher from up near Elko. He got married this—"

Sam cut in with, "But do you know him? From before, I mean?"

"Well, no, but—"

"So how do you know so much about him?"

"He was in here earlier, talking to people, buying everybody drinks, showing off his new little wife—you know."

"Thanks, Chuck." Sam walked out of the bar and down to his table. Pete moved away, so that Sam could take over the stacking. From the stacks of hundred-dollar checks, it was apparent that Premberton had lost a few thousand while Sam had been away. Now the old man handed Harry another five packages of hundred-dollar bills, which went down the slot.

Sam passed two and a half stacks to Harry, who said, "You mind rolling? I'm really beat."

"Sure." As Sam took Harry's place, he glanced at his watch and saw that it was 11:45. In fifteen minutes, the shift would end.

Number 34 came up, and then 6. One of the players had given up his seat to Vikki, who now sat directly across from Sam. "Whatever happened to number twenty-three?" she asked with a smile. It began as a casual smile, but then she glanced up and saw that the old man was engrossed in betting and she looked at Sam and smiled, but directly now. With this smile, all innocence left her eyes.

Sam indicated 23. "I'm afraid it's hidden under all those chips."

"Well, see if you can find it for us."

Sam sent the ball spinning. "I'll do my very best, Mrs. Premberton." The number turned out to be 26. Sam gave the old man thirty-three checks, which Vikki dumped into her bag. There had to be over twenty thousand dollars in that bag by now, but then, almost as much had come out of Premberton's pockets.

The next two numbers were 2 and 12. The old man was out of checks again. "Gimme some of them chips, Vikki, honey."

"Oh, Bert. Don't you think we should stop? It's been a long day and it's almost midnight, and—"

"Jest one more roll. I got a hunch it'll be twenty-three."

Vikki passed a handful of checks to Premberton, who leaned over the table to bet and then silently collapsed and fell onto the table and lay still. When it was plain that he wasn't going to move, Vikki cried out and reached over and touched him.

Others at the table were saying, "Is he dead?" "He's had a heart attack!" "Get a doctor, somebody!"

Pete had already pushed buttons. Two security guards hurried up, herded people aside and got to the old man, who now groaned and opened his eyes and managed to push himself erect. The guards held him up.

"What happened?" Premberton asked.

Mr. Collins hurried up. "Help him to my office," he told the guards. "The hotel doctor is on his way."

"I'm all right," Premberton said. "Jest had a little dizzy spell."

"I insist," said Mr. Collins.

The guards started off with the old man. Vikki followed, but Sam called, "Don't forget your husband's checks, Mrs. Premberton." Sam hadn't started the ball rolling. He picked up the old man's bets and handed them to her.

"Thank you. You're very kind." She hurried off toward Mr. Collins' office.

The table quieted down as Sam started the ball rolling. "How did they do, all told?" Sam asked Harry.

He studied the stacks of checks by the wheel and said, "They're up a hundred. It's getting close to midnight, thank the saints. I'm really beat."

In a few minutes, after the graveyard shift had come onto the floor, Sam and Harry walked up to the higher level, where they met Mr. Collins coming out of his office.

"How's the old man?" Harry asked.

"All right, the doctor says. It was just a faint. His wife tells me he had no dinner and a lot of drinks, and I gathered that they'd spent the afternoon in bed."

"It kind of turns your stomach," Sam said. "That old man and that little girl."

"It may turn yours, sonny boy," Harry said sourly. "But I ain't quite dead yet and it don't turn mine." He walked off.

"They ended a hundred to the good," Sam told Mr. Collins.

"I'm just relieved it was nothing more serious than a faint."

"Do you suppose he can get back to their motel all right?" Sam asked.

"That's for *me* to worry about, Sam," Mr. Collins said in a warning tone.

"Sorry," Sam said and walked away.

In the dealers' room, Sam hung up his apron and chatted with some of the dealers and combed his hair and put on his jacket and then went into the bar and ordered a beer. He enjoyed it, and ordered another, and was starting on that when Mr. Collins came into the bar and up to him.

"Sam, the old man wants to see you."

"Me? Why? How is he?"

"All right. They're about to leave."

Sam followed Mr. Collins into his office, where Premberton was striding around, a highball in hand. Vikki was sitting, also with a drink.

"Hello there, young fella!" the old man said.

"How do you feel, sir?" Sam asked.

"Fit as a fiddle. I'm terrible sorry about causin' all that commotion at your table. And I meant to leave you a little tip. Gimme a hundred, Vikki." She did and the old man handed a check to Sam.

"Thanks very much, sir. And I hope that you and Mrs. Premberton will have a very happy marriage."

Mr. Collins said, "You'll have to excuse me. It's the end of a shift and I have to go and collect the cash from the tables."

"We're jest leavin' ourselves, sir," Premberton said. "Let's go cash in, Vikki honey, and see if we've won anything."

The four left the office together and Sam said good night to the Prembertons, who went off toward the cashier. Mr. Collins said to Sam, "The tip goes in the box."

Sam nodded and smiled and walked down to the floor and dropped the check into the dealers' tip box. Mr. Collins watched this and nodded approval and walked into the cashier's office.

Sam went back up to the bar to finish his beer. Through the archway he saw the Prembertons cashing in. Mr. Collins came out with some empty cashboxes and gave the couple a smile and started off for the tables. Soon Sam saw the old man and the girl walk out of the casino, arm in arm. In a few minutes, Sam finished his beer, left the casino and drove off up the Strip.

After about two miles, he came to the Slumbertime Motel and parked. He got out and walked along a ground-level porch to room 17. A light was on inside. Sam knocked. A man opened the door.

"Yes?" he asked.

Sam frowned. "I'm looking for Mr. Haskins."

"He must be in another room."

"No. He lives here, in seventeen. Or did."

"Well, I checked in here at ten tonight and he wasn't here then."

"I'm sorry to have bothered you," Sam said and hurried down the porch to the office, where he pinged the desk bell. In a moment, a man in a bathrobe came from a rear room. "I'm looking for Mr. Haskins and his granddaughter," Sam said. "They were in seventeen and sixteen."

"They checked out."

"They *did?*"

"About nine tonight."

"Oh. Did—did they leave anything for me? For Sam Miller?"

"Yes, they did." The manager found an envelope and looked at it. "'For Sam Miller.'" Sam took the envelope, thanked him and hurried out to his car. Getting in, he tore open the envelope and found a sheet of paper with writing on it. In order to read it, he flicked on his overhead light. The note read:

> Dear Sammy darling honey. By the time you get this, Grandpa and I will be on our way to somewhere else. I mean, if everything goes OK at your casino tonight. I'm crossing my legs for good luck! Grandpa has decided not to leave you your share, for two reasons. For one thing, he needs the six thousand dollars more than you, because he's an old man and isn't young anymore, like you. Also, he thinks you're a wonderful person and should be straight, and he says he's afraid that if you get your first taste of what he calls ill-gotten gains, it will turn you into a crook like himself for the rest of your life and this he wouldn't like to see. Good-bye. I'll really miss you. You sure are good in bed, Sammy honey.
>
> Love,
> Vikki.

Sam turned off the light and sat in the darkness for a moment. Then fury overcame him and he slammed both hands against his steering wheel again and again, and tears of frustration blurred his eyes.

And then the passenger door opened and the interior light went on and Sam turned to see Mr. Collins standing there.

"Troubles, Sam?" He slid onto the seat and shut the door.

Sam's eyes widened and his mouth fell open. "How? . . . How? . . ."

"I followed you here. I've been sitting in my car over there, and I saw you get turned away from that room, and I saw you get that letter from the manager, and I saw the look on your face when you read it." He brought out a cigarette. "So your friends ran out on you, did they—without giving you your cut?"

"I . . . I . . . don't know what you mean."

"Oh, knock it off, Sam." He lit his cigarette. "You're in serious trouble. Your only hope is to level with me. Where in the name of God did you three manage to *get* a hundred and eighty phony hundred-dollar bills? And what are the old man and his wife to you?"

Sam considered for a moment and then shrugged. "She's his granddaughter. Their name is Haskins." He turned on his overhead light. "Oh, hell." He handed Mr. Collins Vikki's note. "You might as well read this."

Mr. Collins did. "The old man may be selfish, but he's right, you know. That six thousand would have meant the end of you as an honest person." Sam turned off the light. "Where did you meet these two?"

"They were customers of my uncle's liquor store. I got to know Vikki and pretty soon we had a real thing going. Then, when my uncle sold the store, I was out of a job, and one day old Bert asked me how honest I was and I said that depended, and he told me about all these hundreds he had."

"Where did he get them?"

"He'd bought them a long time ago, very cheaply. But he'd never passed any. He had an idea about how they could all be changed in one place at one time—in a casino. He didn't care if he won, you see—he just wanted to change his counterfeits for good money. So he offered me a third if I'd help him and he paid my way through Mr. Ferguson's school. I had to get a job as a dealer up here, so I could find out exactly how things worked in a particular casino."

"Sam, you are a crook. You are a criminal."

"All I did tonight was to keep warning you about the old man and his money."

"You were just setting me up."

"I guess so." Sam sighed. "For all the good it did me."

"Was the old man's faint staged?"

"Yes. He knew he had to stop before midnight, when you'd open the cashboxes and spot his bills. But he figured that if he just stopped right then, you might be suspicious, so he faked a faint."

"And whose idea was it that you should try to *make* me suspicious of them?"

Sam smiled modestly. "Well, it was mostly mine—after I'd met you. I figured that if I questioned the first two thousand and you made sure they were genuine—then you wouldn't have any doubts about the next eighteen thousand. And also, I wanted to be sure you wouldn't connect me with it when it was all over."

Mr. Collins smiled a little. "It was a slick operation, Sam. And it almost worked. But your gamble paid off on the house number—which is double zero for you."

"Where did I go wrong?"

"Well, for one thing, you objected too much and I began to wonder why. And at the end, you wondered if the old man could get back to his *motel*. But meanwhile, the girl had told me they were staying at the Flamingo *Hotel*. I figured something was wrong somewhere. And when I opened your cashbox and found the funny money, it all fell into place."

"What . . . are you going to . . . do about me?"

Mr. Collins shrugged. "Nothing. I expect you back at work tomorrow." Sam looked at him in disbelief. "Sam, unless you're crazy, you'll never try anything funny on me again. And it's my solemn duty to the Nevada gaming industry to make sure you never work for anybody else."

"But . . . but what about the eighteen thousand in phony hundreds you're stuck with?"

"What makes you think so, Sam?"

"Because I saw Vikki cash in before you'd opened the cashboxes. That was good money she walked out with!"

"What makes you think so?"

"I . . . don't understand you."

"Because you'd finally made me suspicious, I'd opened *your* cashbox ten minutes earlier. It was while you were in the dealers' room and the bar. I saw to it that among the twenty thousand your friends walked out with were the same identical one hundred and eighty counterfeit hundreds they'd walked in with." Mr. Collins opened the car door and slid out. "Good night, Sam. See you tomorrow."

So saying, the smartest man in Vegas shut the car door and walked off into the darkness.

Blurred View

JOHN D. MacDONALD

The funeral was a wretched affair. I suppose it was done as tastefully as one would expect. But great gaudy swarms of Gloria's friends from the television industry came up from the Los Angeles area. They were dressed sedately, but still managed to seem like flocks of bright birds, men and women alike, their eyes bright and sharp and questing.

They had been at the inquest too, turning out in numbers which astonished the officials. I had not been surprised. If I learned any one thing from my marriage, it was that those people are incurably gregarious. They had absolutely no appreciation of privacy and decorum. Their ceaseless talk is like the chatter of birds, and largely incomprehensible to the outsider.

After the funeral I settled a few final details before going away. The lawyer had me sign the necessary things. Gloria had managed to squirrel away more than I expected, and she had invested it very shrewdly indeed. My own affairs were in a temporary lull. Bernard, at the gallery, made the usual apology about not being able to move more of my work, and offered his condolences, for the tenth time. I closed the Bay house and flew to the Islands.

Helen's greeting was sweet and humble and adoring. She is a small, plain woman, quite wealthy, a few years older than I. She was most restful after the contentious flamboyance of Gloria. Her figure is rather good. During the weeks we had together she made several shy hints about marriage, but the unexpected size of Gloria's estate gave me the courage to think of Helen as a patron rather than a potential wife.

We returned to Los Angeles by ship, in adjoining staterooms, and parted warmly in that city. She was to return to New York to visit her children and settle some business matters concerning her late husband's estate, then fly back out to San Francisco to be near me.

I moved back into the Bay house and listed it with a good broker. It is a splendid house, set high over the rocks, but a little too expensive to maintain, and a little too conspicuous for the bachelor life I contemplated. Also, there was a silence about it when I was alone there which made me feel uneasy, and made it difficult for me to work in the big studio which Gloria and I had designed together.

After I had been there alone for five days, a seedy little man arrived in the afternoon. He drove up in a battered little car and came to the door carrying a big manila envelope in his hand.

He was trying to say he had something to show me. He was humble, and nervous, and had a little recurring smile like a sudden grimace. He smelled sweaty. Something about him alarmed me. Reluctantly I led him back through the house to the studio.

He said, "Mr. Fletcher, I just want to work something out. That's all. I don't want you should get the wrong idea about anything. It's just one of those things. And we can work something out. The thing is, to talk it over."

I'd had my share of bad dreams about this kind of situation. My voice sounded peculiar to me as I said, "I don't know what you're talking about."

He had put the envelope on a worktable. He said, "What I do, I'm assistant manager, Thrifty Quick. My brother-in-law, he's a doctor, got a home right over there across the way. You can't see it today, it's too misty. The thing is, I was laid up in April. Dropped a case on my foot, and I stayed over there with my sister. I guess I'm what they call a shutterbug. I'm a real nut on photography. It keeps me broke, I'm telling you."

"Mr. Walsik, I haven't the faintest . . ."

"What I was fooling with, long-lens stuff on thirty-five millimeter. I was using a Nikon body and a bunch of adapters, a tripod of course, and I figured it out it came to f/22, sixteen hundred millimeters, and I was using Tri-X. I don't suppose the technical stuff means anything to you, Mr. Fletcher."

"You don't mean anything to me, Mr. Walsik."

"Figuring back, it had to be April tenth. A clear morning and no wind. Wind is bad when you use that much lens. You can't get sharpness. The thing is, I was just experimenting, so I had to find some sharp-edged object at a distance to focus on, so I picked the edge of that terrace out there. I took some shots at different exposures, and after a while I thought I could see somebody moving around on the terrace. I took some more shots. I made notes on exposure times and so on. You know, you have to keep track or you forget."

I sat down upon my work stool. This was the monstrous cliché of all murders, I had thought it a device of scenario writers, the accidental little man, the incongruous flaw. With an effort I brought my attention back to what he was saying.

". . . in the paper that she was all alone here, Mr. Fletcher, and you proved you were somewhere else. Now I got to apologize for the quality of this print. It's sixteen by twenty, which is pretty big to push thirty-five millimeter, and there was some haze, and that fast film is grainy, but here you take a look."

I took the big black-and-white print and studied it. I was at the railing, leaning, arms still extended. He had caught her in free fall toward the rocks, some six feet below my outstretched hands, her fair hair and nylon peignoir rippled upward by the wind of passage. It brought it all back, scooping her up from the drugged and drowsy bed, walking with her slack warm weight, seeing her eyes open and hearing her murmurous question in the instant before I dropped her over the wall. The print was too blurred for me to be recognizable, or Gloria. But it was enough. The unique pattern of the wall was clear. It could no longer be "jumped or fell." And with that picture, they could go back and pry at the rest of it until the whole thing fell apart.

When he took the picture out of my hands I looked up at him. He stepped backward very quickly and said in a shaking voice, "I got the negative in a safe place, with a letter explaining it."

"What do you want?" I asked him.

"Like I said, I just want to work something out, Mr. Fletcher. The way I figure if I try to push too hard what I'll do is spoil everything. What I want is for life to be a little easier. So I could get a little bit better apartment in a handier neighborhood. And there's some lenses and camera equipment I want to buy. I won't be a terrible burden, you understand. But I don't want to sell you the negatives. I want like a permanent-type thing, the way people got an annuity. I've got some bills I want to pay off, so the first bite, believe me, is bigger than the ones I'll want later on. I was figuring it out. If you can get a thousand for me now, then in three or four months I'll come back like for five hundred. I don't see why we can't work it out this way. I want you to be comfortable with it, so you won't try to upset anything."

He was actually pleading with me. And obviously frightened. And I found myself reappraising marriage to Helen. She could more readily afford Mr. Walsik. I had no choice, of course. I had to agree.

He told me where to meet him, and when, and I promised to bring along the thousand dollars in tens and twenties. After he had left I had two stiff drinks and began to feel better. In ridding myself of Gloria I had saddled myself with Walsik, but he seemed a good deal easier to manage.

I found him two nights later exactly where he said he would be, in one of the rear booths of a tiresome little neighborhood bar. I handed him the envelope and he tucked it away. As I got up to leave, two burly chaps grabbed me, snapped steel on my wrist and bustled me out to an official sedan.

They tell me that I held out for fourteen hours before I finally began to give them those answers as deadly to me as the cyanide will be in the gas chamber.

After it was over, they let me sleep. The next afternoon they brought Walsik to see me. He was not seedy. He was not humble. His voice was not the same. He had that odd febrile, animal glitter so typical of Gloria's friends in the industry.

"While you were on the grass-skirt circuit, Frank baby," he said, "we borrowed your pad. We brought the long lenses. We rigged the safety net. A big crew of willing volunteers, baby, all the kids who loved Gloria. We guessed that's how you did it. We took maybe fifty stills of Buddy dropping Nina over the wall. How did you like my performance, sweetie? You bought it good. After you bought it, we brought the law into it, to watch you give me money. Sit right there, Frank baby. Sit there and bug yourself with how stupid you were."

I heard him leave, walking briskly down the corridor, humming a tune. Somebody said something to him. He laughed. A door clanged shut. And I began to go over it all, again and again and again. . . .

The Love of Money

J. I. MWAGOJO

PART ONE

It's quarter to seven in the morning and I am having breakfast with my family, my wife Marrietta . . . our two children Jane and Rachel. Our maid Kasichana is still in the kitchen.

It's Saturday so the children are having their time as there is no hurry, they are not going to school. I am the only one who is in a hurry, I want to be in time in the office . . . at half past seven I say bye to them and enter into my 1968 model of Ford, engage the gear, and start my safari for the office and as I do so all my thoughts go to the office.

My Office Five years are over since I opened up my office under my name of Harry Kidozi. It's Harry Kidozi Investigators, the busiest investigation bureau situated in the centre of the hottest town in Kenya . . . Mombasa.

To take you further back, after my secondary school education I was enlisted in the force, after my course at the training college I was posted to the North Eastern Province where the Shifta war was going on.

My luck was not good . . . After a year or so, I still remember that day . . . It was on a Tuesday, we were escorting a convoy of business lorries which were taking retail goods to Mandera from Garissa. After travelling fifty miles from Garissa our Land-Rover which was at the rear of the convoy was blown up by a land mine which had been planted by the Shiftas . . . Thanks to the mine plate, only two of us died on the spot and the rest of us escaped death with minor injuries, and six months after that incident with the help of my doctor I resigned from the force under medical grounds. Don't ask me why, just figure it out for yourself.

After my resignation I stayed home with no particular work to do for a period of five months, then I decided to get married. It's after the marriage when I opened up the investigation bureau.

I used the balance of the funds which I had been paid during my resignation, with the experience I got while I was in the force I found the going easy. And now it's five years since I opened up the bureau and I am not doing bad at all. I have employed three people to give me a hand in the office work.

Roy, an ex-police Inspector, I employed him as my assistant. Lucy who was working with the law courts as a clerk and later she had to resign on her own grounds which I did not ask when I was employing her. She is my secretary and also she is the one who holds the task of keeping the office work flow with mzee Musa an ex-prison Corporal who can smell an ex-convict a mile away serves as an office messenger . . . so with all these three heads, there is no problem in handling any case . . . an ex-police Inspector, an ex-law courts clerk with an ex-prison Corporal, I got the best brains in the business.

For when we sit together and exchange our ideas, with our past experience boy! . . . you would be surprised the way we crack down our cases.

Besides these three people I have another chap who is also in my payroll, his name is Walter, he works with the Posts and Telecommunication Corporation. We were together in the force, he was working under signals department. He resigned when he came down for his annual leave, by good luck he found an advertisement in the paper that P & T Corporation needed operators with army experience to handle the new equipment the Corporation had bought from Sweden.

With the big pay, free house, a car and the hospital facilities Walter jumped to it and boy! . . . he was lucky enough, they even did not call him on an interview. They only had to see his papers and that's all. He is now getting twice as much as he was being paid in the force, drives the best car and stays in a nice luxury house . . . just because of experience. Brother! . . . who said that experience doesn't grow old? If you happen to meet him say jambo to him. I pay Walter for the services he renders to me here and then.

We sometimes get a call without the caller giving us his name. He threatens us that if we don't drop the case we are handling we goner get a nail in the head. Once we get such a call we only have to contact Walter, give him the time the call was made and in a matter of minutes we know the call was made from such and such number. We inform Inspector Khamis and his boys will rush there to find the fingerprints of the caller and in a matter of hours the caller will find himself behind the bars. That's me, if you try to mess around with my office, I will hit you so fast that you won't know who hit you. I have told you that I have the best brains in the business so never make a call and threaten me even if I am covering your daughter.

I have mentioned the name of Inspector Khamis to you. He is the chap who is in charge of the Crime Department at the Provincial C.I.D. Headquarters and I am in real good terms with him. We have been working together in five or so cases. We all understand each other so well.

Whenever my office needs a hand of a police expert I only have to contact him . . . and brother if you are intending to open up your own investigation bureau the only advice that I can give you is this. Cooperate with your local police inspector, you will last long in the business and find the going easy.

My Client From my residence that is Nyali Estate to my office block is a drive of forty-five minutes. Quarter past eight I swing my car to the parking meter which is outside my office and walk slowly towards my office block, three minutes later I open my private door and walk into my office.

Facing me is a big desk covered with files and newspapers, a bamboo chair is on one side of the desk, another chair by the window. A sofa set special for my clients is on one side of the room and another side is taken up by filing cabinets. I light my Sportsman cigarette and move slowly until I'm behind the desk; I drop the match into the ashtray and sit.

After a minute or so I start with the daily papers. I pick up the *Standard* and go over it carefully; nothing of interest. The headline is about a football match between Gor-Mahia and Horseed, a club from a neighbouring country in a quarterfinals of the African Winners Cup. The daily *Nation* is talking about a club from Sweden which is due to visit the country in two days' time to play with the four top clubs in the country and the match between Gor-Mahia and Horseed has been given a subheading. I relax and pick up the phone.

"Hello . . . good morning, how are you?"

"Fine sir, so you are in?"

"Oh yes . . . I decided to use the private door. Is Roy in yet?"

"No. He has just phoned, he will pass through a bank before he comes."

"OK fine . . . there is nothing important in the papers, you can come and take them for filing." I finish and drop the telephone, take up one of the files and start to go over it.

After a minute the door swings open and Lucy enters into my office with her usual smile on her face which reveals the small-sized teeth in her mouth. She picks up the papers and pauses. The way she is looking at me I know that there is something in her head; without hesitating I say, "Yes?"

"There is a man in the outer office who wants to see you . . . he says he is from Daima Insurance."

"His name?" I ask eagerly.

"He wouldn't give me his name, he says that he is the manager of Daima Insurance."

"OK . . . go back, I will tell you when I am ready to see him." I tell her so and relax on my office chair with my mind busy thinking.

Since I opened up this office never has there come a client to see me without leaving his name with my secretary, this is the first time and let me tell you, there is nothing in this world which I hate more than to talk to a stranger whom I don't know . . . especially in this racket. What if the moment he enters into my office he draws his pistol and shoots me . . . I pick up the phone and dial digit zero for the operator.

"Get me Daima Insurance." I hold on and after a moment a lady's voice replies, "Daima Insurance, can I help you please?"

"Get me Mr. . . ." and then I cough and say, "Sorry! I mean the manager." The cough was just intended to see if my trick of getting the name of the manager will work.

"Who . . . Mr. Ezekiel you mean?" asks the voice.

"The manager," I repeat with a firm voice.

"I am sorry, Mr. Ezekiel has gone out, can you speak to his assistant?"

"No thanks, I will call again," I tell her and drop the phone with a smile on my face . . . so it's obvious that the man who wants to see me is Mr. Ezekiel. I look at my wristwatch . . . it's quarter to nine. I take a pen and write on my desk diary 8.45 *Ezekiel from Daima Insurance.*

After this I tell Lucy to let the gentleman in, at least if he shoots me there is a clue that the police will work on to try to trace him. The door leading to Lucy's office swings open and at the same time I stand to welcome him in with a fixed smile.

"Daima Insurance, you are welcomed, have a chair."

He smiles, "Call me Ezekiel if you like." He slowly sits down and as he does so I observe him carefully. He is around fifty or forty-five years old, tall, about five point four, and he has put on the most expensive clothes. In this town you can only get them on the shops along Digo Road and Moi Avenue, anyone who can afford to buy anything in those shops, don't take him slightly, he earns well and this convinces me that Ezekiel is the manager of Daima Insurance. I let him have his time and then I ask him, "Now can I help you, Mr. Ezekiel?"

The Insurance Policy   "I have come to see you, Mr. Harry, because we are suspecting that one of our clients is taking us for a ride." I nod and he continues. "His name is Andrew Lendu. Last week he came to our office and insured his car for five hundred thousand shillings." He speaks so slowly . . . the way a teacher reads a dictation to his pupils in a class.

"I am with you, Mr. Ezekiel, go on."

"Six days after Andrew insured his car, that was yesterday, he came back claiming that his car is involved in a road accident, he wants our Company to pay him. He further claimed that two of his passengers are seriously injured and are admitted at Bonje Emergency Hospital. We are sure that Andrew is taking us for a ride, that's why we want you to help us."

"Well, Mr. Ezekiel, I real don't see how I can help you . . . with what you have told me I don't see how I can help you.

Forget about Andrew for the moment. Suppose if I pop into your office and insure my car with your company, after a day or so I am involved in an accident . . . won't you pay me as my car is insured with you? . . . or in the right words, for how long were you expecting Andrew to stay without his car being involved in an accident after it was insured with you before you could consider its policy for payment?"

"I see your point, Mr. Harry. One thing which we want you to consider is the amount of the money involved, five hundred thousand shillings is a lot of money, even when Andrew told us that he wants to insure his car for that amount we thought that he was mad in the head . . . we tried to convince him but he wouldn't listen, so when he turned in yesterday with his claim, there is where I realised why he was so eager to insure his car . . . in fact his records are still with us, they have not yet been forwarded to our headquarters in Nairobi. So Mr. Harry, that's why we want you to help us because by Thursday next week if we won't be able to prove that Andrew is taking us for a ride we will have to pay him. I hope you understand me, Mr. Harry."

"I do, Mr. Ezekiel."

He smiles and drops a piece of his cigarette into the ashtray. "I hope you won't let me down Mr. Harry . . . you have seen why we need your help and I think to the best of your knowledge you will accept our case."

I smile and force a laugh. "I accept your case, Mr. Ezekiel, but one thing which you surprise me with, you are approaching me the way Andrew approached you a week ago. There is that urgency in you which you want me to accept your case the way Andrew wanted you to accept his insurance policy."

I pause to let him stare at me so as to make sure that I am not mad in the head.

"And only after a week you suspect him that he is taking you for a ride . . . what about if after I accept your case I find out that there is no Mr. Andrew, what if you are taking me for a ride, Mr. Ezekiel?"

"Oh I would never do that; this is for real, Mr. Harry. I am not taking you for a ride, you can please yourself . . . if you think that I am taking you for a ride you can forget it, I will walk out of your office and try another bureau, I only came here because our first choice was you."

"I have told you that I accept your case. But tell me more about Andrew and his car . . . what type of a car did he insure?"

"Mercedes-Benz 450, registration number MSA 239, blue in colour, chassis numbers are F. 673901. A four-door car with the capacity of carrying five passengers. Front seat two and rear seat three."

"Now tell me . . . this Andrew you are talking about, who is he? Anyone who can afford to drive that car, he must real be in the money."

"Andrew is in the money, but you as a Christian you must remember a verse in the Holy Bible, a verse in Timothy one, chapter six, verse ten which says that 'For the Love of money is a root of all sorts of injurious things.' Andrew is a farmer, he runs his own farm at Rabai. He calls it Maendeleo Farm, he keeps poultry, pigs, and does coconut tapping, all the coconut beer that is being sold in this town is from his farm."

"You said he is from Rabai?"

"Yes . . . Maendeleo Farm Rabai, just before you cross the bridge which is on river Kombeni."

"Have you been there?"

"No! . . . our man has been there."

"OK . . . I will contact you before Thursday next week to tell you how I am going on."

Ezekiel stands up and puts his hand in his rear pocket, he takes out a thousand shillings in hundred-note bills. "Here, take this . . . this is for your fuel and miscellaneous use for our case, we will settle your bill after you have cracked down the case."

"Thanks," I tell him.

"We hope to hear from you soon, though it's Saturday I will remain in the office until six . . . you can contact me there, after six you will get me at my house . . . Kizingo Estate, it won't be difficult for you to trace me in the book."

I thank him again and receive the money. We shake hands, I give him an assurance that I will do all I can to help them and with that assurance he walks out of my office.

PART TWO   Ten minutes past ten I park my car outside

Central Police Station and walk straight to the traffic department. Here is where I expect to get all details about the accident of Andrew Lendu, then after that I will decide what to do next. I ask for Inspector Betty who is in charge of this department and after a delay of ten minutes she lets me in her office.

A Minor Accident   I explain to her that the insurance company is suspecting that Lendu is taking them for a ride . . . she gets the surprise of the year and then she turns to take a file in one of the filing cabinets and starts to read its contents to me.

I explain to her that the insurance company is suspecting that Lendu is taking them for a ride . . . she gets the surprise of the year and then she turns to take a file in one of the filing cabinets and starts to read its contents to me.

"It was just a minor accident. Andrew was driving and the car left the road and slid into a ditch whereby two of his passengers were injured and now are admitted at Bonje Emergency Hospital. Andrew himself was treated for pains and minor injuries."

"Where is the car?" I ask.

"Andrew took it yesterday. It was a minor accident," she insists and continues, "so when Andrew came for it we found out that there is no need of keeping it here with us." She drops the file on the table and stares at me questioningly. Just as if she is telling me that "This is all I can tell you . . . what else do you want?"

"Tell me Inspector. Who is this Andrew? I real don't know him."

She smiles and relaxes on her office chair. "Andrew is a farmer with a steady income, I real don't see any reason why the insurance company should suspect him." I let that pass as if she has told me nothing of importance.

"I see . . . and what do you know about his past life . . . was he just born with everything plus the steady income?"

She forces a smile and says, "Four years ago, Mr. Harry, Andrew was working with Dogo Dogo Motors as a garage foreman, it's after he left them that he started the farming business."

"A garage foreman you mean?" I ask her again.

"Yes . . . what's the surprise about?"

"From what you are telling me it's obvious that Andrew knows a lot about motor vehicles."

"Oh yes."

"What car was he driving?"

"A Benz 450, registration number MSA 239."

"OK thanks, Inspector, for the information, so what do you intend to do with Andrew? I mean what action have you taken against his accident?"

"We only opened an inquiry file . . . which will be heard on Monday morning in the traffic court number four. After that the judge will declare the inquiry closed according to our findings."

I thank her again and walk out of her office to the place where I have parked my car. At least I have learned something . . . so Andrew was a garage foreman. I start the engine and decide to go to the firm Andrew was working with, Dogo Dogo Motors, and as I do so my thoughts go back to what the Inspector has just told me.

"Andrew is a farmer with a steady income and I real don't see any reason why the insurance company should suspect him," and then I recall to what Ezekiel told me when he was in my office.

"Andrew is in the money, but you as a Christian you must remember a verse in the Holy Bible, a verse in Timothy one, chapter six, verse ten . . . 'For the Love of money is a root of all sorts of injurious things.'" I smile and accelerate the speed, I wish the Inspector should have known something about this verse . . . perhaps her attitude towards Lendu's case would have been different.

Quarter to eleven I park my car outside the offices of Dogo Dogo Motors and walk to the reception desk where I find myself face to face with a young lady aged about twenty years.

After introducing myself I tell her that I would like to see the manager, she tells me that he is away to Malindi where he has gone to see some clients who have not settled their bills since last year.

"Your former employee Andrew Lendu was involved in a road accident a few days ago. I have been hired by his lawyers to assist him so as he could be paid something by his insurance company . . . I will pay for the information if you offer to give me that information." I pause and stare at her and by the look of her eyes I see the green light.

"I want to know more about Andrew. His past life and his experience on cars and everything about him." I give her a hundred-shillings note. "This is part of the payment, I will be waiting for you at the Manor Hotel at twelve thirty."

"I will be there . . . the name is Lina," she tells me after putting the note in her purse. I let her stare at me to make sure that she will remember me when she sees me again and then I walk out of the reception desk towards my car.

A Volvo I have an hour before I meet Lina. Why was Andrew so eager to insure his car . . . why he went for it at the traffic department so soon before the inquiry was over? Inspector Betty let him have it because the accident was so minor that she found there's no need of keeping it in the police compound. OK fine.

But what about Andrew, is there anything that he didn't want to be noticed in the car? Is that why he was so eager to take the car away from the police before they could notice that thing? While my mind is busy with all these questions I engage the gear of my Ford and decide to go and see the Registrar of Motor Vehicles and twenty minutes to twelve I find myself outside the offices of the Registrar of Motor Vehicles. After introducing myself to the reception clerk I am directed to the Provincial Officer without any delay.

"What can I do for you, Mr. Kidozi?"

"The usual problem . . . what make is a car, registration number MSA 239, chassis No. F. 673901?"

"Just a moment," he tells me, then he stands and turns to the filing cabinets, he takes out a black register from one of the cabinets and comes with it to the desk. He starts to turn the pages one after the other with his finger moving slowly on the words, followed by his big eyes.

On the centre page he stops and a smile appears on his face.

"Mombasa 239, it's a Volvo," he tells me.

"A Volvo . . . are you sure?"

"Here," he says and turns the register to me, "please yourself." With shy eyes I read the column written MSA 239 and I find out that it's just as he has said. A white Volvo with chassis No. 673901, registered owner being Andrew Lendu of Dogo Dogo Motors. I force a smile and say thanks to him.

"How many blue Mercedes do we have in this town?" He starts to turn the pages again and after a moment he tells me that there are ten.

"And none of them is registered under the name of Andrew Lendu?"

"Oh no . . . Lendu only owns a Volvo."

I thank him again and tell him that I would be grateful if he could arrange to produce a photostat copy of all cars registered under the make of Volvo and Mercedes-Benz. He tells me to send somebody on Monday and he will find the copy ready. We shake hands and then I walk out of his office in a happier mood.

Five minutes to half past twelve I find myself walking into the hotel lobby of the Manor Hotel and to my surprise I see Lina a few steps ahead of me. I join her and we both walk straight to the dining room.

After lunch I take her to the bar which is just opposite the dining hall. I let her have two beers while we talk of this and that to let ourselves familiarize with each other.

I order the third round and then put the question to her. "Now tell me what do you know about Andrew?"

"He worked with us for a period of six years and then he left us. That is four years ago."

"He was working as a what?"

"As a senior foreman in the garage workshop."

"What was the main reason of leaving you?"

"He said that he could not tolerate to be employed forever, just to see somebody making a lot of money through his experience. So he resigned and said that he was going to try his luck by opening an open air garage."

"Did he?" I ask eagerly.

"A year later he did."

"And where is that garage?"

"At his farm . . . Maendeleo Farm Rabai," she tells me.

Any Relation

"Has Andrew got any car?"

"Yes, he has a Volvo . . . he bought it when he was still with us."

"Can you remember its registration number?"

"It's a white Volvo," she pauses and thinks.

"MSA, two thirty . . . two thirty something, I can't remember the last number."

"Could it be two fifty-nine and not two thirty something as you are suggesting?"

A smile appears on her face and she shakes her head. "Oh no . . . it's two thirty-nine . . . I am sure it's two thirty-nine," she tells me.

"How come that the car he was driving was a Benz 239 and not a Volvo?"

"Andrew had only one thing in his mind. He wanted to be rich . . . he was always dreaming of money, that's why he left us and opened up his open air garage at his farm. You have not been there but once you visit him you will know that there are a lot of injurious things going on in that open air garage. He handles stolen motor vehicles, once a stolen car enters into his garage that will be the end of it and if you see it again, you won't recognize it. He changes up its body. If it's a Volkswagen it will be changed into a Ford or something else . . . when it comes to car body-building Andrew is an expert, that is why he was a senior garage foreman when he was with us."

I relax and think deeply all what Lina has told me. I drop my cigarette end in the ashtray and finish up my beer. From what she has told me it's a matter of adding one and two together and then I crack this case down. It's obvious that Andrew changed the body of the Volvo, that is the most important exhibit I need. "I get you so far," I pause so as to attract her attention. "You will agree with me that you cannot change the body of a car using the original body . . . one must have new materials for that type of a work."

"Oh yes."

"If it's so then, where does Andrew keep the original bodies of the cars that he changes then?"

"The garage is just by the riverbank of river Kombeni . . . so he sinks the original bodies into the river."

"So he sinked the body of the Volvo into the river?"

"Yes," she replies.

I order another round and then light a cigarette with my mind busy . . . thinking all what Lina has just told me, then I ask her one more question referring to what she has told me.

"Andrew wanted to be in the money you mean?"

"That's what I have told you."

I smile as if what she has just confirmed is the best joke I have ever heard.

"So after changing the body of his Volvo to resemble the one of a Benz he insured it as Benz 450, the most expensive car in the country and then faked that accident so that he could have the money he was dreaming about."

"It could be so," she says and then I ask her the question I have wanted to ask her since she started to give me all the information about Andrew Lendu.

"Tell me one thing . . . do you have any relation with Andrew, how come that you know more than I was expecting you to know?" She forces a smile and then relaxes on her chair and sips up her beer.

"I have two reasons, why I know more about Andrew . . . more than you were expecting me to know." She pauses and then continues. "First, you offered to pay me for the information and, as you are aware, that where there is money, there is no complication . . . when you offer money you will get everything that you want. So as soon as you left I dug up the information."

"Fine, tell me second reason."

She smiles and then continues, "Andrew is in the same business as we. In order to run your business well you must know how your colleague, who is in the same business with you, how he runs his business. Me as a reception clerk I should know that, it's easy to convince customers. I know which garage is better than us and I know those which we are better than them."

"OK thanks . . ." I tell her, "I will not let you go sister. Andrew is taking the insurance company for a ride, he wants to be paid a half million shillings. Therefore, for your own safety I will take you for a safe custody. I am sure if Andrew learns that you sang that song to me he will harm you. So I don't want to regret later . . . that's why I will take you for a safe custody until Andrew is put behind the bars. Secondly, you will have to sing the same song to the jury when Andrew is put behind the bars. I have a wife and you will be staying with us until then."

"Even if you don't have one . . . I will stay with you until he is put behind the bars, I only let you know that I am engaged to somebody."

"Engaged?" she means . . . and then I recall to what she has told me, "where there is money, there is no complication." That's why she is here with me though she is engaged and that's why she has offered to be staying with me even if I don't have a wife.

At two, we walk out of the bar and I take her to my Nyali residence. I leave her with Marrietta and then I return to town whereby I go to the C.I.D. Headquarters and see Inspector Khamis.

After explaining everything to him, an hour later Inspector Khamis, me and some of his boys, with five divers from the Navy, we find ourselves on the way heading to Andrew's farm.

At the farm, the boys take Andrew's estate into pieces and the divers go to the river. They dive to search the body of the alleged Volvo and after three hours they manage to bring out to the riverbank several car bodies, and the body of the Volvo in question is identified among them. Inspector Khamis and his boys they manage to find several stolen spare parts and cars. Andrew and his chaps are arrested and under heavy escort are taken to the Provincial C.I.D. Headquarters for further questioning before they are charged.

With a relaxed mind I enter into my Ford and start the engine . . . it's quarter to seven in the evening. I am looking forward for a nice dinner at my Nyali residence . . . with Lina around to keep us company it's going to be a special Saturday dinner.

With all the information I have it's now obvious that the Daima Insurance Company won't have to pay Andrew, it's obvious that the inquiry at the traffic court will not take place, Andrew and his chaps will have to face a more serious charge.

Now, I agree with that verse in the Bible. It's quite true that

"*THE LOVE OF MONEY* is a root of all sorts of injurious things," for it's when one thinks of making a lot of money that he finds himself in that Love and it's when he is in that Love that he thinks of the injurious things.

Everywhere in this world, they murder, they hijack planes, they kidnap, they commit burglary, they bribe, they forge, and the only sound reason why they do that, it's because they are in that love . . . *THE LOVE OF MONEY*.

The Man Who Collected "The Shadow"

BILL PRONZINI

Mr. Theodore Conway was a nostalgiac, a collector of memorabilia, a dweller in the simple, uncomplicated days of his adolescence when radio, movie serials, and pulp magazines were the ruling forms of entertainment and super-heroes were the idols of American youth.

At forty-three, he resided alone in a modest four-room apartment on Manhattan's Lower East Side, where he commuted daily by subway to his position of file clerk in the archives of Baylor, Baylor, Leeds and Wadsworth, a well-respected probate law firm. He had no friends to speak of—certainly no one in whom he cared to confide, or who cared to confide in him. He was short and balding and very plump and very nondescript; he did not indulge in any of the vices, minor or major; nor did he have a wife or, euphemistically or otherwise, a girlfriend. (In point of fact, Mr. Conway was that rarest of today's breed, an adult male virgin.) He did not own a television set, did not attend the theater, movies, or any other form of outside amusement. His one and only hobby, his single source of pleasure, his sole purpose in life, was the accumulation of nostalgia in general.

And nostalgia pertaining to that most ubiquitous of all super-heroes, The Shadow, in particular.

Ah, The Shadow! Mr. Conway idolized Lamont Cranston,

loved Margo Lane as he could never love any living woman (psychologically, perhaps, this was the reason why he never married, and seldom dated). Nothing set his blood to racing quite so quickly or so hotly as The Shadow on the scent of an evildoer, utilizing the Power which, as Cranston, he had learned in the mysterious Orient, the Power to cloud men's minds so that they could not see him. Nothing filled Mr. Conway with as much delicious anticipation, as much spine-jellying excitement, as the words spoken by The Shadow prior to the beginning of each radio adventure: *What evil lurks in the hearts of men? The Shadow knows* . . . and the eerie, bloodcurdling laugh, the laugh of Justice triumphant, which followed it. Nothing filled him with as much well-being and security as this ace among aces speaking when the current case was closed, speaking out to all criminals everywhere, words of ominous warning: *The weed of crime bears bitter fruit. Crime does not pay. The Shadow knows!* Nothing gave him more pleasure in the quiet solitude of his apartment than listening to the haunting voice of Orson Welles, capturing The Shadow like no other had over the air; or reading Maxwell Grant's daring, chilling accounts in *The Shadow Magazine;* or slowly, savoringly, leafing through one of the starkly drawn Shadow comic books.

Mr. Conway had begun his collecting of nostalgia in 1944, with a wide range of pulp magazines. He now had well over ten thousand issues, complete sets of *Black Mask* and *Weird Tales*, Vol. 1, No. 1 of 49 different periodicals including *Adventure* and *Dime Detective* and *Detective Fiction Weekly* and *Thrilling Wonder* and *Western Story* and *Doc Savage*. One entire room in his apartment was filled with garish reds and yellows and blues, BEMs and salivating fiends, half-nude girls with too-red lips screaming in the throes of agony, fearless hunters in the hearts of great jungles, stagecoaches outrunning bloodthirsty bands of painted, howling Indians. Then he had gone on to comic books and comic strips (*Walt Disney's Comics and Stories*, *Superman* and *Batman* and *Plastic Man*, *Mutt and Jeff*, *Krazy Kat*, *The Katzenjammer Kids*, a hundred more), and to premiums of every kind and description (decoders and secret-compartment belts and membership cards and message flashlights, spy rings and shoulder patches, outdoor kits and compasses, microscopes and secret pens that wrote in invisible ink so that you had to put lemon juice on the paper to bring out the writing). In the 1950s, he began to accumulate tapes of radio shows—some taken directly off the 16-inch discs upon which they were originally recorded, some recorded live, some recorded off the air (Bob Hope and Jack Benny and Red Skelton and *Allen's Alley*, Ellery Queen and Charlie Chan and *Mr. Keene, Tracer of Lost Persons*, Tom Mix and Hopalong Cassidy and The Lone Ranger, *Buck Rogers in the 25th Century* and Captain Midnight, *Jack Armstrong, the All-American Boy* and *I Love a Mystery*, Dick Powell as Richard Diamond and Howard Duff as *Yours Truly, Johnny Dollar, Bold Venture* with Bogie and Baby, *Fibber McGee and Molly, Inner Sanctum* and *The Whistler* and *Suspense*).

But his favorite, his idol, from the very beginning was unquestionably The Shadow; the others he amassed happily, eagerly, but with none of the almost fanatical fervor with which he pursued the mystique of The Shadow. Hardly a week passed over the years that at least one new arrival did not come by mail, or by United Parcel, or by messenger, or by his own hand from some location in New York or its immediate vicinity. He pored over advertisements in newspapers and magazines and collectors' sheets, wrote letters, made telephone calls, sent cables, spent every penny of his salary that did not go for bare essentials.

And at long last, he succeeded where no other collector had even come close to succeeding. He accomplished a remarkable, an almost superhuman feat.

He collected the complete Shadow.

There was absolutely nothing produced regarding this super-hero, not a written word, not a spoken sentence, not a drawing nor a gadget, that Mr. Conway did not claim as his own.

The final item, the one which had eluded him for twenty-six years—the last two of which, since he had obtained the final radio show on tape, had been spent in an almost desperate search—came to him, oddly enough, by virtue of blind luck (or, if you prefer, fate) on a Saturday evening in late June. He had gone into a tenement area of Manhattan, near the East River, to purchase from a private individual a cartoon strip of *Terry and the Pirates*. Having made the purchase, he had begun to walk toward the subway for the return trip to his apartment when he chanced upon a small, dusty neighborhood bookstore still open in the basement of one of the brownstones. On a whim, he entered and began to examine the cluttered, ill-lighted tables at the rear of the shop.

And there it was.

The October 1931 issue of *The Shadow Magazine*.

Mr. Conway emitted a small cry of sheer ecstasy. He caught the magazine up in trembling hands, stared at it with disbelieving eyes, opened it gingerly, read the contents page, read the date, read it again, ran sweat-slick fingers over the rough, grainy pulp paper. Near-mint condition. Spine unbroken. Colors only slightly faded. And the price—

Fifty cents.

Fifty cents!

Tears of joy rolled unabashedly down Mr. Conway's plump cheeks as he carried his ultimate quest to the bearded man at the cash register. The bearded man looked at him strangely, shrugged, and rang up the sale. Fifty cents. Mr. Conway gave him two quarters, almost embarrassed at the incredibly small sum; he would have paid hundreds, he thought, hundreds . . .

As he went out into the gathering darkness—it was almost nine by this time—he cradled the periodical to his chest as if it were a child (and in a manner of speaking, for Theodore Conway so it was). He could scarcely believe that he had finally done it, that he now possessed the total word, picture, and voice exploits of the most awesome master crime-fighter of them all. His brain reeled dizzyingly. The Shadow was his now; Lamont Cranston and Margo Lane (beautiful Margo!), his, all his, his alone.

Instead of proceeding to the subway, as he would normally have done when circumstances caught him out near nightfall, Mr. Conway impulsively entered a small diner not far from the bookstore and seated himself in a rear booth. He could barely control his excitement, and his fingers moved over the smooth surface of the magazine's cover, tracing each letter of *The Shadow* slowly and rapturously.

When a bored waiter approached the booth, Mr. Conway ordered coffee with cream and sugar in a perfunctory voice; and then he opened the magazine. He had previously read, in reprint form, the story by Maxwell Grant—*The Shadow Laughs!*—but that was not the same as this, no indeed; this was a milestone in the life of Theodore Conway, a day and hour to be treasured, a day and hour of monumental achievement. He began to read the story again, savoring each line, each page, the mounting suspense, the seemingly inescapable traps laid to eliminate The Shadow, the super-hero's wits matched against those of arch-villains Isaac Coffran and Birdie Crull and their insidious counterfeiting plot, Justice emerging triumphant as Justice always did. *The weed of crime bears bitter fruit, crime does not pay* . . .

Mr. Conway lost all track of time, so engrossed was he in the magazine. When at last he came to the end, he sighed blissfully and closed the pages with a certain tenderness. He looked up then, and was somewhat startled to note that the interior of the diner was now deserted, save for the counterman and the single waiter. It had been bustling with activity when he entered. His eyes moved upward to where a clock was mounted on the wall behind the service counter, and his mouth dropped open in surprise. Good heavens! It was past midnight!

He scrambled out of the booth, the pulp magazine pressed under his right arm, and hurriedly paid for his coffee. Once outside, a certain apprehension seized him; the streets were very dark and very deserted, looking ominous and foreboding in the almost nonexistent shine from the quarter moon overhead.

Mr. Conway looked up and down both ways without seeing any sign of life. It was four blocks to the nearest subway kiosk, a short walk in broad daylight—but now, in what was almost the dead of night? Mr. Conway shivered in the cool breeze, moistening his plump lips; he had never liked the darkness, the sounds and smells of the city at night—and then there were the accounts in the papers every morning of muggers and thieves on the prowl. In the evenings, he invariably remained indoors, surrounded by his memorabilia, his only friends.

Four blocks. Well, that really wasn't very far, only a matter of minutes if he walked swiftly. He took a deep breath, gathering his courage, and then started off down the darkened street.

His shoes echoed hollowly on the empty sidewalk, and Mr. Conway could feel his heart pounding in his breast. No cars passed, and his footfalls, except for the distant lament of a ship's horn on the East River, the sibilant whisper of the night wind, were the only sounds.

He had gone two blocks, walking rapidly now, his head darting furtively left and right, when he heard the muffled explosions.

He stopped, the hairs on the back of his neck prickling, a tremor of fear winding icily along his spine. He had drawn abreast of an alleyway—dark and silent—and he peered down it, poising on the balls of his feet preparatory to taking flight. At the end of the alley he could see a thin elongation of pale light, but nothing else.

Mr. Conway's brain was filled with a single thought: *Run!* And yet, curiously, he stood motionless, staring into the black tunnel. Those explosions: gunshots? If so, they meant that danger, sudden death, lurked in that alley, *run, run!*

But Mr. Conway still did not run. Instead, as if compelled, he started forward into the circumscribed blackness. He moved slowly, feeling his way in the absolute ebon expanse, his shoes sliding almost noiselessly over the rough paving. *What am I doing?* he thought confusedly. *I shouldn't be here!* But he continued to move forward, approaching the narrow funnel of light, coming into its glare now.

He saw that it was emanating through the partially open side door to the brick building on his right, an electronics equipment firm, according to the sign over the street entranceway. Cautiously, Mr. Conway put out a hand and eased the door open wider, peering inside. The thudding of his heart seemed as loud as a drum roll in his ears as he stepped over the threshold and entered the murkiness beyond.

The light came from a naked bulb burning above a glass-enclosed cubicle across a wide expanse of concrete flooring.

Dark, shadowy shapes that would be crates of electronics equipment loomed toward the ceiling on either side. He advanced with hesitant, wary steps, seeing no sign of movement in the gloom around him. At last he reached the cubicle, standing in the full cone of light. A watchman's office, he thought, and stepped up to look through the glass.

He stifled the cry which rose in his throat as he saw what lay on the floor within. It was an old man with white hair, supine next to an ancient desk; blood stained the front of his khaki uniform jacket, welling reddish-brown in the dim illumination. The old man was not moving.

He's dead, murdered! Mr. Conway thought fearfully. He had to get out of there, had to telephone the police. He turned—and froze.

The hulking figure of a man stood not three feet away, looking directly at him.

Mr. Conway's knees buckled, and he had to put out a hand against the glass to keep from collapsing. The killer, the murderer! His mind screamed again for him to run, but his legs would not obey; he could only stare back at the man before him with horror-widened eyes, stare at the pinched white face beneath a low-brimmed cloth cap, at the rodent-like eyes and the cruel sneer on the thin-lipped mouth, at the yawning black muzzle of the gun in one tightly clenched fist.

"No!" Mr. Conway cried then. "No, please! Please don't shoot!"

The man dropped into a low crouch, extending the gun out in front of him.

"Don't shoot!" Mr. Conway said again, putting up his hands.

Puzzled surprise, and a sudden trapped fear, twisted the killer's face. "Who is it? Who's there?"

Mr. Conway opened his mouth, and then closed it again abruptly. He could scarcely believe his ears; the man had demanded to know who was there—and yet, he was standing not three feet away from Mr. Conway, looking right at him!

"I don't understand," Mr. Conway said before he could stop the words.

The gun in the killer's hand swung around and the muzzle erupted in flame. The bullet was well wide of the spot where

Mr. Conway was standing, but he jumped convulsively aside and hugged the glass of the cubicle. He continued to stare incredulously at the man—and suddenly, then, with complete clarity, he *did* understand, he knew.

"You can't *see* me," he said.

The gun discharged a second bullet, but Mr. Conway had already moved easily aside. The shot was wild. "Damn you!" the killer screamed. His words were tinged with hysteria now. "Where are you? *Where are you?*"

Mr. Conway remained standing there, clearly outlined in the light, for a moment longer; then he stepped to one side, to where a board broken from a wooden pallet lay on the cement, and caught it up in his hand. Without hesitation, he walked up to the killer and hit him squarely on top of the head, watched dispassionately as he dropped unconscious to the floor.

Mr. Conway kicked the gun away and stood over him; the police would have to be summoned, of course, but there was plenty of time for that now. A slow, grim smile formed at the corners of his mouth. Could it be that the remarkable collecting feat he had performed, his devoted empathy, had stirred some supernatural force into granting him the Power which he now possessed? Well, no matter. His was not to question why; so endowed, his was but to heed the plaintive cry of a world ridden with lawlessness.

A deep, chilling laugh suddenly swept through the warehouse. "The weed of crime bears bitter fruit!" a haunting, Wellesian voice shouted. "Crime does not pay!"

And The Shadow wrapped the cloak of night around himself and went out into the mean streets of the great metropolis . . .

The Adventure of Abraham Lincoln's Clue
ELLERY QUEEN

Fourscore and eighteen years ago, Abraham Lincoln brought forth (in this account) a new notion, conceived in secrecy and

*dedicated to the proposition that even an Honest Abe may
borrow a leaf from Edgar A. Poe.*

*It is altogether fitting and proper that Mr. Lincoln's venture
into the detective story should come to its final resting place in
the files of a man named Queen. For all his life Ellery has con-
secrated Father Abraham as the noblest projection of the
American dream; and, insofar as it has been within his poor
power to add or detract, he has given full measure of devotion,
testing whether that notion, or any notion so conceived and so
dedicated, deserves to endure.*

*Ellery's service in running the Lincoln clue to earth is one
the world has little noted nor, perhaps, will long remember.
That he shall not have served in vain, this account:*

The case began on the outskirts of an upstate-New York city
with the dreadful name of Eulalia, behind the flaking shutters
of a fat and curlicued house with architectural dandruff, recall-
ing for all the world some blowsy ex-Bloomer Girl from the
Gay Nineties of its origin.

The owner, a formerly wealthy man named DiCampo, possessed a grandeur not shared by his property, although it was
no less fallen into ruin. His falcon's face, more Florentine than
Victorian, was—like the house—ravaged by time and the in-
clemencies of fortune; but haughtily so, and indeed DiCampo
wore his scruffy purple velvet house jacket like the prince he
was entitled to call himself, but did not. He was proud, and
stubborn, and useless; and he had a lovely daughter named
Bianca, who taught at a Eulalia grade school and, through
marvels of economy, supported them both.

How Lorenzo San Marco Borghese-Ruffo DiCampo came to
this decayed estate is no concern of ours. The presence there
this day of a man named Harbidger and a man named Tungston, however, is to the point: they had come, Harbidger from
Chicago, Tungston from Philadelphia, to buy something each
wanted very much, and DiCampo had summoned them in
order to sell it. The two visitors were collectors, Harbidger's
passion being Lincoln, Tungston's Poe.

The Lincoln collector, an elderly man who looked like a mi-
grant fruit picker, had plucked his fruits well: Harbidger was

worth about forty million dollars, every dollar of which was at the beck of his mania for Lincolniana. Tungston, who was almost as rich, had the aging body of a poet and the eyes of a starving panther, armament that had served him well in the wars of Poeana.

"I must say, Mr. DiCampo," remarked Harbidger, "that your letter surprised me." He paused to savor the wine his host had poured from an ancient and honorable bottle (DiCampo had filled it with California claret before their arrival). "May I ask what has finally induced you to offer the book and document for sale?"

"To quote Lincoln in another context, Mr. Harbidger," said DiCampo with a shrug of his wasted shoulders, "'the dogmas of the quiet past are inadequate to the stormy present.' In short, a hungry man sells his blood."

"Only if it's of the right type," said old Tungston, unmoved. "You've made that book and document less accessible to collectors and historians, DiCampo, than the gold in Fort Knox. Have you got them here? I'd like to examine them."

"No other hand will ever touch them except by right of ownership," Lorenzo DiCampo replied bitterly. He had taken a miser's glee in his lucky finds, vowing never to part with them; now forced by his need to sell them, he was like a suspicion-caked old prospector who, stumbling at last on pay dirt, draws cryptic maps to keep the world from stealing the secret of its location. "As I informed you gentlemen, I represent the book as bearing the signatures of Poe and Lincoln, and the document as being in Lincoln's hand; I am offering them with customary proviso that they are returnable if they should prove to be not as represented; and if this does not satisfy you," and the old prince actually rose, "let us terminate our business here and now."

"Sit down, sit down, Mr. DiCampo," Harbidger said.

"No one is questioning your integrity," snapped old Tungston. "It's just that I'm not used to buying sight unseen. If there's a money-back guarantee, we'll do it your way."

Lorenzo DiCampo reseated himself stiffly. "Very well, gentlemen. Then I take it you are both prepared to buy?"

"Oh, yes!" said Harbidger. "What is your price?"

"Oh, no," said DiCampo. "What is your bid?"

The Lincoln collector cleared his throat, which was full of slaver. "If the book and document are as represented, Mr. DiCampo, you might hope to get from a dealer or realize at auction—oh—fifty thousand dollars. I offer you fifty-five thousand dollars."

"Fifty-six thousand dollars," said Tungston.

"Fifty-seven thousand dollars," said Harbidger.

Tungston showed his fangs.

"Sixty thousand dollars," he said.

Harbidger fell silent, and DiCampo waited. He did not expect miracles. To these men, five times sixty thousand dollars was of less moment than the undistinguished wine they were smacking their lips over; but they were veterans of many a hard auction-room campaign, and a collector's victory tasted very nearly as sweet for the price as for the prize.

So the impoverished prince was not surprised when the Lincoln collector suddenly said, "Would you be good enough to allow Mr. Tungston and me to talk privately for a moment?"

DiCampo rose and strolled out of the room, to gaze somberly through a cracked window at the jungle growth that had once been his Italian formal gardens.

It was the Poe collector who summoned him back. "Harbidger has convinced me that for the two of us to try to outbid each other would simply run the price up out of all reason. We're going to make you a sporting proposition."

"I've proposed to Mr. Tungston, and he has agreed," nodded Harbidger, "that our bid for the book and document be sixty-five thousand dollars. Each of us is prepared to pay that sum, and not a single penny more."

"So that is how the screws are turned," said DiCampo, smiling. "But I do not understand. If each of you makes the identical bid, which of you gets the book and document?"

"Ah," grinned the Poe man, "that's where the sporting proposition comes in."

"You see, Mr. DiCampo," said the Lincoln man, "we are going to leave that decision to you."

Even the old prince, who had seen more than his share of the astonishing, was astonished. He looked at the two rich men really for the first time. "I must confess," he murmured, "that your compact is an amusement. Permit me?" He sank into thought while the two collectors sat expectantly. When the old man looked up he was smiling like a fox. "The very thing, gentlemen! From the typewritten copies of the document I sent you, you both know that Lincoln himself left a clue to a theoretical hiding place for the book which he never explained. Some time ago I arrived at a possible solution to the President's little mystery. I propose to hide the book and document in accordance with it."

"You mean whichever of us figures out your interpretation of the Lincoln clue and finds the book and document where you will hide them, Mr. DiCampo, gets both for the agreed price?"

"That is it exactly."

The Lincoln collector looked dubious. "I don't know . . ."

"Oh, come, Harbidger," said Tungston, eyes glittering. "A deal is a deal. We accept, DiCampo! Now what?"

"You gentlemen will of course have to give me a little time. Shall we say three days?"

Ellery let himself into the Queen apartment, tossed his suitcase aside, and set about opening windows. He had been out of town for a week on a case, and Inspector Queen was in Atlantic City attending a police convention.

Breathable air having been restored, Ellery sat down to the week's accumulation of mail. One envelope made him pause. It had come by airmail special delivery, it was postmarked four days earlier, and in the lower left corner, in red, flamed the word *URGENT*. The printed return address on the flap said: *L.S.M.B-R. DiCampo, Post Office Box 69, Southern District, Eulalia, N.Y.* The initials of the name had been crossed out and "Bianca" written above them.

The enclosure, in a large agitated female hand on inexpensive notepaper, said:

Dear Mr. Queen,

The most important detective book in the world has disappeared. Will you please find it for me?

Phone me on arrival at the Eulalia RR station or airport
and I will pick you up.   Bianca DiCampo

A yellow envelope then caught his eye. It was a telegram,
dated the previous day:

WHY HAVE I NOT HEARD FROM YOU STOP AM IN DESPERATE
NEED OF YOUR SERVICES   BIANCA DICAMPO

He had no sooner finished reading the telegram than the
telephone on his desk trilled. It was a long-distance call.

"Mr. Queen?" throbbed a contralto voice. "Thank heaven
I've finally got through to you! I've been calling all day—"

"I've been away," said Ellery, "and you would be Miss
Bianca DiCampo of Eulalia. In two words, Miss DiCampo:
Why me?"

"In two words, Mr. Queen: Abraham Lincoln."

Ellery was startled. "You plead a persuasive case," he chuck-
led. "It's true. I'm an incurable Lincoln addict. How did you
find out? Well, never mind. Your letter refers to a book, Miss
DiCampo. Which book?"

The husky voice told him, and certain other provocative
things as well. "So will you come, Mr. Queen?"

"Tonight if I could! Suppose I drive up first thing in the
morning. I ought to make Eulalia by noon. Harbidger and
Tungston are still around, I take it?"

"Oh, yes. They're staying at a motel downtown."

"Would you ask them to be there?"

The moment he hung up Ellery leaped to his bookshelves.
He snatched out his volume of *Murder for Pleasure,* the historical work on detective stories by his good friend Howard Hay-
craft, and found what he was looking for on page 26:

And . . . young William Dean Howells thought it
significant praise to assert of a nominee for President of
the United States:

The bent of his mind is mathematical and meta-
physical, and he is therefore pleased with the absolute
and logical method of Poe's tales and sketches, in
which the problem of mystery is given, and wrought
out into everyday facts by processes of cunning anal-

ysis. It is said that he suffers no year to pass without
a perusal of this author.

Abraham Lincoln subsequently confirmed this statement, which appeared in his little known "campaign biography" by Howells in 1860 . . . The instance is chiefly no-
table, of course, for its revelation of a little suspected
affinity between two great Americans . . .

Very early the next morning Ellery gathered some papers
from his files, stuffed them into his briefcase, scribbled a note
for his father, and ran for his car, Eulalia-bound . . .

He was enchanted by the DiCampo house, which looked
like something out of Poe by Charles Addams; and, for other
reasons, by Bianca, who turned out to be a genetic product
supreme of northern Italy, with titian hair and Mediterranean
blue eyes and a figure that needed only some solid steaks to
qualify her for Miss Universe competition. Also, she was in
deep mourning; so her conquest of the Queen heart was immediate and complete.

"He died of a cerebral hemorrhage, Mr. Queen," Bianca
said, dabbing at her absurd little nose. "In the middle of the
second night after his session with Mr. Harbidger and Mr.
Tungston."

So Lorenzo San Marco Borghese-Ruffo DiCampo was unex-
pectedly dead, bequeathing the lovely Bianca near destitution
and a mystery.

"The only things of value father really left me are that book
and the Lincoln document. The sixty-five thousand dollars
they now represent would pay off father's debts and give me a
fresh start. But I can't find them, Mr. Queen, and neither can
Mr. Harbidger and Mr. Tungston—who'll be here soon, by the
way. Father hid the two things, as he told them he would; but
where? We've ransacked the place."

"Tell me more about the book, Miss DiCampo."

"As I said over the phone, it's called *The Gift: 1845*. The
Christmas annual that contained the earliest appearance of
Edgar Allan Poe's 'The Purloined Letter.'"

"Published in Philadelphia by Carey & Hart? Bound in red?"
At Bianca's nod Ellery said, "You understand that an ordinary

copy of *The Gift: 1845* isn't worth more than about fifty dollars. What makes your father's copy unique is that double autograph you mentioned."

"That's what he said, Mr. Queen. I wish I had the book here to show you—that beautifully handwritten *Edgar Allan Poe* on the flyleaf, and under Poe's signature the signature *Abraham Lincoln*."

"Poe's own copy, once owned, signed, and read by Lincoln," Ellery said slowly. "Yes, that would be a collector's item for the ages. By the way, Miss DiCampo, what's the story behind the other piece—the Lincoln document?"

Bianca told him what her father had told her.

One morning in the spring of 1865, Abraham Lincoln opened the rosewood door of his bedroom in the southwest corner of the second floor of the White House and stepped out into the red-carpeted hall at the unusually late hour—for him—of 7:00 A.M.; he was more accustomed to beginning his workday at six.

But (as Lorenzo DiCampo had reconstructed events) Mr. Lincoln that morning had lingered in his bedchamber. He had awakened at his usual hour but, instead of leaving for his office immediately on dressing, he had pulled one of the cane chairs over to the round table, with its gas-fed reading lamp, and sat down to reread Poe's "The Purloined Letter" in his copy of the 1845 annual; it was a dreary morning, and the natural light was poor. The President was alone; the folding doors to Mrs. Lincoln's bedroom remained closed.

Impressed as always with Poe's tale, Mr. Lincoln on this occasion was struck by a whimsical thought; and, apparently finding no paper handy, he took an envelope from his pocket, discarded its enclosure, slit the two short edges so that the envelope opened out into a single sheet, and began to write in a careful hand on the blank side.

"Describe it to me, please."

"It's a long envelope, one that must have contained a bulky letter. It is addressed to the White House, but there is no return address, and father was never able to identify the sender from the handwriting. We do know that the letter came through the regular mails, because there are two Lincoln stamps on it, lightly but unmistakably cancelled."

"May I see your father's transcript of what Lincoln wrote out that morning on the inside of the envelope?"

Bianca handed him a typewritten copy and, in spite of himself, Ellery felt gooseflesh rise as he read:

> Apr. 14, 1865
>
> Mr. Poe's The Purloined Letter is a work of singular originality. Its simplicity is a master-stroke of cunning, which never fails to arouse my wonder.
>
> Reading the tale over this morning has given me a "notion." Suppose I wished to hide a book, this very book, perhaps? Where best to do so? Well, as Mr. Poe in his tale hid a letter *among letters*, might not a book be hidden *among books*? Why, if this very copy of the tale were to be deposited in a library and on purpose not recorded—would not the Library of Congress make a prime depository!—well might it repose there, undiscovered, for a generation.
>
> On the other hand, let us regard Mr. Poe's "notion" turn about: suppose the book were to be placed, not amongst other books, but *where no book would reasonably be expected?* (I may follow the example of Mr. Poe, and, myself, compose a tale of "ratiocination"!)
>
> The "notion" beguiles me, it is nearly seven o'clock. Later to-day, if the vultures and my appointments leave me a few moments of leisure, I may write further of my imagined hiding-place.
>
> In self-reminder: the hiding-place of the book is in 30d, which

Ellery looked up. "The document ends there?"

"Father said that Mr. Lincoln must have glanced again at his watch, and shamefacedly jumped up to go to his office, leaving the sentence unfinished. Evidently he never found the time to get back to it."

Ellery brooded. Evidently indeed. From the moment when Abraham Lincoln stepped out of his bedroom that Good Friday morning, fingering his thick gold watch on its vest chain, to bid the still-unrelieved night guard his customary courteous "Good morning" and make for his office at the other end of the hall, his day was spoken for. The usual patient push through the clutching crowd of favor-seekers, many of whom had bedded down all night on the hall carpet; sanctuary in his sprawling office, where he read official correspondence; by 8 A.M. having breakfast with his family—Mrs. Lincoln chattering away about plans for the evening, twelve-year-old Tad of the cleft palate lisping a complaint that "nobody asked me to go," and young Robert Lincoln, just returned from duty, bubbling with stories about his hero Ulysses Grant and the last days of the war; then back to the presidential office to look over the morning newspapers (which Lincoln had once remarked he "never" read, but these were happy days, with good news everywhere), sign two documents, and signal the soldier at the door to admit the morning's first caller, Speaker of the House Schuyler Colfax (who was angling for a Cabinet post and had to be tactfully handled); and so on throughout the day—the historic Cabinet meeting at 11 A.M., attended by General Grant himself, that stretched well into the afternoon; a hurried lunch at almost half-past two with Mrs. Lincoln (had this forty-five-pounds-underweight man eaten his usual midday meal of a biscuit, a glass of milk, and an apple?); more visitors to see in his office (including the unscheduled Mrs. Nancy Bushrod, escaped slave and wife of an escaped slave and mother of three small children, weeping that Tom, a soldier in the Army of the Potomac, was no longer getting his pay: "You are entitled to your husband's pay. Come this time tomorrow," and the tall President escorted her to the door, bowing her out "like I was a natural-born lady"); the late afternoon drive in the barouche to the Navy Yard and back with Mrs. Lincoln; more work, more visitors, into the evening . . . until finally, at five minutes past 8 P.M., Abraham Lincoln stepped into the White House formal coach after his wife, waved, and sank back to be driven off to see a play he did not much want to see, *Our American Cousin,* at Ford's Theatre . . .

Ellery mused over that black day in silence. And, like a relative hanging on the specialist's yet undelivered diagnosis, Bianca DiCampo sat watching him with anxiety.

Harbidger and Tungston arrived in a taxi to greet Ellery with the fervor of two castaways waving at a smudge of smoke on the horizon.

"As I understand it, gentlemen," Ellery said when he had calmed them down, "neither of you has been able to solve Mr. DiCampo's interpretation of the Lincoln clue. If I succeed in finding the book and paper where DiCampo hid them, which of you gets them?"

"We intend to split the sixty-five-thousand-dollar payment to Miss DiCampo," said Harbidger, "and take joint ownership of the two pieces."

"An arrangement," growled old Tungston, "I'm against on principle, in practice, and by plain horse sense."

"So am I," sighed the Lincoln collector, "but what else can we do?"

"Well," and the Poe man regarded Bianca DiCampo with the icy intimacy of the cat that long ago marked the bird as its prey, "Miss DiCampo, who now owns the two pieces, is quite free to renegotiate a sale on her own terms."

"Miss DiCampo," said Miss DiCampo, giving Tungston stare for stare, "considers herself bound by her father's wishes. His terms stand."

"In all likelihood, then," said the other millionaire, "one of us will retain the book, the other the document, and we'll exchange them every year, or some such thing." Harbidger sounded unhappy.

"Only practical arrangement under the circumstances," grunted Tungston, and *he* sounded unhappy. "But all this is academic, Queen, unless and until the book and document are found."

Ellery nodded. "The problem, then, is to fathom DiCampo's interpretation of that *3od* in the document. 3od . . . I notice, Miss DiCampo—or, may I? Bianca?—that your father's typewritten copy of the Lincoln holograph text runs the *3* and *o* and *d* together—no spacing in between. Is that the way it occurs in the longhand?"

"Yes."

"Hmm. Still . . . 3od . . . Could *d* stand for *days* . . . or the

British *pence* . . . or *died,* as used in obituaries? Does any of these make sense to you, Bianca?"

"No."

"Did your father have any special interest in, say, pharmacology? chemistry? physics? algebra? electricity? Small *d* is an abbreviation used in all those." But Bianca shook her splendid head. "Banking? Small *d* for *dollars, dividends?*"

"Hardly," the girl said with a sad smile.

"How about theatricals? Was your father ever involved in a play production? Small *d* stands for *door* in stage directions."

"Mr. Queen, I've gone through every darned abbreviation my dictionary lists, and I haven't found one that has a point of contact with any interest of my father's."

Ellery scowled. "At that—I assume the typewritten copy is accurate—the manuscript shows no period after the *d,* making an abbreviation unlikely. 30d . . . let's concentrate on the number. Does the number 30 have any significance for you?"

"Yes, indeed," said Bianca, making all three men sit up. But then they sank back. "In a few years it will represent my age, and that has enormous significance. But only for me, I'm afraid."

"You'll be drawing wolf whistles at twice thirty," quoth Ellery warmly. "However! Could the number have cross-referred to anything in your father's life or habits?"

"None that I can think of, Mr. Queen. And," Bianca said, having grown roses in her cheeks, "thank you."

"I think," said old Tungston testily, "we had better stick to the subject."

"Just the same, Bianca, let me run over some 'thirty' associations as they come to mind. Stop me if one of them hits a nerve. The Thirty Tyrants—was your father interested in classical Athens? Thirty Years War—in seventeenth century European history? Thirty all—did he play or follow tennis? Or . . . did he ever live at an address that included the number 30?"

Ellery went on and on, but to each suggestion Bianca Di-Campo could only shake her head.

"The lack of spacing, come to think of it, doesn't necessarily mean that Mr. DiCampo chose to view the clue that way," said

Ellery thoughtfully. "He might have interpreted it arbitrarily as 3-space-o-*d*."

"Three od?" echoed old Tungston. "What the devil could that mean?"

"Od? Od is the hypothetical force or power claimed by Baron von Reichenbach—in 1850, wasn't it?—to pervade the whole of nature. Manifests itself in magnets, crystals, and such, which according to the excited baron explained animal magnetism and mesmerism. Was your father by any chance interested in hypnosis, Bianca? Or the occult?"

"Not in the slightest."

"Mr. Queen," exclaimed Harbidger, "are you serious about all this—this semantic sludge?"

"Why, I don't know," said Ellery. "I never know till I stumble over something. Od . . . the word was used with prefixes, too—*biod,* the force of animal life; *elod,* the force of electricity; and so forth. *Three* od . . . or *triod,* the triune force—it's all right, Mr. Harbidger, it's not ignorance on your part, I just coined the word. But it does rather suggest the Trinity, doesn't it? Bianca, did your father tie up to the Church in a personal, scholarly, or any other way? No? That's too bad, really, because Od—capitalized—has been a minced form of the word God since the sixteenth century. Or . . . you wouldn't happen to have three Bibles on the premises, would you? Because—"

Ellery stopped with the smashing abruptness of an ordinary force meeting an absolutely immovable object. The girl and the two collectors gawked. Bianca had idly picked up the typewritten copy of the Lincoln document. She was not reading it, she was simply holding it on her knees; but Ellery, sitting opposite her, had shot forward in a crouch, rather like a pointer, and he was regarding the paper in her lap with a glare of pure discovery.

"That's it!" he cried.

"What's it, Mr. Queen?" the girl asked, bewildered.

"Please—the transcript!" He plucked the paper from her. "Of course. Hear this: 'On the other hand, let us regard Mr. Poe's "notion" turn-about.' *Turn-about.* Look at the 3od 'turn-about'—as I just saw it!"

He turned the Lincoln message upside down for their inspection. In that position the 30d became:

ᴘᴏƐ

"*Poe!*" exploded Tungston.

"Yes, crude but recognizable," Ellery said swiftly. "So now we read the Lincoln clue as: 'The hiding-place of the book is in *Poe*'!"

There was a silence.

"In Poe," said Harbidger blankly.

"In Poe?" muttered Tungston. "There are only a couple of trade editions of Poe in DiCampo's library, Harbidger, and we went through those. We looked in every book here."

"He might have meant among the Poe books in the *public* library. Miss DiCampo—"

"Wait." Bianca sped away. But when she came back she was drooping. "It isn't. We have two public libraries in Eulalia, and I know the head librarian in both. I just called them. Father didn't visit either library."

Ellery gnawed a fingernail. "Is there a bust of Poe in the house, Bianca? Or any other Poe-associated object, aside from books?"

"I'm afraid not."

"Queer," he mumbled. "Yet I'm positive your father interpreted 'the hiding-place of the book' as being 'in Poe.' So he'd have hidden it 'in Poe' . . ."

Ellery's mumbling dribbled away into a tormented sort of silence: his eyebrows worked up and down, Groucho Marx-fashion; he pinched the tip of his nose until it was scarlet; he yanked at his unoffending ears; he munched on his lip . . . until, all at once, his face cleared; and he sprang to his feet. "Bianca, may I use your phone?"

The girl could only nod, and Ellery dashed. They heard him telephoning in the entrance hall, although they could not make out the words. He was back in two minutes.

"One thing more," he said briskly, "and we're out of the woods. I suppose your father had a key ring or a key case, Bianca? May I have it, please?"

She fetched a key case. To the two millionaires it seemed the sorriest of objects, a scuffed and dirty tan leatherette case. But

Ellery received it from the girl as if it were an artifact of historic importance from a newly discovered IV Dynasty tomb. He unsnapped it with concentrated love; he fingered its contents like a scientist. Finally he decided on a certain key.

"Wait here!" Thus Mr. Queen; and exit, running.

"I can't decide," old Tungston said after a while, "whether that fellow is a genius or an escaped lunatic."

Neither Harbidger nor Bianca replied. Apparently they could not decide, either.

They waited through twenty elongated minutes; at the twenty-first they heard his car, champing. All three were in the front doorway as Ellery strode up the walk.

He was carrying a book with a red cover, and smiling. It was a compassionate smile, but none of them noticed.

"You—" said Bianca. "—found—" said Tungston. "—the book!" shouted Harbidger. "Is the Lincoln holograph in it?"

"It is," said Ellery. "Shall we all go into the house, where we may mourn in decent privacy?"

"Because," Ellery said to Bianca and the two quivering collectors as they sat across a refectory table from him, "I have foul news. Mr. Tungston, I believe you have never actually seen Mr. DiCampo's book. Will you now look at the Poe signature on the flyleaf?"

The panther claws leaped. There, toward the top of the flyleaf, in faded inkscript, was the signature *Edgar Allan Poe*.

The claws curled, and old Tungston looked up sharply. "DiCampo never mentioned that it's a full autograph—he kept referring to it as 'the Poe signature.' Edgar *Allan* Poe . . . Why, I don't know of a single instance after his West Point days when Poe wrote out his middle name in an autograph! And the earliest he could have signed this 1845 edition is obviously when it was published, which was around the fall of 1844. In 1844 he'd surely have abbreviated the 'Allan,' signing 'Edgar A. Poe,' the way he signed everything! This is a forgery."

"My God," murmured Bianca, clearly intending no impiety; she was as pale as Poe's Lenore. "Is that true, Mr. Queen?"

"I'm afraid it is," Ellery said sadly. "I was suspicious the moment you told me the Poe signature on the flyleaf contained the 'Allan.' And if the Poe signature is a forgery, the book itself can hardly be considered Poe's own copy."

Harbidger was moaning. "And the Lincoln signature underneath the Poe, Mr. Queen! DiCampo never told me it reads *Abraham* Lincoln—the full Christian name. Except on official documents, Lincoln practically always signed his name 'A. Lincoln.' Don't tell me this Lincoln autograph is a forgery, too?"

Ellery forbore to look at poor Bianca. "I was struck by the 'Abraham' as well, Mr. Harbidger, when Miss DiCampo mentioned it to me, and I came equipped to test it. I have here—" and Ellery tapped the pile of documents he had taken from his briefcase "—facsimiles of Lincoln signatures from the most frequently reproduced of the historic documents he signed. Now I'm going to make a precise tracing of the Lincoln signature on the flyleaf of the book—" he proceeded to do so "—and I shall superimpose the tracing on the various signatures of the authentic Lincoln documents. So."

He worked rapidly. On his third superimposition Ellery looked up. "Yes. See here. The tracing of the purported Lincoln signature from the flyleaf fits in minutest detail over the authentic Lincoln signature on this facsimile of the Emancipation Proclamation. It's a fact of life that's tripped many a forger that *nobody ever writes his name exactly the same way twice*. There are always variations. If two signatures are identical, then, one must be a tracing of the other. So the 'Abraham Lincoln' signed on this flyleaf can be dismissed without further consideration as a forgery also. It's a tracing of the Emancipation Proclamation signature.

"Not only was this book not Poe's own copy; it was never signed—and therefore probably never owned—by Lincoln. However your father came into possession of the book, Bianca, he was swindled."

It was the measure of Bianca DiCampo's quality that she said quietly, "Poor, poor father," nothing more.

Harbidger was poring over the worn old envelope on whose inside appeared the dearly beloved handscript of the martyr President. "At least," he muttered, "we have *this*."

"Do we?" asked Ellery gently. "Turn it over, Mr. Harbidger."

Harbidger looked up, scowling. "No! You're not going to deprive me of this, too!"

"Turn it over," Ellery repeated in the same gentle way. The Lincoln collector obeyed reluctantly. "What do you see?"

"An authentic envelope of the period! With two authentic Lincoln stamps!"

"Exactly. And the United States has never issued postage stamps depicting living Americans; you have to be dead to qualify. The earliest U.S. stamp showing a portrait of Lincoln went on sale April 15, 1866—a year to the day after his death. Then a living Lincoln could scarcely have used this envelope, with these stamps on it, as writing paper. The document is spurious, too. I am so very sorry, Bianca."

Incredibly, Lorenzo DiCampo's daughter managed a smile with her *"Non importa, signor."* He could have wept for her. As for the two collectors, Harbidger was in shock; but old Tungston managed to croak, "Where the devil did DiCampo hide the book, Queen? And how did you know?"

"Oh, that," said Ellery, wishing the two old men would go away so that he might comfort this admirable creature. "I was convinced that DiCampo interpreted what we now know was the forger's, not Lincoln's, clue, as 30d read upside down; or, crudely, ᴘᴏ℥. But 'the hiding-place of the book is in Poe' led nowhere.

"So I reconsidered. P, o, e. If those three letters of the alphabet didn't mean Poe, what could they mean? Then I remembered something about the letter you wrote me, Bianca. You'd used one of your father's envelopes, on the flap of which appeared his address: *Post Office Box 69, Southern District, Eulalia, N.Y.* If there was a Southern District in Eulalia, it seemed reasonable to conclude that there were post offices for other points of the compass, too. As, for instance, an Eastern District. Post Office Eastern, P.O. East. P.O.E."

"Poe!" cried Bianca.

"To answer your question, Mr. Tungston: I phoned the main post office, confirmed the existence of a Post Office East, got directions as to how to get there, looked for a postal box key in Mr. DiCampo's key case, found the right one, located the box DiCampo had rented especially for the occasion, unlocked it—and there was the book." He added, hopefully, "And that is that."

"And that *is* that," Bianca said when she returned from seeing the two collectors off. "I'm not going to cry over an empty milk bottle, Mr. Queen. I'll straighten out father's affairs somehow. Right now all I can think of is how glad I am he didn't live to see the signatures and documents declared forgeries publicly, as they would surely have been when they were expertized."

"I think you'll find there's still some milk in the bottle, Bianca."

"I beg your pardon?" said Bianca.

Ellery tapped the pseudo-Lincolnian envelope. "You know, you didn't do a very good job describing this envelope to me. All you said was that there were two cancelled Lincoln stamps on it."

"Well, there are."

"I can see you misspent your childhood. No, little girls don't collect things, do they? Why, if you'll examine these 'two cancelled Lincoln stamps,' you'll see that they're a great deal more than that. In the first place, they're not separate stamps. They're a vertical pair—that is, one stamp is joined to the other at the horizontal edges. Now look at this upper stamp of the pair."

The Mediterranean eyes widened. "It's upside down, isn't it?"

"Yes, it's upside down," said Ellery, "and what's more, while the pair have perforations all around, there are no perforations between them, where they're joined.

"What you have here, young lady—and what our unknown forger didn't realize when he fished around for an authentic White House cover of the period on which to perpetrate the Lincoln forgery—is what stamp collectors might call a double printing error: a pair of 1866 black 15-cent Lincolns imperforate horizontally, with one of the pair printed upside down. No such error of the Lincoln issue has ever been reported. You're the owner, Bianca, of what may well be the rarest item in U.S. philately, and the most valuable."

The world will little note, nor long remember.

But don't try to prove it by Bianca DiCampo.

Counselor at Law

AL NUSSBAUM

Her blond hair had a shine to it and a trace of warm colors—amber, red, and orange. That's the first thing David Morgan noticed. Then he saw that she was at least ten years younger than his thirty-five, about four inches taller than his five foot eight, and as pretty and as slim as a *Vogue* model.

There were several stepped-upon cigarette ends outside his office door. He was returning from a quick lunch, and they hadn't been there when he left. If they were all hers, she was extremely nervous. The way she was unconsciously twisting her large handbag seemed to confirm that diagnosis.

He slipped his key into the lock of his door. The frosted glass was lettered:

David Morgan,
Counselor at Law

The other attorneys in the building all had their doors lettered *Attorney at Law*. Morgan liked to think that the difference indicated was one of style, not quality. He preferred to aid his clients without resorting to briefs, courtrooms, or even the mildest legal mumbo jumbo.

"Mr. Morgan?" she asked. She had a husky voice.

"Yes?" he replied, pushing open the door.

The office was a mess. Papers and open law books covered almost every available surface. He picked up a stack of papers from the seat of the chair beside the desk and added it to the pile on one of the bookcases.

"Everything is in chronological order," he explained, offering her the seat with a wave of the hand. "The first things I dropped are on the bottom, the last ones are on top."

She didn't crack a smile. She just looked confused and sat down, clutching her large handbag on her lap with both hands like a child with a security blanket.

Morgan took his place behind the desk and sat back. When she said nothing, he raised his eyebrows quizzically and waited a few more beats. More silence.

Finally, he asked, "What brings you here, Miss . . . Miss?"

"Heller . . . Louise Heller," she said. "I . . . I saw your name in the newspaper a month ago. I . . . I figured any lawyer who would file over a hundred pre-trial motions in a misdemeanor case had to be a fighter."

It had been a tactic to insure that plea bargaining would be less difficult in the future. No one wanted to go through that again, least of all himself. He didn't tell her this, though, nor that his client in that case had been found guilty, anyhow, and that the judge had reprimanded him for causing the state unnecessary court costs. Instead, he asked, "You mean you remembered my name all this time?"

"I wrote it down so I wouldn't forget."

Morgan smiled. "Then you must have known a month ago that you would be needing an attorney. Why didn't you see me then?"

"Well . . . I hoped I wouldn't need you." She gripped her bag tighter and her knuckles whitened. Then the words poured out in a rush. "I hoped by some miracle I'd be able to put the money back, but I couldn't. And the bank examiners will be there tomorrow morning."

Morgan decided to take a shortcut through what promised to be a long story. "Do you work in a bank?" he asked.

Louise nodded.

"And your accounts are short?"

She nodded again.

"How short?"

"Ten thousand dollars. Can you help me?"

He sat up and pulled his chair closer to the desk. Then he asked, "How much money do you have?"

She fumbled with the catch on her handbag. "I have two hundred dollars," she said, reaching inside.

"Don't you have any savings?"

She stopped with her hand inside the bag. "No."

"How about friends and relatives. Don't you have a few of

them who would be willing to lend you some money to help you out of this mess?"

She hung her head. "There's no one."

"Come on, Louise. You're an attractive woman. You must have a boyfriend or two who would be willing to help you with a small loan."

A muffled, "No."

Morgan drummed his fingers, searching for an inspiration, while she stacked some small bills on the edge of the desk.

"No boyfriends? None at all?" he asked.

"No. I . . . I took the money to . . . to help a man get started in a business, but it failed and he left town."

That piece of information surprised Morgan. She looked smarter than that. He got out of his chair and paced up and down between the desk and the window. Every once in a while he'd look over at her and shake his head.

At last he said, "Do you know the penalty for embezzlement in this state?"

She shook her head no.

"It's two to ten years," he told her. "And your good looks won't save you. Women's Lib has ended those days forever."

"Can't you help me?" A tear ran down her cheek, leaving a shiny trail.

"That depends upon you. Do you always do whatever a man asks of you?"

"Yes. Most of the time."

Morgan went back to his chair and sat down. "What bank did you take the money from?"

"The Merchant's National."

"And you still work there?"

"Yes."

"All right," he said. "I want you to go back to work this afternoon. Make some excuse for being late. Then take another ninety thousand dollars and bring it here."

She started to say something, but he cut her off. "If following orders got you into this mess, you can follow mine to get out. Now, you'd better get going. I'll wait for you."

An hour passed and then another. It was almost four o'clock

when she returned. She still clutched her large handbag with both hands, but now its sides bulged and her face was flushed with excitement and apprehension.

"Did you have any trouble?" he asked.

"Oh, no!" Her voice showed the surprise she felt. "It was easy. All of the bank officers were having a meeting. I just walked into the vault and took ninety thousand from the emergency cash reserve." She opened her bag and stacked bundles of neatly wrapped fifty- and hundred-dollar bills on Morgan's desk.

"Give me the telephone number of the bank," he said. "And the president's name." While the phone was ringing, he asked her, "How would you like to go to Las Vegas this weekend?"

The phone was answered, and the call had to be routed from the switchboard to the man's secretary and then to him. Louise was sitting on the edge of her chair, hanging on every word. The frightened look she had worn when she arrived earlier in the day was no longer in evidence.

Then the bank president was on the line. Morgan introduced himself and told the man, "One of your employees, Miss Louise Heller, is in my office. She has embezzled one hundred thousand dollars from your bank, a fact the examiners will soon confirm." He waited for the banker to stop sputtering at the other end of the line, then said, "If the bank will agree not to prosecute or publicize this loss, my client will return *half* the money."

There was more sputtering.

"Otherwise, it will be needed for bail and legal expenses."

David Morgan, Counselor at Law, sat back and smiled at Louise, confident that even if the bank president wanted to refuse the partial restitution, his insurance company wouldn't let him.

The lawyer smiled at his lovely client. "You'll like Vegas," he told her.

Her sudden smile told Morgan that *he* was going to like it, too.

The Iron Collar

FRANK SISK

The two old men appeared to have nothing in common except their incredibly great age. Both were in their late eighties, if you believed those who drank a morning beer in the plazuela of the Hotel Reforma. Their days ran far back into the hazy distance where life begins to merge with history.

The one known as Miguel Solaz possessed a serious and quiet dignity always adorned with a grayish straw hat and a shiny black suit with fraying velvet lapels. The other, known only as Vicente, was a voluble man with a small stock of self-deprecating, shoulder-shrugging gestures. His flat-backed head was generally protected from the sun by a checkered kerchief.

It seemed to be Miguel's custom to arrive in the plazuela just as I was sweetening a second cup of coffee. He came slowly, on legs as stiff and unbending as the white cane which contributed to his support. For all practical purposes he was blind. That is why, probably, he invariably sat at the small round table near the fountain, to enjoy the faint spray and the cool sound.

The sole waiter, who never rushed under any conditions, treated the arrival of Miguel Solaz as an event unnoticed.

The old man would sit there counting his fingers. You could almost hear him. *Uno, dos, tres, cuatro* . . . A petal from the nearby bougainvillea sometimes drifted down on the brim of his hat. He waited with finger-counting patience.

Vicente usually appeared about ten minutes after Miguel. He was accompanied by an elderly burro which pulled a two-wheeled cart of the sort called *carretilla de mano*. It was the only pushcart in the city, I believe, that was not man-powered.

Though Vicente was supposed to be the same age as Miguel, he acted as if he were younger and inferior. He approached the table as a son approaching a father.

Vicente sold loaves of bread, shaped like turtles whose heads have been withdrawn and legs left out. From his cart Vicente would take two of the smaller loaves and move with age-halted gait to the table at which Miguel sat. He would not quite bend a knee in obeisance or touch the non-existent fore-lock under the kerchief, but he still managed to give the impression of vassal importuning lord.

Miguel acknowledged his presence with a grave inclination of the head that sent a petal fluttering from his hat. Vicente sat then, at the side of the table farthest from the fountain's light spray, holding the loaves upright in either hand.

Only then did the slow waiter accommodate that area to his point of view. When he finally approached the table, his gaze always rested on Vicente, and Vicente always held up the two loaves of bread in silent signification of his habitual order, a pot of coffee for Miguel, a bottle of beer for himself and a jar of cheese between them. It was apparent who had the money if not the dignity.

After the waiter had served them, Vicente would lift his stein to nose level as if in homage to Miguel, who always took an unconscionably long time in finding the handle of his cup. Yet Vicente would wait patiently until Miguel had sipped before sliding the beer under his own scraggly mustache.

Each morning for five days I witnessed this companionable scene, and each morning I grew more mystified and more curious. On the sixth morning I was joined at breakfast by an attorney, Juan de Luega, who was arranging certain import-export contracts for my company.

As second coffees were being served, Miguel Solaz took his seat at the table by the fountain. Interrupting the business subject of our conversation, I asked Señor de Luega the identity of the dignified old man.

"Miguel Solaz? He is a retired public official. He has been retired for many years now."

"Does he have a pension?"

"A negligible one."

"That accounts for the condition of his clothes then. In the States we call it shabby genteel. What sort of public official was he?"

"An honest one, I imagine," the attorney said with a smile.

"Otherwise he would not be what you call shabby genteel, no?"

"Perhaps. But what I meant was the capacity in which he served as a public official."

"He served in several capacities, I believe," the attorney said. He removed his dark glasses and commenced to polish them. "He dates long before my time. Before the time of my father even. You must appreciate that."

"I appreciate it all right. I just wondered what the old man did when he was younger."

"He served in several capacities, I understand."

"So you have already said, Señor de Luega."

"I beg your pardon, my friend, but I seem to remember only one of these several capacities. And it is one I would much prefer to forget."

"It's really of no importance," I said to hide my curiosity. "Put it aside, amigo."

The attorney returned the dark glasses to the upper half of his face. "No," he said. "Why should I hide an aspect of local color from a client? If you really wish to know, Miguel Solaz is remembered best in his public capacity as El Verdugo."

"El Verdugo?" I searched among my sparse Spanish assets and failed to find an English equivalent. "El Verdugo?"

"The executioner," said the attorney softly. "Miguel Solaz was once the public executioner."

I looked more intently at the finger-counting old man. "A public executioner. Appearances are most deceiving, aren't they?"

"At that age, my friend, appearances are hardly revealing," said the attorney.

"And with a name like Solaz. Doesn't it mean something like solace?"

"Solace, yes, or comfort. Ease. But of course it is not his true patronymic. That, I think, is something like Santomarco or Santomarino. I cannot be sure."

"Why would he drop his family name?"

"Well, Miguel's life goes far back to the First Revolution. In those times it was customary for the activists to adopt a *nombre de guerra* to protect relatives against possible reprisals."

"Solaz, though, for an executioner? Isn't that a bit ironic?"

"Not entirely, if you consider that it is the common hope that death will bring relief from the trials of the temporal world. In the case of Miguel it carried a further meaning. Or so I am told."

"May I ask what further meaning, señor?"

"I am told that Miguel Solaz was not only an executioner, but also an inventor."

I was about to ask what Miguel had invented when Vicente and his burro-pulled pushcart came leisurely around the corner of wall that half hid the plazuela from the street. "Here's what really interests me," I said to the attorney. "The old peasant kowtowing to the retired revolutionist. There's certainly a sample of irony for you."

Señor de Luega offered me a cigarro saying, "There is more irony here than meets the eye of a casual observer, my friend." He produced a lighter and leaned across the table with the flame. "The so-called peasant was once a prosperous man of business. He is now known simply as Vicente. His family name I do not know. At any rate, he has not used it in a long while. If one really wishes to underline historical absurdity, one might say that the capitalist is bringing votary offerings to the revolutionary peasant. For Miguel Solaz comes from the soil. What is taken in him for dignity is actually the fatalism of the peasant."

Intrigued, I asked, "How long has the old man of business been coming here like this with his loaves of bread?"

"Longer than I can remember," the attorney said.

"And what is his reason?"

The attorney studied the new ash of his cigar through the dark glasses. "I don't know. Probably Miguel doesn't know. Even Vicente may not know. But whatever the reason, it had its birth back in the days of the First Revolution."

"The Revolution was evidently a success?" I asked.

"All our revolutions are a success," said the attorney with a smile. "But the first is always the first. As the story goes in this locality, Vicente at that time bought and sold most of the grain produced in this province. Nowadays we describe such a man as a monopolist."

Through a haze of aromatic smoke I watched Vicente humbly seating himself at the table over which Miguel Solaz silently presided. He had the two loaves and now he had the eye of the waiter.

Señor de Luega's voice continued: "All this grain, hundreds of tons of it, was kept in a large warehouse in this city. When the revolutionists seized control they quickly impounded that warehouse. It represented, in those days, a good portion of the area's resources. For the provisionary government in the city it meant added power, economic power, which is always the ultimate.

"Exact records of what followed seizure of the granary are not obtainable. But this much is known. A few months after the expropriation, the granary was burned to the ground with its contents a total loss. It was a serious blow to the revolutionary government. A determination of arson was made—arson by counterrevolutionists. And presently the culprit was found; or the alleged culprit, I should say, for in such unsettled times it is essential to fasten the guilt on somebody quickly, guilty or not. Presumably a tribunal sat on some sort of quasi-legal proceeding. However, no records of it exist. What I am telling you, therefore, is not very reliable as fact. Still it is somewhat more reliable than folklore because two of the principals are still alive and sitting within earshot."

"Then the alleged culprit was Vicente," I said.

"No," said the attorney. "It was Vicente's son, a boy of sixteen, his only son. But it brought disgrace to the family name."

"He was found guilty?"

"Yes. Of treason."

"And the sentence was death, I suppose?"

"By the garotte, in those times."

"And now I must conclude that the executioner was Miguel Solaz. Is that it?"

"You are correct."

I stared at the two old men breaking bread in the warm morning sunlight. "Why does the father come here each day to sit with the man who executed his only boy?"

The attorney gave just the suggestion of a shrug. "As I've said, he may no longer know the answer to that himself. But it is generally believed that Vicente regards Miguel Solaz as a benefactor. Do not kick that word away until you hear the rest of the story."

I smiled. I said nothing.

"The garotte, my friend, do you know what it is?" the attorney asked.

"An instrument of strangulation, isn't it?"

"Correct. In our country it was the official instrument of execution until we abolished capital punishment thirty years ago. To die by the garotte, until certain refinements were introduced, was a slow and painful death. Some of the instruments are preserved in the museums. Have you ever seen one?"

"A garotte? No."

"Let me describe it. The concept was based on two semicircular pieces of iron designed to fit the neck like a collar. A large-handled screw actuated the constricting movement. As the screw was turned, the rear half of the collar pushed against the back of the victim's neck and the front half moved toward the windpipe. The garotte, in those days, was usually affixed to a wooden post at a level which permitted the victim to sit on the ground. He was usually tied to the post too, but not always. Some executioners liked to give the victim a chance to thrash around. The death agony often lasted five minutes."

"I get the picture," I said, my eyes still on the table by the fountain. Vicente's kerchief-wrapped head was bent deferentially to one side, aslant of the raised stein of beer, as he waited for Miguel to take that first sip of coffee. "And that's the way the boy died, Vicente's boy?"

"But with a significant difference," the attorney said. "If there are any really significant differences in the way death comes."

"It's hard to make a choice," I remarked.

"Well, whatever the difference in the case of Vicente's son, Miguel Solaz made it. The story which has been passed down says that Miguel lost a close relative to the garotte at the hands of a bungling executioner, and ever after felt that the instrument should be made more humane. Hence, when he became

El Verdugo, he put to work a native ingenuity and eventually produced a garotte which accomplished its task with comparative speed."

"Then *this* is where his claim to invention rests?"

"Correct," the attorney said. "A most simple improvement. He fitted the inside of the back collar with a thin, very sharp blade about two inches deep. Now when the screw was turned, the blade quickly passed between two bones in the back of the neck and severed the spinal column."

"Some invention!"

"It earned Miguel the name of Solaz," the attorney continued. "It brought the solace of death swiftly to the condemned man. It made the execution a bit less painful for the relatives who had to bear witness."

"I suppose so," I said. "Did Vicente witness his only son die by this improved method?"

"Yes. It was quite an event, for it was the first time the new garotte was officially used. And it is said to have performed perfectly, the boy twitching only once at the critical severance. Yes, Vicente was there, with his wife and daughters. Attendance was compulsory. Public executions then, as always, were supposed to serve as warnings."

My gaze was again back at the fountain table. "Vicente seems to have learned his lesson well."

The attorney was also looking at that table, meditatively. "He learned it well but too late. The old ones, his contemporaries who are no longer with us, used to say that Vicente gained an iron collar when he lost his good name. They said that was why he always wore a kerchief around his neck—to conceal the iron collar."

"He wears the same old kerchief around his head now," I said, "judging from its looks."

"Perhaps he feels he has nothing to conceal from Miguel. Notice the way he holds his head forward and to one side even when he drinks the beer."

"I've noticed. Deferential."

"It isn't that entirely, or so the old ones used to say. It's the feel of the old-style garotte around his neck. It has been stran-

gling him for more than sixty years, slowly and most agoniz-
ingly, and he is not dead yet."

"But why?"

Señor de Luega seemed suddenly sad. "The death of his son
was a miscarriage of justice. The boy was innocent of setting
the granary afire. Many weeks after the execution the truth
gradually became manifest."

"In that case, I should think that long ago Vicente would
have brought a knife for Miguel's throat, instead of bread and
deference."

The attorney's voice carried an undertone of sadness. "No, it
was no fault of Miguel. Vicente knows that. Miguel was simply
doing his duty. He did it as mercifully as possible. Vicente rev-
erences him for that. It is himself that he cannot abide. You
see, it was Vicente who set the fire."

The Poisoned Pawn

HENRY SLESAR

If it weren't for the state of his own health (his stomach felt
lined with broken green bottle glass), Milo Bloom would have
giggled at the sight of his roommate in the six-bed ward on the
third floor of Misercordia Hospital. Both of his arms were in
casts, giving them the appearance of two chubby white sau-
sages; the left arm dangled from a pulley in a complex traction
arrangement that somehow included his left leg. Later, he
learned that his companion (Dietz was his name), had fallen
from a loading platform. Milo's hospital admittance record told
a far more dramatic story. He had been poisoned.

"And I'll tell you something," Milo said, shaking his head
sadly and making the broken glass jiggle, "I learned a lesson
from it. I was lying under my own dining table, and my whole
life flashed in front of my eyes, and you know what it looked
like? One long chess game. I saw myself born on QB4, a

white pawn wrapped in a baby blanket, and here I was, dying, caught in a zugzwang and about to be checkmated . . ."

Of course, Milo was still under sedation and wasn't expected to talk coherently. An hour later, however, he was able to express himself more clearly.

"Never again," he said solemnly. "Never, never again will I play another game of chess. I'll never touch another piece, never read another chess column. You say the name 'Bobby Fischer' to me, I'll put my hands over my ears. For thirty years I was a prisoner of that miserable board, but now I'm through. You call that a game? That's an obsession! And look where it got me. Just look!"

What he really meant, of course, was "listen," which is what Dietz, who had no other plans that day, was perfectly willing to do.

My father cared very little about chess. When he proudly displayed me to the membership of the Greenpoint Chess Club, and mockingly promoted a match with Kupperman, its champion, it wasn't for love of the game; just hate for Kupperman. I was eleven years old, Kupperman was forty-five. The thought of my tiny hands strangling Kupperman's King filled him with ecstasy.

I sat opposite Kupperman's hulking body and ignored the heavy-jowled sneer that had terrified other opponents, confident that I was a prodigy, whose ability Kupperman would underestimate. Then zip! wham! thud! the pieces came together in the center of the board. Bang! Kupperman's Queen lashed out in an unorthodox early attack. *Whoosh!* came his black Knights in a double assault that made me whimper. Then *crash!* my defense crumpled and my King was running for his life, only to fall dead ignobly at the feet of a Rook Pawn. Unbelievable. In seventeen moves, most of them textbook-defying, Kupperman had crushed me. Guess who didn't get ice cream that night?

Of course, I was humiliated by Kupperman's victory. I had bested every opponent in my peer group, and thought I was ready for prodigy-type encounters. I didn't realize at the time how very good Kupperman was. The fact that he was Number

One in a small Brooklyn chess club gave no real measure of the man's talent, his extraordinary, Petrosian-like play.

I learned a great deal more about that talent in the next two decades, because that wasn't the last Bloom-Kupperman match; it was only the first of many.

Kupperman refused to play me again until four years later, when I was not only a ripe fifteen, but had already proved my worth by winning the Junior Championship of Brooklyn. I was bristling with self-confidence then, but when I faced the 49-year-old Kupperman across the table, and once again witnessed the strange, slashing style, the wild romping of his Knights, the long-delayed castling, the baffling retreat of well-developed pieces, surprising *Zwischenzuge*—in-between moves with no apparent purpose—and most disturbing of all, little stabbing moves of his Pawns, pinpricks from both sides of the board, nibbling at my presumably solid center, panic set in and my brain fogged over, to say nothing of my glasses from the steam of my own accelerated breathing. Yes, I lost that game, too; but it wasn't to be my last loss to Kupperman, even though he abruptly decided to leave not only the Greenpoint Chess Club, but the East Coast itself.

I never knew for certain why Kupperman decided to leave. My father theorized that he was an asthma victim who had been advised to bask in the drying sunshine of Arizona or some other western state. Actually, the first postmark I saw from a Kupperman correspondence was a town called Kenton, Illinois. He had sent a letter to the Greenpoint Chess Club, offering to play its current champion by mail. I suppose he was homesick for Brooklyn. Now, guess who was current champion? Milo Bloom.

I was twenty-two then, past the age of prodigy, but smug in my dominance of the neighborhood *potzers*, and pantingly eager to face the Kupperman unorthodoxy again, certain that nobody could break so many rules and still come out on top consistently. I replied to Kupperman at once, special delivery no less, and told him with becoming modesty of my ascension in the club and my gracious willingness to play him by mail.

A week later, I received his reply, a written scowl is what it was, and an opening move—N-KB3! Obviously, Kupperman hadn't changed too much in the intervening seven years.

Well, I might as well get it over with and admit that Kupperman defeated me in that game and, if anything, the defeat was more shattering than the head-to-head encounters of the past. Incredibly, Kupperman posted most of his pieces on the back rank. Then came a Knight sacrifice, a pinned Queen, and a neatly executed check.

Foreseeing the slaughter ahead, I resigned, despite the fact that I was actually ahead by one Pawn.

Obviously, my early resignation didn't fully satisfy Kupperman (I could just visualize him, his unshaven cheeks quivering in a fleshy frown, as he tore open my letter and growled in chagrin at my reply). Almost the next day, I received a letter asking me why I hadn't sent my White opening for the next game.

I finally did: P-Q4. He replied with N-KB3. I moved my own Knight. He responded by moving his Pawn to the Queen's third square. I moved my Knight to the Bishop's third square, and he promptly pinned it with *his* Bishop, contrary to all common sense. Then he proceeded to let me have both Bishops and bring up my Queen. I should have known that I was doomed then and there. He smothered my Bishops, made an aggressive castling move, and needled me with Pawns until my position was hopeless.

A month went by before Kupperman sent me the next opening move (this time, his letter was postmarked Tyler, Kansas) and we were launched into the third game of what was to become a lifetime of humiliating encounters.

Yes, that's correct. *I never won a game from Kupperman.* Yet, despite my continuing chagrin and, one might think, despite Kupperman's boredom, our games-by-mail were played for a period of *nineteen years*. The only real variations were in Kupperman's postmarks; he seemed to change his residence monthly. Otherwise the pattern remained the same: Kupperman's unorthodox, Petrosian-like style invariably bested my solid, self-righteous, textbook game. As you can imagine, beating Kupperman became the primary challenge, then, of my life.

Then he sent me The Letter.

It was the first time Kupperman's correspondence consisted of anything but chess notations. It was postmarked from New Mexico, and the handwriting looked as if it had been scrawled out with a screwdriver dipped in axle grease.

"*Dear Grand Master,*" it said, with heavy irony. "*Please be advised that the present score is ninety-seven games to nothing. Please be advised that upon my hundredth victory, we play no more. Yours respectfully, A. Kupperman.*"

I don't know how to describe the effect of that letter upon me. I couldn't have been more staggered if my family doctor had diagnosed a terminal illness. Yes, I knew full well that the score was 97 to 0, although I hadn't realized that Kupperman kept such scrupulous records; but the humiliation that lay ahead of me, the hundredth defeat, the *final* defeat, was almost too much for me to bear. Suddenly, I knew that if I didn't beat Kupperman at least *once* before that deadline, my life would be lived out in shame and total frustration.

It was no use returning to the textbooks; I had studied thousands of games (*all* of Petrosian's, until I knew each move by rote) without finding the secret of overcoming Kupperman's singular style. If anything, his use of Knights and Pawns was even wilder and more distinctive than Petrosian's. It was no use hoping for a sudden failure of Kupperman's play; not with only three games left. In fact, it was no use believing in miracles of any kind.

I walked about in a daze, unable to decide whether to send Kupperman the opening move of the ninety-eighth game. My employer (the accounting firm of Bernard & Yerkes) began to complain bitterly about frequent errors in my work. The young woman I had been dating for almost two years took personal affront at my attitude and severed our relationship.

Then, one day, the solution to my problem appeared almost magically before my eyes.

Strangely enough, I had seen the very same advertisement in *Chess Review* for almost a dozen years, and it never assumed the significance it did that evening.

The advertisement read: "*Grand Master willing to play for*

*small fee, by mail. Guaranteed credentials. Fee returned in
case of draw or mate. Yankovich, Box 87."*

I had never been tempted to clash with any other player by
mail except Kupperman; I had certainly never been willing to
lose money in such encounters.

I stared at the small print of the advertisement, and my
brain seemed flooded with brilliant light. It was as if a voice, a
basso profundo voice, was speaking to me and saying: Why
not let someone *else* beat Kupperman?

The simple beauty of the idea thrilled me, and completely
obliterated all ethical doubts. Who said chess was a game of
ethics, anyway? Chess players are notorious for their killer instincts. Half the sport lay in rattling your opponent. Who can
deny the malevolent effects of Fischer's gamesmanship on
Boris Spassky? Yes, this would be different; this would be a
blatant falsehood. If I gained a victory, it would be a false one;
but if I could beat Kupperman, even a phantom victory would
do.

That night I addressed a letter to the Grand Master's box
number, and within two days received a reply. Yankovich's fee
was a mere twenty-five dollars, he wrote. He required the
money in advance, but promised to return it after the con-
clusion of the game, in the event of a draw or a defeat. He
wished me luck, and on the assumption that I would be interested, sent me his opening move: P-Q4.

With a feeling of rising excitement, I sent off two letters that
day. One to Yankovich, Box 87, and one to A. Kupperman in
New Mexico. The letter to Yankovich contained twenty-five
dollars, and a brief note explaining that I would send my coun-
termove by return mail. The letter to Kupperman was briefer.
It merely said: *"P-Q4."*

Within two days, I had Kupperman's reply: *"N-KB3."*

I wasted no time in writing to Yankovich. *"N-KB3,"* my letter said.

Yankovich was equally prompt. *"N-KB3,"* he said.

I wrote Kupperman: *"N-KB3."*

Kupperman replied: *"P-B4."*

I wrote Yankovich: *"P-B4. "*

By the sixth move, Yankovich-Bloom's Bishop had captured

Kupperman's Knight, and Kupperman's King's Pawn took possession of our Bishop. (I had begun to think of the White forces as *ours*.) True to form, Kupperman *didn't* capture toward the center. This fact seemed to give Yankovich pause, because his next letter arrived two days later than usual. He responded with a Pawn move, as did Kupperman, who then gave up a Pawn. I felt a momentary sense of triumph, which was diminished a dozen moves later when I realized that Kupperman, once again poising his pieces on the *back* rank, was up to his old tricks. I fervently hoped that Grand Master Yankovich wouldn't be as bemused by this tactic as I was.

Unfortunately, he was. It took Kupperman forty moves to beat him into submission, but after battering at Yankovich-Bloom's King side, he suddenly switched his attack to the Queen's, and . . . *we* had to resign.

Believe me, I took no pleasure in the letter Yankovich sent me, congratulating me on my victory and returning my twenty-five dollars.

Nor was there much pleasure in the grudging note that Kupperman penned in his screwdriver style to the bottom of his next missive, which read: *"Good game. P-K4."*

I decided, however, that the experiment was worth continuing. Perhaps Yankovich had simply been unprepared for so unorthodox a style as Kupperman's. Surely, in the next round he would be much warier. So I returned the twenty-five dollars to Box 87, and sent Yankovich my opening move: *"P-K4."*

Yankovich took an extra day to respond with P-K3.

I don't know how to describe the rest of that game. Some chess games almost defy description. Their sweep and grandeur can only be compared to symphonies, or epic novels. Yes, that would be more appropriate to describe my ninety-ninth game with Kupperman. (By the fourteenth move, I stopped calling it Yankovich-Bloom, and simply thought of it as "mine.")

The game was full of plots and counterplots, much like the famous Bogoljubow-Alekhine match at Hastings in 1922. As we passed the fortieth move, with neither side boasting a clear advantage, I began to recognize that even if my next-to-last game with Kupperman might not be a victory, it would be no less than a Draw.

Finally, on the fifty-first move, an obviously admiring Yankovich offered the Draw to Kupperman-Bloom. In turn, I offered it to Kupperman, and waited anxiously for his rejection or acceptance.

Kupperman wrote back: *"Draw accepted."* He added, in a greasy postscript, *"Send opening move to new address—Box 991, General Post Office, Chicago, Ill."*

My heart was pounding when I addressed my next letter to Yankovich, asking him to retain the twenty-five dollars, and to send me *his* White move for what was to be my final match— with Yankovich, with Kupperman, or with anyone else.

Yankovich replied with a P-K4.

I wrote to Kupperman, and across the top of the page, I inscribed the words: *"Match No. 100—P-K4."*

Kupperman answered with an identical move, and the Last Battle was joined.

Then a strange thing happened. Despite the fact that I was still the intermediary, the shadow player, the very existence of Yankovich began to recede in my mind. Yes, the letters continued to arrive from Box 87, and it was Yankovich's hand still inscribing the White moves, but now each move seemed to emanate from my own brain, and Yankovich seemed as insubstantial as Thought itself. In the Chess Journal of my mind, this one-hundredth match would be recorded forever as Bloom vs. Kupperman, win, lose, or draw.

If the previous match had been a masterpiece, this one was a monument.

I won't claim it was the greatest chess game ever played, but for its sheer wild inventiveness, its incredible twists and turns, it was unmatched in either my experience or my reading.

If anything, Kupperman was out-Petrosianing Petrosian in the daring mystery of his maneuvers. Like a Petrosian-Spassky game I particularly admired, it was impossible to see a truly decisive series of moves until thirty plays had been made, and suddenly, two glorious armies seemed opposed to each other on the crest of a mountain. With each letter in my mailbox, the rhythm of my heartbeats accelerated, until I began to wonder how I could bear so much suspense—suspense *doubled* by virtue of receiving both sides of the game from the two battling champions, one of whom I had completely identified as myself. Impatiently, I waited to see how *I* was going to respond to Kupperman's late castling, how *I* was going to defend against his romping Knights, how *I* was going to withstand the pinpricks of his Pawns.

Then it happened.

With explosive suddenness, there were four captures of major pieces, and only Pawns and Rooks and Kings remained in action. Then, my King moved against both Kupperman's Rook and Pawn, and Kupperman saw the inevitable.

He resigned.

Yes, you can imagine my sense of joy and triumph and fulfillment. I was so elated that I neglected to send my own resignation to Yankovich; not that he required formal notification. Yankovich, however, was gracious to his defeated foe, not realizing that my defeat was actually victory. He wrote me a letter, congratulating me on the extraordinary game I had played against him, and while he could not return the twenty-five-dollar fee according to the rules of our agreement, he *could* send me a fine bottle of wine to thank me for a most rewarding experience.

The wine was magnificent. It was a Chateau Latour, '59. I drank it all down with a fine dinner-for-one in my apartment, not willing to share this moment with anyone. I recall toasting my invisible chess player across the table, and that was the last thing I recalled. The next thing I saw was the tube of a stomach pump.

No, there wasn't any way I could help the police locate Yankovich. He was as phantomlike as I had been myself. The name was a pseudonym, the box number was abandoned after the wine had been dispatched to me, and the *Review* could provide no clues to the identity of the box holder. The reason for his poisoning attempt was made clear only when Kupperman himself read that I was hospitalized, and wrote me a brief letter of explanation.

Yankovich's real name was Schlagel, Kupperman said. Forty

years ago, Schlagel and Kupperman (his name, too, was an alias) had been cell mates in a Siberian prison. They had made five years pass more swiftly by playing more than two thousand games of chess. Schlagel had the advantage when the series ended with Kupperman's release.

Kupperman then took a different kind of advantage. Schlagel had charged him with seeking out the beautiful young wife Schlagel had left behind. Kupperman found her, and gave her Schlagel's best. He also gave her Kupperman's best. Six months later, she and Kupperman headed for the United States.

Like so many romances, the ending was tragicomic. Schlagel's wife developed into a fat shrew who finally died of overweight. No matter; Schlagel still wanted revenge, and came to the States to seek it after his release. He knew Kupperman would have changed his name, of course, but he wouldn't change his chess style.

Consequently, year after year, Schlagel-Yankovich ran his advertisement in the chess journals, hoping to find the player whose method Schlagel would recognize in an instant . . .

"Well, that's what happened," Milo Bloom told his roommate at Misercordia Hospital. "Believe me, if I didn't have a nosy landlady, I would be dead now. Luckily, she called the ambulance in time.

"Sure, it was a terrible thing to happen to anybody. But at least I've learned my lesson. Life wasn't meant to be spent pushing funny-looking pieces around a checkered board. But maybe you've never even tried the game . . ."

The man in traction mumbled something.

"What was that?" Milo asked.

"I play," Dietz said. "I play chess. I've even got a pocket set with me."

Milo, merely curious to see what the set looked like, eased himself out of bed and removed it from the bedside table. It was a nice little one, all leather and ivory.

"It's not a bad way to pass the time," Dietz said cautiously. "I mean, I know you said you'd never play anymore, but—if you wanted to try just *one* game . . ."

Milo looked at his casts, and said, "Even if I wanted to play —how could *you?*"

Dietz smiled shyly, and showed him. He picked up the pieces with his teeth. In the face of a dedication matching his own, how could Milo refuse? He moved the Pawn to P-K4.

The Canarsie Cannonball

GERALD TOMLINSON

His poise on the mound was steady and unshakable. From an exuberant young righthander at Canarsie High School, Brooklyn, in the spring of 1951, he had become by late summer of 1952 a canny and consistent Class A starting pitcher, Elm City, Allegheny League, with 17 wins, 2 losses, and an earned run average of 1.92.

"Hey, Lew," I said to him that night—the night he went after win number 18—"keep it fast and low to Tillray. The guy's no Musial, but he won himself some of Fred's threads a week ago on a pretty fair change-up you gave him."

Lew Knebel grinned. "No mackerels tonight, Skipper. Zoom, zoom, zoom. Tillray can't hit the drop."

I drew a pattern in baseline dust with the spikes of my right foot. Looking past Lew's square shoulders out toward the "Hit this sign on the fly and win a suit from Fred's" billboard in centerfield, I said, "Just one of your zooms now and then, Lew. Don't use the drop any more than you have to."

His so-called drop wasn't the old-fashioned kind. It wasn't just a garden-variety curve that fell off the table. It was a spitball, and a beauty. It came in fast without a spin, then dived like a kamikaze. Nobody but a golfer with a canoe paddle could hit it. The trouble was, tonight's plate umpire, Babe Francesco, was on to the pitch, and I didn't want any spitball fuss this late in the season.

I was in my second year as Elm City's manager. A one-time utility infielder with the Dodgers, brought up after a couple of so-so seasons with Fort Worth in the Texas League, I'd gone into managing rather than going down to the minors as a player or back to the Ford assembly line as a riveter.

My first year as a manager had been less than brilliant. I'd led a pretty fair Elm City team to a next-to-last-place finish, a finish that didn't impress the Dodger front office. Important heads wagged.

They weren't wagging any more. This year I had a pitching sensation in Lew Knebel, in a pair of Brooklyn-bound returnees, in a young team fired with enthusiasm, with a good shot at the Allegheny League pennant.

Knebel brought major-league class to minor-league Elm City. He was a tall skinny kid whose father, a tailor, had wanted Lew to follow in his footsteps. But when the boy ambled out to the mound and struck out all but four of the opposing hitters in his debut at Canarsie High (losing the game 2–1 on a three-base error) his father began to reconsider. Two years later Lew got a four-thousand-dollar bonus offer, the highest allowed at the time, and that settled the issue.

His father was now his second-staunchest fan. I was Number One. I could already see myself as an old hot-stover saying, "That's right, son. I managed Lew Knebel in his one and only year of minor-league ball. The first day I saw him pitch at Vero Beach, I figured, 'Now there's a kid heading for the big time. A long career with the Dodgers. A great career. Then after fifteen seasons, twenty if he's lucky, he'll join the Cooperstown immortals.'"

And the spitter was a part of that glittering promise. A big part. Not that we talked much about it, since the spitter was, and is, an illegal pitch.

Of course a pitcher can't survive on just one pitch, no matter how good it is. Lew Knebel, a virtuoso from sandlot days, had four pitches: the spitter, a slider, a change-up, and a fast ball. His fast ball was Powder River, the best in the league. It inspired an Elm City sportswriter to christen him "The Canarsie Cannonball."

We drew a good crowd that night. Gardner Municipal Stadium, built ten years before, was a decent ballpark for a small city. It had better-than-average lighting, a conscientious grounds keeper, a friendly concessionaire, and a seating capacity of 6,200. Tonight it was about two thirds filled. Lew Knebel on the mound must have brought in an extra 1,000 or 1,500 people this late in the season, even with the new and hard-to-resist lure of television. After all, they'd probably be seeing Lew Knebel himself on TV next year, right along with Sid Caesar.

My Elm City team, the Hawks, stood second in the league, a few percentage points from the top.

The weather was stifling, the way Lew liked it. He'd pitched his two best games, both of them one-hitters, in this kind of muggy heat. Warming up, he looked unbeatable.

I watched my ballplayers closely. Studied them. That's what the Dodgers paid me to do. To look; to recognize the potential stars and develop them; to diagnose players' weaknesses and, if possible, correct them. If I won my Class A pennant, fine. If not, it didn't matter a lot to the front office. My main job was to identify and nurture the major leaguers on my roster. If my has-beens, like Arnie Hunter in the bullpen, or my never-to-be's, like Doc Bettinger at third base, happened to approve of my managing, fine. If not—well, they were nice guys, they'd never scare Leo Durocher.

There we were, 1952, the year Eisenhower won the presidency. A good year. I was trying hard to instruct and encourage my young players, especially Lew Knebel and Sandy Estes. I intended to succeed as a manager, and I intended to start succeeding this year. Even though I wasn't a pitching coach, I thought I'd handled Lew pretty well. Of course that 17–2 record of his and the great ERA had more to do with the boy's talent and instincts than with my advice. He knew that, I knew that. He was what the poets call a natural.

So was Sandy Estes at shortstop, but with a difference. I'd managed Sandy in Elm City in '51, and he'd fielded like a seven-gloved octopus, equal to the best in the business. But he'd hit a puny .170. Only my toe-to-toe pleading with Fresco Thompson, the Dodger VP, in spring training had ticketed him for Elm City in '52 instead of down to Class C, Greenwood.

Score one for Larry Carver—that's me—because in '52 Sandy Estes hit everything but the jackpot at Monte Carlo. He raised

his batting average more than a hundred and fifty points, to
.328. He was voted the league's all-star shortstop, fielding even
better than the year before. Estes would go to Triple-A next
spring—Pee Wee Reese's job being unavailable at the moment.
I liked Sandy, and took some of the credit for his improvement.

That's how it was in the minors in those days, back when we
had a long alphabet of leagues below the majors. Most teams,
at least the ones Class B or better, had a couple of future major
leaguers like Lew Knebel or Sandy Estes. They also had a
whole rafter of turkeys like Doc Bettinger, my third baseman.

A strange guy, Bettinger. Sandy Estes called him "The
Loser," and that's what he was, but I never really knew why.
He could have been a pretty good third baseman. He had the
quick moves, he could usually hit the curve, and he was our
smartest man on the bases, though not our fastest. A college
student in the off-season, as well as a part-time researcher at
Doyle-Kindon Labs in New Jersey, he'd been working toward
a degree in pharmacy at NYU. That's how he got the nickname
"Doc." It was just as well he had a drugstore in his future, I
figured, because at age twenty-seven, hitting .233 in Class A,
he wasn't about to replace Billy Cox in the Dodger starting
lineup.

Erratic. That's the word I'd use, and did use, to describe
Doc Bettinger. He'd dive like the ghost of Pie Traynor to stop
a sure ground single on one play. Then he'd misjudge an easy
pop fly on the next. He'd time a sharp curve perfectly on one
pitch, swinging after the break, and line a base hit to right
field. The next time up he'd take a third called strike on a fast
ball that bisected the plate. In nine years of pro ball he'd never
been higher than Class A, and he never would be.

He was erratic in other ways too. Bettinger wasn't exactly
superstitious. You wouldn't expect a graduate student in pharmacy to buy a whole lot of baseball superstition—the ballplayers' usual rites, ritual, and rigamarole—and he didn't. But
superstitious or not, he was forever changing his equipment or
his playing habits—changing his bat, changing his glove,
changing his stance, changing his grip, changing his moves.

Nothing worked for him, not even my repeated advice to stop it, to settle down.

Tonight, after the ball had been whipped around the infield, Bettinger had started something new. Carefully and for no reason I could see, he began to deliver the ball in person to Lew Knebel. Instead of tossing it twenty or thirty feet to the pitcher the way he'd done for the past one hundred and ten games, he trotted over to the mound, carrying the horsehide like a sacred offering, said a few words to Knebel, and plopped the ball into Lew's glove.

Maybe he thought the personal touch would help. That's about the only thing I could figure, but it didn't jibe with Bettinger's personality. Say-hey he wasn't. Besides, any concern he had, if he had any, seemed pretty unnecessary—Lew Knebel was mowing down the Hartsfield Chiefs inning after inning. When the top of the third ended, Knebel had five strikeouts, including Tillray on a drop, and our Hawk outfielders hadn't had to worry about making a putout. Lew and the infield had done it all. We were leading 2–0.

But something was wrong.

When Lew Knebel trotted back to the dugout after the top of the third, he looked a little confused, a little hesitant. His movements were jerky, and he acted as if he wondered whether he was welcome on his own bench. He sat down and hunched his shoulders. This wasn't the tough, aggressive Lew Knebel I'd come to know and respect.

I got up and walked over to him. "Anything the matter, kid?"

He shook his head and shivered. He tugged at the peak of his cap. "Damn lights," he muttered without looking up. "Damn lights."

"The floodlights?"

"Yeah. Haven't you—noticed?"

"Noticed what?"

He gave a long-drawn-out whistle. Then he giggled. That wasn't like him either. And it didn't go with his glum expression.

"Are the lights bothering you, Lew? What's up?"

He waved a hand across his face, like a man brushing away

cobwebs. His voice sounded far away. "Don't worry, Skipper. I'll be—okay."

I had to leave it at that, because just as he finished saying "okay," four thousand fans rose from their seats at Gardner Stadium, voices also rising, heads swiveling. I looked toward the field in time to see an arcing Sandy Estes drive rattle off the wall in deep left center, dotting the "i" on the Pepsi-Cola sign. The left fielder and the center fielder played it like bushers, and by the time C. J. Kenny, the Chiefs' rookie in center, got his hands on the ball, Sandy was streaking toward third base.

Arnie Hunter, coaching at third tonight, gauged the situation right, saw the opportunity, took the odds-on gamble, and began waving his left arm like a windmill in a hurricane. Sandy never broke stride. He rounded third at full throttle, leaning into the night air, and raced toward home. The Chiefs' shortstop, a freckled stringbean, pirouetted and fired the ball to home plate.

It was a good throw, a little off to the left. A major-league catcher would have made the tag. But Sandy Estes was sliding this year as if he'd been reading an inspirational biography of Ty Cobb. He nicked home plate with a dazzling hook slide, and Babe Francesco's arms leveled straight out above the August dust, palms down. Safe. An inside-the-park home run.

We led 3–0.

Sandy came charging toward the bench, gleeful. "How about that, Doc?" he shouted. "How about that?"

Jumping into the dugout, he made a place for himself between Bettinger and me. "That'll cost you twenty-five iron men, Doc."

I tapped Sandy on the shoulder. When he glanced toward me, I stared at him, hard. "I don't want to know about any twenty-five-dollar bet, Sandy. I don't want to hear about it. Understand? Neither do the folks up there in the box seats. Keep it to yourself."

Actually, I'd already heard about it. I knew too much about it. So did everybody else on the team. You can't travel by bus from city to city, state to state, staying overnight for three or four days each at seven different downtown hotels, and not get to know your teammates about as well as you know your own family.

Doc Bettinger, our third baseman and pharmacist, was also a gambler. A losing gambler. I think he was what they call a compulsive gambler. He'd bet on anything the mind could dream up, especially if you'd let him set the odds. And four times out of five he'd lose.

I could imagine what must have been the story on the Sandy Estes home run. Doc speaking: "Five'll get you twenty-five you don't hit another inside-the-park homer this year, Sandy."

A pretty safe bet, as Doc's bets went. It was now the third week of August. Sandy Estes had belted six inside-the-park home runs this season, an Allegheny League record. He'd hit three of those homers at the Chiefs' Wennick Stadium in Hartsfield, where you needed a telescope to see the center field fence; it was 510 feet to the wall in dead center, the same as at the Polo Grounds.

The way Bettinger must have figured it, with only a dozen games left, Estes' chances of earning those twenty-five bucks were pretty slim. Sandy needed Class D outfielding on a long triple in a big ballpark. He got it.

Gambling. It was a part of all our lives. It was too much a part of Bettinger's.

Poker games took up a lot of Doc's leisure time. On weekday nights after the game Doc's hotel room, which he shared with Arnie Hunter, turned into a smoke-filled card parlor, with beer, potato chips, Slim Jims, and half a dozen seven-card-stud regulars, including Lew Knebel and Sandy Estes. I knew about the games, but I hadn't taken any action to stop them. I knew that Fresco Thompson didn't like gambling, but I don't think many of his minor-league managers outlawed it. I didn't. Better the pasteboards, I figured, than too many real live girls.

Of course there were those, too, and I'd conducted a few mad-scramble bed checks in May and June. I'd walked in on Knebel with Miss Elm City of 1951, a black-eyed blonde, a photographers' model. Twice I'd caught Bettinger with the ticket manager's wife, a restless redhead whose shapely shadow briefly clouded Doc's image as a loser. But mostly we had a sedate team—at least, that's what I told the front office.

The scoreboard clock—"It's Flaherty's for Fine Watches"—read 8:55.

Lew Knebel tripped and stumbled as he left the dugout for the top of the fourth inning. Stumbled and almost fell. What the hell did that mean? Lew Knebel tripping? Stumbling?

"Hey, Lew," I called after him, suddenly concerned, but Knebel didn't look back. He ambled toward the mound, head down, a skinny kid pounding the pocket of his glove as if the future of Western civilization depended on his super-drop.

I motioned toward Arnie Hunter, and the old reliefer came over and sat down. "What do you think's the matter with Lew?"

Arnie Hunter, a balding moon-faced man with a growing paunch, had thrown a two-hit shutout at the Chicago Cubs many years ago, fanning Big Bill Nicholson three times. He never bragged about it. But he'd never do anything like it again. At thirty-four his arm was gone, and he was lucky to last a couple or three innings against a run-of-the-mill Class A lineup. This would be his last year as a player. He knew it, and he felt pretty bad about it. He wanted to manage, but I doubted he'd make it. Too easygoing.

Arnie picked his teeth with the edge of a matchbook cover. "Dunno, Larry," he said at last.

"Thanks, Arnie," I said solemnly. "I knew you'd have the answer."

He spat on the concrete floor of the dugout. "Yeah, Larry."

The top of the fourth inning, Gardner Stadium, Elm City, August 22, 1952: a night that isn't likely to be forgotten by any of the 4,108 fans who had pushed their way through the turnstiles. I know I won't forget it.

After getting an o and 2 count on C. J. Kenny, the leadoff hitter, Lew Knebel turned wild. Wild as dandelions.

First he bounced a spitball off the plate for ball one. That pitch by itself wasn't too surprising. Any low-flying spitter is apt to crash in the dirt.

Lew examined the new ball for a long time. Then, as if to make up for his bouncing drop, he wound up very deliberately and threw a high change-up. I mean high. It cleared the batter's head by at least five feet and carried all the way to the screen. The fans let out a worried groan.

2 and 2.

Del Rhodes caught for us that year. He was an Allegheny all-star like Estes, one of those slow-talking Southerners, a boy from Milledgeville, Georgia, whose manner alone could calm an earthquake. He called time, trudged out to the mound, handed Knebel the ball, said a few words to him, and glanced toward the dugout. He motioned Bettinger over from third and stood talking for a while with the two of them. He jogged back toward home plate when Babe Francesco, halfway to the mound, began lobbing threats at him.

Knebel's next pitch, a fast ball, was probably the wildest pitch ever thrown in Gardner Stadium. It took off at right angles to the plate, Lew having stumbled off the rubber as he threw it. A bullet to the grandstand. It hit John R. Flaherty, an Elm City jeweler, on the left shoulder with a loud crack, breaking his collarbone.

Flaherty, a tiny pink-faced man with a hearing aid, was sitting with his two teenaged sons in Box 5-C, directly behind the visiting team's dugout. Jolted by the pitch, he half rose from his seat, howled something I think was an obscenity, and sat down again. Despite his outcry, he looked more surprised than hurt.

No one retrieved the ball. The stands were strangely quiet, as if the fans couldn't believe what had happened.

Half a dozen Hawks, led by me, sprinted toward the mound. The Chiefs' manager, Ed Jenkins, a grinning gorilla on most occasions, came out of his dugout at a lope, with no grin. Three umpires also converged on the derailed Canarsie Cannonball.

The object of all this attention peered uncertainly in the direction of Box 5-C. He didn't move an inch from where his follow-through had left him. By the time I got to the mound, he'd given up watching the grandstand. Instead he was studying the webbing of his glove with the intensity of a medieval scholar at work on an illuminated manuscript. He stood there, head down, mute, as our small but excited crowd milled around him, buzzing like so many defective floodlights.

"Hey, Lew," I said, and the buzzing stopped. I had the opening, but I didn't know what to do with it. All I said was, "What's the matter?"

Something was decidedly the matter. Knebel, sweating, stared fixedly at his glove. "Don't you—hear—the lights?" He said it softly, dragging out the question a good ten seconds.

There was absolute silence even in the stands, except for the slight rustling as a pair of ushers escorted John R. Flaherty toward an exit. The old man, dazed and dough-faced, was supported by a son on either side.

"What do you mean?" Sandy Estes asked before I could find my tongue.

A long pause. "Purple," Knebel said, his gray eyes dreamy. "Fantastic—it's—music."

"Talk sense," I snapped. "What the hell's going on?" I started to lay a hand on his shoulder.

He screamed—a shrill drawn-out scream that echoed through the stadium, rebounded off the Allegheny hills, and chilled the night air. The crowd gasped.

"What's the matter, Lew?"

"Don't touch me!"

"Aw, c'mon, Lew." It was Arnie Hunter, trying to console the youngster who'd become his protégé. He said, "Everybody gets wild now and then. Even Spahn."

"Stay away from me!"

"C'mon, kid. Take it easy. Here's a little Slippery Elm for your nerves. It'll make you feel better." He tried to feed Knebel a Thayers Slippery Elm tablet, the spitballers' constant companion. I couldn't believe it. Slippery Elm, with three umpires looking on. Poor Arnie Hunter, a spitballer himself, must have been more upset than he looked.

I will say this for Babe Francesco and the other two umps: they were charitable. They cleared their throats in unison and focused their attention on a scuffle in the bleachers.

"Leave me alone!" Knebel shouted. "Get away from me!" He waved his arms awkwardly.

"Why, Lew?"

"Why? Why?" It ended in a sob.

I looked toward Doc Bettinger, who looked fascinated.

"Better take him out," Doc said. "He hasn't got the good stuff tonight. Who's warming up?"

I turned to Hunter. "Warm up."

Arnie left for the bullpen.

I turned to Babe Francesco, the plate umpire, who seemed almost as bewildered as John R. Flaherty. "Get a doctor," I said.

"A doctor?"

"A doctor."

"What the hell do you think he wants?" Bettinger muttered. "A compass?"

I said to Del Rhodes, "Go get Sergeant Schrag from the stands. He'll be somewhere back of third base unless he went over to check the Flaherty box."

"He's a cop?"

"That's right, Del. I think Lew's got himself a dose of something. Maybe peyote."

"Peyote?"

"Yeah. God knows where he could've got it. Maybe Mexico. You ever been to Mexico? Ever tried peyote?"

Rhodes shook his head. He'd been from Milledgeville to Elm City, and that was about it.

"I have," Sandy Estes said. "I tried it one summer, three or four years ago, when I was playing semipro in Alpine, Texas. But I don't think this is peyote. It all happened too fast. Something like peyote maybe. Or maybe Lew's just flipped."

"Lew wouldn't just flip," I said, watching the tall, talented pitcher who'd been hearing purple and who, for no apparent reason, had wheeled and fired a 90-mph fast ball at Elm City's leading credit jeweler.

At that point Lew Knebel flipped.

He swayed off the mound, banging into the first-base umpire as if he didn't see him, then ricocheted off Ed Jenkins, the Chiefs' skipper, who grunted, "Whoa, there," but didn't try to rein him in.

Lew kept right on going, past first base, through a door in the low green wall behind it, and up the cinder path between the grandstand and the bleachers. He dissolved in the gloom.

Knebel wasn't going very fast or very straight, but it took me almost a minute to recover my senses. Finally I said, "Sandy, you'd better go after him."

Without a word Sandy Estes raced toward the cinder path.

Paul Gosling, our big first baseman, followed him, showing more speed than he had since spring training. Paul, a Triple-A veteran down from St. Paul, told me later he figured Sandy might be overmatched by the six-foot-three Canarsie Cannonball.

A few of the fans were starting to stomp. They'd come to watch Lew Knebel and a ball game, and they weren't seeing either one. Too bad for them. I wasn't about to bring in Arnie Hunter, no wins and five losses, and two banjo-hitting bushers from the bench. Not yet.

I'd seen peyote work. I myself had once heard a symphony orchestra play a version of the rainbow down in Nuevo Laredo. I'd seen the twisted stick figures of my friends and teammates. But Sandy might be right. This drug, whatever it was, seemed a lot quicker and meaner than peyote. But it was a drug all the same. And illegal. I knew that much.

I turned to Bettinger. "You want to tell me about it, Doc?"

Bettinger scowled, his black eyebrows almost meeting above a broad sunburnt nose. "Tell you about it?" He feigned innocence. "Me?"

"Yeah, Doc. You. You're the druggist here. What's Lew high on?"

Bettinger shrugged. "Some hallucinogen maybe. Could be mescaline. Could be psilocybin. I wouldn't know. It's out of my line."

"I think it is in your line, Doc. You owe Knebel quite a bit of gambling money, I hear. Six, seven hundred dollars. That's the scuttlebutt. Is it true?"

He shrugged again.

"Doc," I said, "you can start answering my questions or you can start packing for Ponca City. Understand?"

Bettinger rearranged the dirt on the mound with his toe. He looked as if he'd like to take a swing at me. But all he said was, "Yeah, Skip. I understand. I owed Lew a little poker money. It's no secret."

"Seven hundred?"

"Eight fifty."

"You had a bet on tonight's game? Double or nothing—something like that? I'm guessing. Was there a bundle riding on tonight's game?"

Bettinger fiddled nervously with his glove. Sunburn and all, he looked a little pale. "I won't answer that, Skip."

"You just did. Tell me about the peyote. Was it your insurance against Lew winning his eighteenth?"

Defiantly: "Look, I don't know peyote from peanut butter. I'm not an Aztec medicine man. I'm a pharmacist."

At this moment Sergeant Schrag of the Elm City Police Department elbowed his way into the group. A burly man with a neck like a pro tackle, he wore a plaid sports jacket with wide lapels, Fred's threads from the forties, under which there were a couple of unnatural bulges. I knew Schrag to speak to, mainly because our wives were friends.

"What's the matter with Knebel?" Schrag asked. "Hooch?"

I said, "I think you've got a drug case on your hands, Sergeant. You might call it a practical joke. A joke that's also a crime. I'd like you to take a look at our third baseman." I pointed. "Barry Bettinger. I think he's carrying dope."

"You want me to search him?"

"That's right."

"You'll take the responsibility?"

"He's my boy, Sergeant."

Schrag, a dull man with a keen sense of duty, nodded and said to Bettinger, "Okay, kid, if you got the stuff on you, let's have it. No need for a lot of noise. Otherwise we'll go back and take a look in the showers."

I had a sudden thought. "Try his right back pocket."

Bettinger didn't swear very often, but he swore now. He hurled his glove to the ground and stamped around like Leo Durocher in a rage. "Thanks a lot, Skip. Thanks for everything." He plunged his hand into his right back pocket and pulled out a small white cube that looked like sugar.

Schrag blinked. "Say, that's pretty good, Carver. How'd you figure it out?"

"I'm paid to watch my ballplayers," I said. "I watch 'em. Like Hawks."

Schrag didn't smile. Neither did I.

I asked Babe Francesco for a new ball. He gave it to me, and I rubbed Bettinger's white cube back and forth on the horsehide, making sure it crossed the stitches. I'd seen Doc go to his back pocket a few times that night and then rub up the baseball.

I handed the rubbed ball to Bettinger—handed it to him, just the way he'd handed it to Lew Knebel.

"Show us Lew's best pitch," I said.

"The fast ball?" Bettinger was still trying to act innocent, but he was no better at acting than he was at filling inside straights.

"The drop. Knebel's drop."

"Hey, wait a minute, Skip. If you're talking about an illegal pitch, forget it. Arnie Hunter may throw the spitter, I don't know if he does or not, but Lew's on the up-and-up. Lew wouldn't throw it."

"Pretend he would."

Bettinger aimed a stream of tobacco juice at my feet. "Go to hell." He thrust the ball back at me, dropping it in my right hand. He rubbed his fingers briskly on his shirt to get rid of the powder. "You're the genius, Skip, why don't you show us?"

"And hear purple sing? Or watch Babe Francesco turn into a pretzel?"

But I did show them. I slowly touched two fingers of my left hand, the uncontaminated hand, to my tongue. I did it a second time for good measure, staring all the while at the plate umpire. "This is Lew's best pitch, Babe. The spitter. Loaded up and ready to dive. Does that come as a big surprise to you?"

Francesco grunted. "What do you think? Last game he pitched I seen spit flying for sixty feet. Damn ball hit the catcher's mitt like a busted watermelon. But Del Rhodes here, he could of caught old Burleigh Grimes. He protects his boy real good. Gets that spit off the ball one way or the other."

Sergeant Schrag studied the white cube. "You mean Bettinger rubbed a few specks of this stuff on the dry ball—then Knebel grabbed the ball and gave his fingers one or two licks before throwing the spitter—and that did it?"

"That's right."

"Holy Christmas, this stuff must be murder. What do you call it, Bettinger?"

"LSD. Lysergic acid diethylamide. Five thousand micrograms in a sugar cube. There's plenty of it down at the lab. No big deal. It's just another hallucinogen."

By now the fans were in full revolt. Cigar and cigarette smoke hung like an angry thundercloud below the floodlights. Even the box-seat fans were on their feet, shouting. Two knock-down-drag-out fights had flared up in the bleachers. Beer cans and pop bottles had started to litter the field.

I was in no mood to go on with the game. My pitcher was flying high. My third baseman was on his way to the slammer for drug possession. My shortstop and first baseman were somewhere out in the night. I could guess how the front office was going to react.

At this point only Arnie Hunter, faithful Arnie, down in the bullpen, was ready to go.

The umpires—the Three Stooges I'd always called them— were right on top of the action for once. They could see my dilemma. They'd been pretty understanding, too, but they were starting to get restless.

Francesco said, "Two minutes from now, Carver, I want nine of your men on the field."

But at the instant he shouted, "Play ball!" Sandy Estes and Paul Gosling came charging through the low green gate. They were sweating, and they looked grim.

"Hold it!" Sandy yelled. His shout sounded more like a wail.

Our small crowd reassembled at the mound, Francesco's mouth forming a line like a crowbar.

"Lew got to his car before we could catch up with him," Sandy said. "We borrowed the ticket manager's car."

Knebel had bought a convertible in the spring with his four-thousand-dollar bonus. "It's class," he'd said. "Not flashy, but classy." Lew, at eighteen, was the only player on the team who didn't travel mostly by bus. I'd permitted him to take his car on the road after he won six straight in May.

"He drove out Route 324," Sandy went on. "Through Southport, past Victory Gardens. Toward Shelby's Bridge."

"He drove like a maniac. All over the road."

"We chased him, but he must have had that convertible to ninety by the time he hit the bridge. We were pretty far behind when it happened."

"When what happened?"

There was a pause. Gosling kicked a beer can toward the first-base coaching box.

Sandy answered, his voice frayed and angry. "I told you what happened, Skipper. *He hit the bridge.*"

"Hell, he climbed the bridge," Gosling said in a tone as quiet as death. "His car went right up the steel superstructure and flipped. It landed topside down in the middle of the road."

For a moment we all looked blankly at each other. I saw Sergeant Schrag pull the handcuffs from inside his jacket.

"Lew?—" I began.

No one spoke. Sandy Estes made the sign of the cross. Paul Gosling closed his eyes and lowered his head.

Sergeant Schrag snapped the cuffs on Doc Bettinger's unresisting wrists.

"Lew was a great pitcher," Ed Jenkins murmured.

"Shut up," I said. I don't know why I said it, but I guess it made as much sense as anything else.

Schrag, numbly leading Bettinger toward the cinder path, kept glancing back at us, as if he wanted to explain something, but didn't quite know what it was.

"The DA should be able to figure out a charge," he said at last.

A Matter of Kicks

LAWRENCE TREAT AND RICHARD PLOTZ

Nobody in his right mind would have taken Chief Dan Moorhead of Morgan County for a dancer. He was solid as a banquet table and plump as a mooring buoy. Still, like Zero Mostel, he was light enough on his feet to move with the best of them in an old-fashioned square dance, or a Yugoslav line dance, or a Scandinavian turning dance, or even a Bulgarian line dance with eleven-sixteenth rhythm and belt holds. So, quite naturally, he was at the international dance festival on the high school athletic field when it all happened.

There had been some drinking, and it ended up in a kind of wild jamboree where nobody bothered with partners but just picked whoever was nearest and went through the steps. But that shouldn't have been done with a Hopak, which is difficult to learn and has to be timed to a nicety. Otherwise the turns and jumps and kicks can get out of hand. As, apparently, they did.

Dan was making the most of that last, furious round. He did a squat-and-kick routine with a sturdy little girl whom he figured for a high-school cheerleader. Then, out of the semidarkness of the athletic field, a tall Amazon with wide shoulders and a big floppy hat appeared. Somehow she pushed the bouncy little cheerleader aside and began dancing at Dan, and then with him.

She seemed to sense his rhythm and his timing, and then to challenge him to some kind of a contest, which he took up with a will. The fancier his step, the better she liked it. She had speed, grace, and balance. Slap your hips, then your ankles—wheel, turn, jump, hop, whirl me, spin me, and dance me. She seemed determined to prove she was as good as Dan, and maybe better.

Briefly, under the flapping hat, he caught a flash of eyes and a glimpse of parted lips in a shadowy oval face. Then, at the height of their dance, Dan heard a yell and saw a group standing at the edge of the ball field bending over something or someone.

Dan broke off at once. "Got to see," he said and left his mysterious partner.

He was certain she had no idea who he was, because here, at a festival like this, if anybody even bothered calling him by name, it was only Dan. From the two or three times he'd attended the series of summer folk dances, he recognized some of the regulars who showed up faithfully every week. But he had no idea what any of them did apart from folk dancing.

It was simply as Dan, then, rather than as the Morgan County Police Chief, that he strode over to the group surrounding the still figure of a man. Nevertheless, Dan conveyed the stamp of authority in manner and voice. He took charge at once and checked the man's vital signs, after which he looked up. "Someone had better get a doctor," he said.

A minute or so later a stocky man, broad in nose and lip, came rushing over. He stopped short when he recognized the man on the ground.

"It's Howard Lieb!" he exclaimed. "Howie—" He dropped to his knees, felt Howard's pulse, and put his ear to Howard's chest. Then he straightened up. "He's dead," he announced somberly, and shaking his head he gave his diagnosis. "A coronary. Not much doubt about that."

"What about the blood on his forehead?" Dan asked.

"He probably hit his forehead when he fell."

"He fell on his forehead?" Dan said.

The stocky man faced him, as well as a man can face someone a good eight inches taller. "I," he said, "am Dr. Amos Kolodny. Maybe you know more about this than I do."

"I wish I did," Dan said. "I'm Chief Moorhead, Morgan County Police. Would somebody put in a call to the Medical Examiner's office? Maybe the autopsy can pin this down, but right now—" He turned to the group clustered around. "How did this happen? Did anyone see?"

There were no clear answers. In the confusion, in the semi-darkness where you could barely recognize your best friend, no one remembered seeing Howard Lieb or even knew whether he'd been dancing.

Dan tried to get a few facts from the organizers of the festival, who turned out to be Dr. Kolodny and a couple named Spelt. Lily Spelt was a quick, dark little woman with a long high-bridged nose and a mouth that seemed constantly to be exploding into a smile. Whatever she said was preceded and followed by a smile, as if it somehow gave a point to her words. Her husband, Phil, had a shorter nose and a longer face, and he seemed to speak out of a perpetual gloom. He even spoke with the sepulchral tones of someone entering a funeral parlor.

"Everybody knew Howard," he announced sadly.

Lily smiled brightly. "He just wrote a book about folk dancing. He'd studied it all over the world."

"We gave him some photographs for the book," Phil said regretfully.

"I helped him with it too," Dr. Kolodny said. "A number of his friends did."

"He was an authority," Lily said. "Everybody respected him."

"Without him," Phil said mournfully, "we wouldn't have had the dance this evening."

"Why not?" Dan asked.

"The school didn't want us to use their field. But Howard managed to override their objections. He argued that folk dancing is not only an art, but excellent exercise and very good for the health."

"As the school physician and a member of the Board of Health," Kolodny said, "I backed him up."

"Did Lieb have a heart condition that you know of?" Dan asked.

"He came to see me some time ago," Kolodny said, "complaining of migraines."

"What did you do?"

"What I did," Kolodny said, "was strictly between doctor and patient. Not that I'd withhold anything—far from it—but in these days of malpractice suits, I've learned to keep my mouth shut. Let me just say I found nothing seriously wrong with him and advised him to consult a specialist."

"Did you recommend someone?" Dan asked.

"No, he said he had somebody in mind, and I let it go at that."

Flashing lights and the wail of a siren interrupted Dan's questioning, and he walked over to the ambulance and identified himself. "He's been certified as dead," he said, "by Dr. Kolodny over there. Check it out with him."

"We'll do that."

"But first let me have another look at the body under that spotlight of yours."

In the glare, Dan examined Lieb's forehead. He saw a bump and a small amount of blood that had receded, apparently from gravity, with the body on its back.

Later that evening, in the Right Side Bar & Grill where Dan

was in the habit of meeting Willy Wharton, his counterpart across the state line, Dan outlined the case. Willy dwarfed Dan by at least half an inch, but lost out on pounds.

"It was a mess," Dan said. "With sixty or seventy people dancing, plenty of beer, poor light, and music that set you going—how the hell can you do more than guess what really happened? Maybe Lieb tripped, maybe he got a kick in the head or banged into somebody—it could have been anything."

"This dancing—is it strenuous?" asked Willy.

"Plenty. And a good folk dancer has to be something of an athlete. The timing can be tricky."

"You said something about Lieb maybe getting kicked," Willy said. "How hard a kick could somebody have given him?"

Dan slid out of the booth and called out to Maxie, behind the bar. "Maxie, have you got some good old-fashioned music in that juke box of yours?"

"Sure, Dan. How about an Irish jig?" the bartender called back.

"Fine. Just the thing to show Willy something."

Everybody who was at the Right Side Bar & Grill, so named because it was on the right side of the state line, where liquor taxes and prices were lower, would remember that evening. Dan Moorhead put on a show of stamp and clap and kick, and the kick hit the hook of a clothes rack and shot the whole works up to the ceiling. The consequent applause rattled the glasses behind the bar. Dan grinned and sat down.

"That," he told Willy, "is how hard a kick somebody could have given him."

Willy rubbed his nose, which was strong, high, and irregular. "Quite a kick," he said, "but it would take a powerful man to do it."

"I know a woman who could do it," Dan said. "I just don't know her name."

He got the autopsy report by phone the next morning. Although the M.E. couched it in the usual medical jargon, it boiled down to the fact that Howard Lieb had had a previous arteriovenous malformation, which is a lesion that can compress the surrounding brain tissue.

"A sharp impact could easily be fatal," said the M.E., "and as far as I can judge from the wound, it resulted from some kind of a blow. Not with a sharp instrument, although the skin was indented. There were no splinters in the wound, so the object was probably metal or plastic."

"Would the edge of a shoe do it?" Dan asked.

"Perhaps, although I'd guess the instrument was more rounded. Rounded, say, like a watch."

"How about the tip of a woman's shoe? Say a toe with a steel tip?"

"That would certainly do it, although I think the angle of impact would indicate a blow from the side."

"Thanks," Dan said, thinking that you could kick from the side if you were tall enough.

He assigned three men to the job of tracing Howard Lieb's movements during the twenty-four hours preceding his death. Meanwhile, he went back to the athletic field where the dancing had taken place.

He knew where Lieb had collapsed, but he had to guess where Lieb had been hit. He combed the area inch by inch, expecting nothing and finding nothing, except what seemed to be a plastic watch crystal. It was a large one, a full inch and a half in diameter. He put it into a small cardboard box, labeled it for the state lab to examine, and sat down to think things out.

A wristwatch whipped on the end of its leather band? A blow of a wrist armed with the metal casing of a watch? A hard-toed shoe? Even, perhaps, a tap such as tap dancers wore? They were all possibilities. So who had a wristwatch with a missing crystal? And who had the kind of shoe he was looking for—and where was she?

He discussed the problem with Willy that evening, along with the rest of the day's findings. "Lieb had a CAT scan at Dundee Memorial Hospital the day before the festival, and the next day he was told he had an AV malformation," Dan said. "As far as I can find out, Lieb told nobody about the X ray or its results."

"Don't go technical on me," Willy said. "What's an AV malformation? What's a CAT scan?"

"AV stands for arteriovenous. An arteriovenous malformation means his blood vessels were mixed up inside his head and were very fragile. I'm told a few people are born that way, and it usually never gives them any trouble beyond occasional migraines, which Lieb had. But a blow to the head could have caused this one to bleed into his brain. The M.E. says that's probably what killed him."

"Do you think Lieb knew about it?" asked Willy.

"Probably not. Chances are he'd never have known about the malformation except for the CAT scan. They're pretty rare. The CAT is a new kind of X-ray machine that can see things like AV malformations that older machines couldn't catch. The CATs are expensive, so you don't find many of them around. Lieb was lucky the hospital had one—that is, he would have been lucky if he'd lived. The M.E. says an operation could have cured him."

"But you still don't know whether his death was an accident?" Willy said.

"That's the trouble. Unless I find someone who knew about that vulnerable spot of his, I have no case."

"Better forget it," Willy said.

"The last dance number bothers me too," Dan said. "They had a nicely programmed group of dances, everything going fine, then all of a sudden there was this free-for-all, with everybody going wild. I can't put my finger on who put the Hopak record on the machine. We'd played it earlier in the evening and we'd just had a Zweifacher, which is a combination pivot dance and waltz, ending up in three stamps. Then suddenly this second Hopak. Somebody must have planned it."

"Any idea who?"

"It's hard to tell. In the general confusion, anybody could have walked up to the phonograph, picked up the record he wanted, and put it on the turntable."

"What about a motive—if it is a homicide?"

"I don't know that either. But before I give up on this, there's somebody I have to talk to."

"Who?"

Dan shrugged. "I don't even know her name. For that matter, I hardly saw her face."

"You're nuts," Willy said.

If business had been brisk the next morning, Dan would have had to forget the whole Lieb business. An accidental kick was a perfectly reasonable hypothesis. He'd spent a whole day on a case that was no case at all, but it so happened that crime in Morgan County was in the doldrums. Nobody had been robbed or mugged, no drunks had been driving cars, no teen-agers had failed to make a turn. Dan could have taken the morning off, but instead he went hunting shoemakers.

There were none listed in the yellow pages. These days, when shoe fashions change every season, you throw out the old and buy the new—who bothers repairing a shoe that's out of style? Still, there were a couple of repair shops in Morganville, and they told him of a place in Bullock and one in Red Hill. Steel toes were common enough, though the shoemakers Dan spoke to didn't know of any tap dancers and one wasn't entirely sure what a tap dancer was. Dan showed him in a two-minute performance that shook the walls of the shop and knocked an ashtray off the counter.

After that, slightly out of breath and realizing that the cobbler shops weren't likely to solve his problem, he decided to have a look at Lieb's apartment.

It was on the ground floor of a two-family house on the outskirts of Morganville. Scouting it from the outside, Dan found a screen that had been slashed and left on the ground just below a broken window. Between that and the shards of glass lying on the carpet inside, it was pretty obvious that somebody had raised the window, climbed inside, and lowered the sash. Dan, expecting to follow the same procedure, found he was too big to squeeze through the window without cutting himself on the jagged glass.

Frustrated, he rang the bell to the upstairs apartment. His identification got him nothing but antagonism, and it took a shouting match with a rather deaf but determined woman to convince her that he had a right to the key to the downstairs apartment, and that he had no evil designs on her person.

She opened the door grudgingly and Dan stepped inside. With the door still open he said, loud enough for anyone in the apartment to hear but too low for the deaf woman to catch,

"Never mind, I won't go in after all." And, without leaving, he slammed the door shut.

Both the idea and its execution were fine. He figured it would smoke out anybody who still happened to be in the apartment, but he didn't figure on the dog.

A small, playful edition of a Welsh terrier came scampering down the corridor and jumped up on Dan in a spasm of sheer happiness. Automatically Dan said, "Down!" The dog obeyed.

Lieb's dog? Probably. But if anyone was still here, Dan had given away his presence. He walked forward cautiously.

The small desk in the corner of the living room had been ransacked. The drawers were open and papers were strewn among the pieces of glass from the broken window.

Dan picked up a couple of sheets of paper and examined them. Bills. A carbon of a letter to a dance group in France. A playbill from Los Angeles. A letter from his publisher concerning Lieb's book.

The dog had disappeared, but Dan found it in the kitchen lapping at a newly filled dish of dog food. The kitchen was a large one, with two doors in addition to the entry through which Dan had come. The back door and, he assumed, a pantry door.

He walked over to the latter and opened it, but ducked fast as a can whammed past him. A jar of pickles followed. It smashed against a chair, and a tornado in black erupted from the pantry. Dan hooked the charging figure with one swoop of his arm, but he reeled back under the slap-and-scratch attack that ripped a couple of buttons off his shirt and dug into his neck. Then he grabbed her arm and twisted, and Lily Spelt screamed.

"Let me go!" she yelled. "You're hurting me—let me go!" She bared her teeth in what more or less resembled a grin. When Dan eased up, the grin became the artificial smile with which Lily punctuated every other sentence.

"Police," Dan said. "Remember me?"

"You assaulted me! You have no right to use force!" She smiled again. Whereupon the dog, which had been running around madly and yapping mostly for the fun of it, sat down and proceeded to the business of straight uninterrupted barking. Dan took Lily by the arm and towed her into the living room.

"Sit down," he ordered, pointing to a chair, "and tell me what you're doing here."

"I want my manuscript."

"What manuscript?"

"The one Howard stole. I sent him an article on Swedish folk dancing and he published it under his own name. He stole it. I'm going to sue and I need the original manuscript—with my handwriting—to prove it was mine."

"So you broke in and went through his things and took what?"

"Just the manuscript and some photographs."

"Larceny. Breaking and entering."

"I came to feed the dog," she said, smiling. "I didn't want it to starve, and while I happened to be here I looked for the manuscript."

"Lieb's dog?" Dan said.

"Yes. I was worried about him."

"Breaking and entering," Dan said again.

"You wouldn't really, would you? Everybody would be on my side. Everybody hated Howie. He stole articles and pictures and used them as if they were his."

"Where's your wristwatch?" Dan said.

She reached into the pocket of her slacks and took out a small square watch. "Here. I took it off when I broke the window. Why?"

"Lily," Dan said, "do you think anybody hated Howard Lieb enough to have murdered him?"

"Murder?" she said, and whatever surprise or fear she had was covered up by her grin. "Everybody would have loved to murder him. He was overbearing, egotistical, and conscienceless. He stole every single article in his book."

"When I spoke to you at the dance festival, you were full of praise for him."

"Would I stand there in front of a dead man and say I hated him?" She looked toward the kitchen where the dog was still barking. "I'd like to take the dog home with me and take care of it."

"Go ahead," Dan said. "At least it should keep you out of trouble for a while."

Dan figured he'd spend the rest of the day checking jewelers, but he only got as far as the first one because as he entered the store, a customer turned around and they recognized each other.

In the daylight, her hair was golden, her face was polished perfection, and her eyes were blue and clear. She was wearing her floppy hat, and she was buying a new crystal for her wristwatch.

"It must have come off the other night when I was dancing," she said, holding up her watch. It was round, and large for a woman's.

Dan told Willy about it. "It was murder after all," Dan said. "And pure luck that I was right there when it happened. But it's over and done with now, wrapped up with airtight evidence and a full confession. Even the DA seems satisfied."

"What was the motive?" Willy said.

"He swiped a lot of people's articles and a lot of people had that motive. Lieb wasn't the great expert on folk dancing he pretended to be. Every single piece in that book of his had been given to him with the understanding that he'd pay and credit the contributors, only he never did."

"So that's why Lily Spelt killed him?" Willy said.

"You're way ahead of me," Dan said. "Lily Spelt didn't break the case. It was a woman named Sandra Jorgensen. I call her Sandy. Her folks come from Sweden, which is why she's so blonde."

"Sounds romantic," Willy said drily. "You were saying?"

"Last week Sandy discovered Lieb had stolen her article, so she phoned him long distance and demanded payment. When he put her off, she came to Morganville to collect. She had trouble getting in touch with him, so she came to the festival to have it out with him.

"She's a strong girl, Willy, and a talented folk dancer. She *could* have kicked him in the forehead and killed him. But when she saw him on the ball field and started over to speak to him, something came over her—the idea that she could come so close to killing him was too much for her—and she fainted dead away. When she came to, Amos Kolodny was leaning over her, examining her. He took her pulse and listened to her heart with his stethoscope. And that did it."

"Did what?"

"Gave me my case. I was there when he examined Lieb, and I remember that Kolodny hadn't used a stethoscope. That told me. That and his fast diagnosis when he said it was a coronary, right off, just like that.

"It got me thinking, Willy. The plastic cover on the stethoscope head is about an inch and a half in diameter, just like the cover of a watch. Suppose he swung the metal head by the rubber tube that holds it? With that leverage, if you hit a lesion such as Lieb had, the blow could be fatal, and Kolodny knew it.

"I'd already sent that plastic cover up to the lab. They found a fleck of blood on it, and the type matched Lieb's. When I went to see Kolodny and found he had a stethoscope with a missing cover for the head and with what looked like a shred of skin caught on the serrated inside edge, I had him cold. He broke down and confessed."

"I guess he knew about that whatever-you-call-it."

"The malformation. Right. He'd examined Lieb a couple of months ago and he could hear the blood rushing through the area when he listened to Lieb's head—with the same stethoscope he later used to kill him.

"From then on, Kolodny thought often about how easy it would be to kill Lieb with a blow to the forehead, and how it would seem like an accident. Then, the other night, the big chance came. Kolodny happened to be alone with Lieb for a few seconds, out of sight of the crowd. Lieb made some crack about what a lousy article Kolodny had written and Kolodny got sore. He tore the stethoscope out of his pocket and whammed Lieb on the forehead. Lieb kind of staggered and Kolodny walked away, but Lieb didn't collapse until ten or fifteen minutes later."

"What about the girl?" asked Willy.

"Her? Best Hopaker I ever came across, and she went back to Minnesota—to her husband." Dan heaved the sigh of a man who has lost his all.